A Village Scandal

Diane Allen was born in Leeds, but raised at her family's farm deep in the Yorkshire Dales. After working as a glass engraver, raising a family and looking after an ill father, she found her true niche in life, joining a large-print publishing firm in 1990. She now concentrates on her writing full time. Diane's novels include *Secrets in the Dales*, *Wartime in the Dales* and *The Yorkshire Farm Girl*.

Diane and her husband Ronnie live in the Dales market town of Settle, and have two children and four beautiful grandchildren.

By Diane Allen

For the Sake of Her Family
For a Mother's Sins
For a Father's Pride
Like Father, Like Son
The Mistress of Windfell Manor
The Windfell Family Secrets
Daughter of the Dales
The Miner's Wife
The Girl from the Tanner's Yard
A Precious Daughter
A Child of the Dales
The Yorkshire Farm Girl
Wartime in the Dales
Secrets in the Dales
A Village Scandal

DIANE ALLEN

A Village Scandal

PAN BOOKS

First published 2026 by Pan Books an imprint of Pan Macmillan

The Smithson, 6 Briset Street, London EC1M 5NR
EU representative: Macmillan Publishers Ireland Ltd, 1st Floor,
The Liffey Trust Centre, 117–126 Sheriff Street Upper,
Dublin 1 D01 YC43
Associated companies throughout the world

ISBN 978-1-0350-5030-7

1 3 5 7 9 8 6 4 2

A CIP catalogue record for this book is available from the British Library.

Typeset by Palimpsest Book Production Ltd, Falkirk, Stirlingshire
Printed and bound by CPI Group (UK) Ltd, Croydon, CR0 4YY

For all my amazing readers and the people of the Yorkshire Dales.

Chapter 1

Giggleswick, Yorkshire Dales, 26 May 1941

'Come back to bed – come and stay with me just a minute or two longer. I love you so much.'

Flora Whitaker, landlady of the Cunning Vixen, pulled gently on her husband's arm and looked up at him with pleading eyes. 'Come on, you know you have the time . . .' Flora's long auburn hair cascaded over the pillow as she lay half-naked in bed, gazing up at her handsome, dark-haired man. He was showing signs of his age but was still fit and energetic.

Bill sighed and looked around their homely double bedroom. He was going to miss the everyday things – the love of his wife, the comfort of an eiderdown on the bed, even the sound of the annoying church bells outside the bedroom window.

'Now, you know I'd love to, but the lads will be here in an hour. I can't be late. The sergeant major wouldn't be too happy if he heard they had to wait for me while I finished having nookie with my wife.' He pulled on his trousers and pulled his braces up over his vest. 'I'll be back before you know it. I'll try to get leave to come home and help you with the pub as soon as I can.' He paused, seeing Flora's expression. 'Now, don't make that face. You know I can't stand behind that bar pulling pints while most men my age are out fighting for our country. I'm sorry, love. I have to go.' Bill's tone was gentle. More than anything, he was going to miss his wife, and he hoped she would be true to him while he was away.

'Oh, Bill, I don't want you to go. I don't know what possessed you to sign up; there was no need for it. You should have told them about your back. You're not so young anymore, and we have this business.' Flora sighed, knowing full well that nothing could have stopped her husband volunteering to join his old regiment and fight for his country. He had to prove to the world that he was still a red-blooded man, despite being over forty now.

'I couldn't stand by and do nowt, not when my country needs me. I don't want to be like some of them we serve over that bar, talking a good talk but doing nothing about it. Not when I'm already a crack shot and still fit.' Bill watched as Flora got up, stripping off her flimsy nightdress. She pulled on her brassiere and knickers and reached for her underskirt. 'That's it, get a move on, woman. Let's have a decent breakfast together, proper eggs and bacon before I have to start on army rations. That's one thing I will miss, your cooking.'

'But you're *not* fit, Bill. No matter what you say, you still have pain from the last time you served.' Flora was frowning but then, looking into the bedroom mirror as she fastened her hand-knit cardigan, she grinned at his reflection. 'Oh, and so you won't miss anything else about me except my cooking, Bill Whitaker? I hope you remember those words when you curl up with your rifle in your bunk bed instead of me. A gun won't keep you so warm and satisfied.'

'Aye, but it will keep me safe. Now, will I be safe leaving you behind on your own behind that bar? No flirting with half the men of Giggleswick while I'm away.' He patted her bottom as she opened the bedroom door to make her way down to the kitchen. She waited a moment as he picked up his kitbag to check the contents before returning to his old unit at Catterick.

'You know me, I'm always true to you. I might talk to everyone, that's part of being a barmaid, but I'll always be yours. I just wish you weren't leaving me.' Flora brushed away a tear as she watched him put his hair cream, razor and soap into the bag. She and Bill had been married ten years and were used to one another's company even though she was a typical landlady, always ready to entertain her guests with a winning smile and a twinkle in her eye.

'Aye, lass, stop blubbing – I'm not going anywhere except to the barracks for the next fortnight. I might even get back to see you again before they send me abroad. Even then, I'll be fine. I'm longer in the tooth than some of the young lads I'll be with. I know when to keep my head down.'

He gave her a quick hug and kissed her cheek, then followed her down the stairs with the kitbag on his back and set it down on the floor as she went into the pantry. 'Here, I'll get the fire going. Young May will be in shortly, and you know how she likes a cuppa before she cleans the bar. Don't let her catch you crying, else she'll start, and then we'll never hear the last of it.' He bent over the ancient Yorkshire range that kept the kitchen warm. Flora often still made a hotpot pie or rice pudding in its oven instead of using the new electric Baby Belling he'd invested in a few months earlier.

Once the flames had taken to a few pieces of the dry kindling that was always stored in a brass box next to the fire, Bill put the already filled pot-black kettle onto the burning coals. 'No need to use electricity when it can boil on here. A penny saved here and there, lass – now, don't forget that when I'm not here.' He smiled and sat down at the small kitchen table.

The pub's living quarters were cramped but adequate for a couple, although the building was old and constantly in need of repairs. Bill had installed electricity as soon as it came to the village – only in the essential rooms at first, but when he got home from the war he intended to run spurs off from the main box and add lights and sockets to the places he hadn't yet been able to afford. So far, it had been a boon to the small pub: the electric lighting in the bar, replacing the old gas lamps, had even attracted one or two new customers.

'It's quicker with the electric kettle,' Flora smiled back at him as he settled into his chair. 'A watched kettle never boils.' She placed a frying pan on the ring of her pride and joy, the cooker, put in two rashers of bacon and waited for them to sizzle before adding two eggs. 'I've agreed with Bernard Fowler that he'll supply us with a butchered pig this back-end, providing we keep it fed with the pub scraps and pay for its upkeep. And keep our mouths shut to the ministry,' Flora added, as she put the breakfast plate in front of her husband.

'Only one egg? This might be the last one I get for a while.' Bill sighed and watched as she gave her egg to him.

'See, that's how much I love you. Can't have my man going hungry,' Flora said, and decided to make her bacon into a sandwich. The kettle on the fire finally boiled, and she filled the teapot.

They ate their breakfast in silence, occasionally looking across at one another. Flora could feel the tears welling up again at the thought that this could be the last meal they shared, for all Bill's positive attitude to the war against Hitler and his followers. It was Bill, despite his moods and temper, who kept her spirits high. He was always there when she needed him, a consistent presence behind the bar, serving the locals, making sure neither of them went without anything. Now she'd have to do everything for herself. He had no real idea how much she was going to miss him.

'That's grand, my lass.' Bill looked across at his wife and knew she was near tears. 'Now, we covered everything last night, didn't we? The brewery always delivers on a Tuesday. Get the drayman to take it down to the cellar for you. Pay them once a month. You might have a little bother getting hold of any spirits, but folk will just have to drink beer. Besides, there's always our friend the milkman, who will keep you supplied until he gets caught with his extra deliveries of golden nectar. Our customers should know there's a war on and stuff is hard to get hold of. Don't stay open any longer than midnight, and make sure the door's locked with no sign of a light, especially after eleven. They should think themselves lucky we can get away with a lock-in at all these days. If anyone gives you any bother, go for Jack next door. They'll soon behave themselves once he steps into the pub.'

Jack was Bill's drinking partner, but Flora privately hoped he would stay away while Bill was at the barracks. She didn't like him, and he never came to her aid when Bill was in a mood. She would not be calling for him, and she didn't expect to see Jack stopping in at the pub without Bill there to slip him free drinks.

'I'll be fine, don't worry about me.' Flora attempted a smile. 'Just look after yourself. I wish you weren't going.' She blew her nose on her handkerchief, then quickly composed herself as she saw a figure pass the kitchen window.

A moment later the door opened and May, their cleaner, let the early morning sunshine into the low-set kitchen along with her usual smile. She was a pretty lass of eighteen with blonde hair and a clear complexion, well liked by everyone in the village.

'Morning; how lovely it is out there! You'd never think

there was a war on.' May beamed at her employers as she stepped inside and turned to close the door. Then she caught sight of the packed kitbag and remembered that this was the morning Bill was joining his old regiment, despite the old injuries he'd avoided mentioning during his examination. 'Sorry, Mr Whitaker – I forgot that today's your leaving day. Are you all packed and ready?'

'I am, May. Are you ready to help Flora run this place? I'm counting on you to do those extra jobs while I'm away.' Bill stood and picked up his army jacket – which he had lovingly cared for since his discharge during the previous war – from the back of his chair. He put it on, straightened it over his stomach and adjusted his tie, then picked up his battalion cap.

'Oh, my, don't you look smart! I'd hardly have recognized you. Of course, it goes without saying that I'll help whenever I can. Everyone has to do their bit. My mam says she really admires you for going back to the army. She says that the country should have more men like you.' May blushed and looked at Flora.

'He's an idiot, May, but I know why he's doing it. And I'm proud of him.' Flora stood up and walked to Bill's side, brushing imaginary fluff away from his khaki jacket just so that she could put her hands on him. 'He's got to take care and come back to us. This pub can't function without him for long, and neither can I.' As she kissed him gently on the cheek, the nearby church clock began to strike eight, and her stomach churned.

'I'd better go out and wait for the lorry. They're picking

some cadets up from Giggleswick School first and then stopping for me at the village cross.' Bill reached across to shake hands with May. 'You take care of yourself, May. And like I say, help Flora out as much as you can.' He held the young woman's hand tightly and looked her in the eye. He'd known her since she was in a pram, and it was for her and others like her that he'd decided to join up again. 'I'll be back before they send me over to fight. Of that I'm sure.'

'You take care, Mr Whitaker, and don't you worry about Flora. The pub's in good hands.' May watched as Flora threaded her hand through her husband's arm and they left the house by the back door. She sighed, feeling sad for them – especially for Flora, who was being left with everything to run.

Stepping closer to the kitchen window, she watched the couple walk down the yard to the main road, where an ancient cross stood outside the church. 'Please let him be all right; let him return,' she whispered under her breath, then started to clear the breakfast table and make herself a cuppa with rationed tea. Better to keep her mind busy than dwell on the war and Bill Whitaker going to fight.

May was prepared to do anything Flora asked of her. Her employer was a kind, clever woman, and she was sure that they would manage to run the pub between them. In fact, it would probably be easier while Bill was away. He drank a lot of the profits, and everyone knew that he was sometimes unkind to Flora when his jealous streak got the better of him.

'You've got everything?' Flora asked Bill, as he stood with his kitbag at his feet in the bright morning sunshine.

'Aye, everything I need for now. No doubt they'll kit me up once I'm at Catterick.' Bill looked up at the clear blue sky and watched the swifts and swallows diving and screeching through the air. Another few weeks and it would be the sound of Messerschmitts and Spitfires in the air above his head. He'd be fighting for his life and the lives of others around him. He was scared, but he wouldn't let Flora know.

At his age, and with pre-existing war wounds, there had been no need for him to go and fight, but the more he'd read the papers and listened to the news, he'd known that he had to. He'd fought for the final year of what was supposed to be 'the war to end all wars', until the Germans had been forced to surrender. This time, after sitting back for two years of the current war and watching the madman Hitler and his evil ways, he'd felt he had to do something more than live a quiet life running a Yorkshire Dales pub.

'I'm sorry, Flora; you know I have to go.' He pulled his wife to him and kissed her as he heard the gears of the army lorry crunching down the steep hill from Giggleswick School. It was an ancient and upper-class establishment, known for its army cadets and top-class sportsmen as well as being one of the most academically rigorous schools in the country.

'I know.' Flora put both her hands to his face and kissed him as the lorry covered with a tarpaulin pulled up beside them. A soldier in full army dress climbed out of the cab, holding a clipboard.

'I'll write as soon as I get there. You behave yourself, and I'll be back before you know it. No flirting, do you hear?' Bill held onto her hand as long as he could while the soldier took down his details and pulled back the tarpaulin, directing him to climb into the back with six fresh-faced schoolboys.

He gazed at the young lads. They knew nothing: they had never seen a dead man or watched a friend die. He wished they didn't have to do it now. He climbed up beside them and sat down on the wooden bench that ran along the length of the lorry, holding back the tarp long enough to wave to Flora one last time as the lorry revved its engine and started with a jolt. Flora stood by the ancient cross with tears running down her face, but she was still trying to smile as she waved to him while the lorry made its way up the steep hill and out of Giggleswick.

This was the second time he had left the sleepy village of his birth. Last time, he had been saved by the war coming to an end; hopefully, this time he would be just as lucky. He was already regretting his decision as he sat back, closed his eyes and thought of his wife and the nights they had spent with friends at the Cunning Vixen. It would still be there when he came home; Flora would make sure of that. She was a canny lass, and ten times the businessman he was. All he needed to do was survive the war.

Flora stood waving for a long time as the lorry took Bill away from her, then sank down onto the steps of the ancient market cross. *The stupid man*, she thought, wiping her eyes. Why couldn't he stay with her? Let the younger ones fight the war.

At the same time, she was proud of him – proud of how much he loved his country, and proud of his willingness to fight for its freedom. She remembered seeing a newspaper report that said men up to the age of thirty-six were to be conscripted. She'd been so grateful that Bill, now over forty, would not be among them. And then he had returned from Settle, the market town that intertwined with Giggleswick, and told her he'd lied about his age and attended a conscription campaign at the town hall. He'd been determined to show his worth, no matter his age and the old injury that gave him trouble in his back. There was shrapnel still embedded next to his spine.

Flora sighed and dropped her head. Now it was up to her to keep the pub going and to be strong for when he came back to her. After all, the war couldn't go on for ever. It had already been raging for two years; surely it would end soon.

She looked over at the Cunning Vixen, not yet ready to go back inside. May would be having her usual morning brew and then going in to clean the bar area. Flora was in no mood for the young woman's chatter about the village lads or what she was going to wear that weekend. What Flora needed was to talk to her mother and have a good cry. Her mother would understand.

She made her way along the village and over the large slate stone that crossed the bubbling beck, following the path to Tems Beck cottages. She knocked gently at number three before opening the door into the house where she had been born and that she still called home, despite living at the pub for the last eleven years. The row of cottages had originally been mill houses; they were old and dark inside, no matter how bright the day outside.

Flora blinked as her eyes adjusted, searching the small front room for her mother. 'Mam, are you in? I just thought I'd pop by. I've just said bye to Bill.'

The two Windsor chairs with their handmade cushions stood empty at either side of the Yorkshire fireplace. Flora noticed a bunch of bluebells in a jug on the oak dresser. 'Mam!'

'I'm through here, in the garden. I'm just planting some lettuce out. Doing as the government tells me to do – not that they're worth listening to half the time,' Mary Towler shouted from the back kitchen garden. She straightened up, wiping the dirt from her hands on her already filthy apron. She didn't need the War Ag to tell her to grow vegetables in her garden; she had always done so. Fred, her late husband, had kept it all neatly maintained until his death, and then she had taken over, being even more dependent on her own produce.

'Don't you be doing too much,' Flora said as she crossed the small back kitchen and stepped out into the sunshine.

'It keeps me busy, and besides, it will help you out with vegetables at that pub of yours. You'll be needing them, the way the world is going.' Mary put her hands on her hips and looked at her only daughter. 'Well! Has the idiot gone? Why he wants to leave a quiet life running the pub and put himself back in the line of fire beats me.'

'Oh, Mam, don't. I've come for a bit of sympathy, not a lecture.' Flora shook her head at her mother. Mary was a strong woman, in more ways than one. Although she was in her mid-sixties, she still had a good figure and her looks had not yet left her; apart from the greying of her hair, you would never have known her true age.

'Well, the silly fool. The country would have survived without him joining up. He should have left it to the young 'uns. Anyway, never mind him. How are you?' Mary tucked a stray lock of her daughter's hair away from her face and looked closely at her.

'I'm all right. Don't know how I'm going to cope with everything, but I'll manage. I'm not daft, and folk in Giggleswick are a good lot. All my regulars will just have to bear with me until I get into my stride.' Flora pushed her hands into the pockets of her cardigan and stared down at the path that ran the length of the garden.

'It'll not make much difference, not having Bill about. He never did a lot. Cleaned the cellar and looked busy all the time, when he was really doing nothing. You could have done a lot better for yourself. I just wish that you'd kept on with . . .'

'Mam, stop it. Before you even mention Johnny Cowperthwaite – he's a good man, but I would never have made a farmer's wife. He's happy where he's at, on his own farming on that godforsaken moor. You have never liked Bill, and you always make it obvious to him – that's why I hardly come here! You make it impossible for me.' Flora sighed, remembering the day when Bill had come to ask for her hand after she, by herself, had moved into the Cunning Vixen. That visit had been followed by a curt lecture from her mother once he had gone, about how she could do a lot better and to forget being a landlady. Since that day, Mary had repeatedly reminded her daughter that she could have made better choices for herself.

'Well – a shop boy, that's all he was. If it hadn't been for you getting the Vixen, you'd be penniless, so I'm not worried that you will struggle without him. Anyway, never mind, what's done is done. Do you want a brew? I'm going to have one, and then I'll walk up into Settle.' Mary pushed her garden fork into the rich, dark soil and walked past Flora into the kitchen.

Flora could have done with her mother putting her arms around her and holding her close, but Mary was not that sort. Left with Flora to bring up after the Great War had taken Flora's father, she had become practical and a little bit hard.

'No, I'm all right, thanks, Mam. I'll have to get back to see what May is doing. I want her to clean the brass round the bar before we open at twelve. She'll not do it if she thinks she can get out of it. Another time.'

'I'll perhaps see a bit more of you, now he's away? I hope so. You know I'm always here for you, no matter what,' Mary said as she looked out of her kitchen window, not wanting to show Flora her true feelings.

'I know, Mam; and I'm here for you. Come and sit in the snug and have a sherry. You used to always go across to the Vixen on a Saturday night with your friend Lottie when I was young. I wish you were still friends with her – I still don't know why you fell out.' Flora made her way towards the front door.

'Oh, I don't know; she mixes more with Jenny Moon and that lot. I can't be doing with all their gossiping.' Mary followed her daughter to the door. 'Have you seen the baby ducklings on the beck? They do make me smile. I just hope nobody pinches them now that meat is on ration.'

Mother and daughter paused in the doorway, gazing out across the cobbles to the small, clear beck that ran through the heart of Giggleswick. In summer it caused no problems, but in the winter months the cottages along its banks were always under threat of flooding. That was when all the neighbours on the row pulled together to keep the waters from pouring in through their doors.

'Yes, I saw them the other day when they'd only just hatched. They should be all right unless a mink or a fox gets them. There are a few families – there are some on the Ribble as well. They were sunning themselves on Queen's Rock when I walked into Settle the other day. It must be summer coming, no matter what state the world is in.' Flora smiled at her mother. 'Right, I'll have to go, Mam. Got a lot to do.'

'Aye, take care, my lass. I might bethink myself to come for a sherry some Saturday, if I can be bothered. But on my own, I think.' Mary shook her head.

'Do, Mam. It'll be good to have you supporting me. There's still that nice seat in the corner.'

Chapter 2

'I know it's not my place to ask, but are you all right, Flora? My mam says I should be there for you if you need me, and I can see that you look a bit miserable this morning. I would if my man had just gone off to war, so I know how you feel.' Young May shook the tin of Brasso and smeared it onto the brass rail that ran all around the main bar.

'I don't know what I am, May. I can't seem to settle this morning. I keep wanting to cry, and then I tell myself to get a grip on things. Thousands of men have gone to fight and have left their wives and families.'

'Yes, and he's at least not going to be on the beaches like they were at Normandy the other year. That must have been awful – pinned down with not a chance in the world to escape. Although all our lads and men are so brave, no matter where they're fighting.' May started polishing hard with her yellow duster, getting rid of the white streaks and making the gleaming brass shine through.

'You've a great way of cheering people up, May,' Flora said ironically, but she smiled. 'But as you say, at least I know he's not in France, that the Green Howards are going to the Middle East once they've finished training. He'll be warm if nothing else.' She checked the large wall clock: it showed eleven forty-five. 'Nearly time to open up. Have you done? All looks tidy enough, and I've some cooked ham if anybody needs a sandwich making. Heaven knows how long I'll be able to serve meals and beer, everything's that scarce, but so far we're all right.'

'Yes, all done for another day. I'll be back in the morning. If you need my help, I'm only across the way. I can help serve if you want me to?' May asked, but she already knew the answer.

'No, I can manage, thanks. Through the day isn't bad; it's the evenings when I'll need your help behind the bar. I'm not letting Bill come home to find I've not been coping without him. This has always been my pub, and I can run it with one hand tied behind my back, no matter what he thinks. Now, you get yourself home. And prop the main doors open on your way out . . .' Flora watched as May did as she was told. 'Thank you! Thank you. I know you're only wanting to help,' she shouted, as the young lass walked out into the bright sunshine.

'See you later on. Dominoes night – get ready for the rowdy lot!' May called back.

Flora stood behind the bar and looked around her, reminding herself again that she could cope on her own. She pulled a test pint and inspected its clarity. The last thing she wanted was a reputation for serving cloudy beer, and she knew there would be those who'd try it on with her. Especially some of the old regulars who always liked to sit in the same spot and chew over the village's happenings. She smiled at the thought. They invariably started with a list of people who had died, either naturally or in the war; then progressed to what was wrong with the world; and finally finished on any fresh bit of scandal they might have heard. They looked up to Bill – Flora was just the barmaid in their eyes, but she would keep them in line. After all, as she'd said, it was her pub. Her name was above the door as they entered, so they were answerable to her.

'Now, then, Flora. Has he got away, then? I thought about you this morning,' Frank Capstick greeted her as he walked into the pub. Limping over the stone flags and leaning on the bar, he pulled his pipe out of his pocket to smoke with his first pint of the day.

'He has. There was no talking him out of it, no matter how I tried. I don't know how he got past the doctor's examination, but he did.' Flora shook her head. 'I love him, but I think he's a fool to go. He won't last five minutes if his back starts playing up.' She smiled at the old man, whom she'd known all her life; he, too, suffered pain when walking after years of kneeling and bending, tending the gardens of Giggleswick School. 'Pint of the usual?'

'Aye, well, I know I'll not be joining your fella. Far too long in the tooth. Aye, a pint of that there bitter, just an odd'en. It passes the day. Although I thought I might go and sit down by King's Mill and watch the world go by for an hour or two, keep out of the way of the missus. She's got three of her mates round knitting gloves and balaclavas. I keep telling her they aren't needed this time, in this war, but she's not for listening.'

'I'm sure there will be a soldier somewhere grateful for them, especially when winter comes. I can't see the war ending any time soon; else my fella wouldn't have gone.' Flora leaned on the bar and watched as Frank took his first sip and wiped his mouth.

'They need to send my old woman and the three that are knitting and nattering at our house. All the hot air that comes out of them, they could gas bloody Hitler with. They never shut up, especially that nosy Jenny Moon. What she doesn't know, she makes up. I can't be doing with her. Folks that live in glass houses shouldn't throw stones, and she's no angel by a long way. I remember what she was like when she was younger, and she sometimes forgets that.'

Frank lit his pipe and then headed for his usual corner by the window, where he liked to sit and gaze across at the village shop. Everyone in Giggleswick stopped there for necessities rather than walking the half-mile into Settle, and the Giggleswick School pupils relied on it to keep them supplied with sweets.

'They're struggling, aren't they? Can't get any toffees or half the things they used to stock. Bloody Jerry, bombing our supplies and drowning our lads. I thought they would have learned the last time they got put in their places.' Frank nodded to the little shop, squeezed into a row of cottages.

'I know, everybody is struggling. I hold my breath when our beer supply comes. Barley is so scarce, and beer production's been cut; little pubs up here like us don't stand a chance.' Flora leaned on the bar.

'You'll have to make your own. You've got a good fresh stream running past your door and plenty of outhouses. Keep it to yourself, don't let on to them that snoop, and you could make a good profit.' Frank's tanned face broke into a grin, and he spat a mouthful of black saliva down into the spittoon near his feet.

'I think the War Ag would find out soon enough, Frank, once I started ordering in oats and barley. They don't miss a thing. Besides, try and hide that from Jenny Moon! She would smell the first brewing straight away.' Flora reached for some glasses and started to wipe them, thinking that she could do with more than just Frank drinking today. But the evening would be busier; it was dominoes night, as May had reminded her. Quite a few men, and even a few women, would fill up the bar later.

'She's just a nosy old devil. I keep telling my Madge not to encourage her, but she hangs around like a bad smell. The only peace I get is when I go for a walk or when I go to my allotment. Mentioning which, if you need any vegetables, just tip me the wink. Perhaps we could come to an agreement: vegetables for beer? Providing you don't let my Madge know. I've some cabbage ready now if you want some.'

'I'd be happy to do that, Frank. I'd pay you in beer or money. Everything is getting so scarce, I don't know what I'm going to feed folk. I've managed to boil a ham hock for tonight that I'll make up into sandwiches for the domino teams. Times are hard.' Flora glanced up as two more locals entered the pub. Hopefully it would pay its way this afternoon after all.

'Well, we'll do that, then. I'll let you know what I can supply you with, and you let me know what you want.' Frank smiled. 'You'll manage, lass. Locals will stand by you. We can't have our pub closing just when we need a place to sit and enjoy a pint and try to forget the real world out there.'

'You aren't closing, are you, Flora? I know Bill has gone, but I thought you were carrying on?' Robert Pitcher, who lived just a stone's throw from the pub, asked her with concern on his face.

'No, I'm not closing. Just finding it difficult to get what I need to keep the business going, but I won't be closing. I love my pub. You'd have to see me in my grave before I leave this place.' Flora pulled a pint each for Robert and his mate Graham Windle, passed them across the bar and took the much-needed payment.

'If you want some music one night, we can both come round with our guitars and sing. Cheer folk up, even though there's nowt to be cheerful about. You've got to keep your spirits up one way or another.' Graham took a sip and brushed the white head of froth off his moustache. 'Bloody Jerries, bloody government. Nobody wanted this war, but we're all in it and we all have to stand by one another. You let us know, no charge. It would make a good night.'

'Thanks, Graham, that might be an idea. Something

cheery so that everyone can have a sing-along, providing the ARP warden doesn't come in and spoil it. He struts about down here like a little Hitler. He's teetotal, so he thinks this place is hell itself and that I'm after all your souls. And that nobody will ever fight anybody or work because of their love of evil drink.' Flora shook her head. She would invite the men to play, but probably not for a little while yet; not until she had things more in hand.

'He's just a hypocrite,' said Robert. 'I remember when he was a young fella. He used to trail home from the King Billy in Settle in the early hours of the morning, absolutely legless. Only gave it up when his old fella drowned in the Ribble after falling over the mill bridge, drunk. His mother, Ma Rawlinson – now she was a stickler. She'd take your last penny off you when she ran the lock-up at Langcliffe. Her beer was rubbish as well.' He sighed and leaned on the bar.

'I'd forgotten his mother had the lock-up. I can just remember my dad talking about it. And he has the nerve to preach to me?' Flora gasped.

'Aye; they had a cottage in Langcliffe with a window that opened up towards the street. If she knew you, she used to serve you no matter what time you knocked on the door or window. She'd come and ask for your brass and then serve you this home-brew in anything you brought to take it away in. It was blinking lethal. A pint of that and you were anybody's. I remember having one when I'd just started drinking, I was ill for days after.' Robert gave a wan smile and turned to Frank Capstick, pointing at the stool next to him, before he and Graham went to join him by the window.

'Them that have the most to hide, lass, are always the worst. Remember that.' Frank sat back and drew on his pipe, smiling at the two men. He'd stop for another pint instead of that walk, now he had company. Perhaps either Robert or Graham would buy him one if he supped slowly.

'He's right there, Flora. Take no notice of the warden. The authority has gone to his head. We're living in the Yorkshire Dales, not Buckingham Palace.' Robert grinned. Everybody disliked George Rawlinson; he was one of those men who walked with a certain air about him, as if he had a bad smell under his nose. He always knew best, no matter what you said, and now that he was ARP warden he was relishing his position of power.

'Oh, he wastes his breath on me, stupid little man. Let's put it this way, I have bigger things to worry about than a blind not being pulled tight enough.' Flora sighed. She wasn't joking; she had more worries than she'd ever anticipated. And now she was on her own to face them.

'Aye, he wants to think on that a lot of us have lads out there fighting. I was talking to Lottie Taylor today. Her lad's out in the Atlantic on his ship. She never said anything, but it sounded like she thought he was in a battle. Poor soul filled up and cried when I asked how he was.' Robert sank the half-pint remaining in his glass and stood up to get another.

'What ship is he on?' Graham asked, still nursing his first pint.

'I shouldn't say. You aren't supposed to tell anybody in case those bloody Jerry spies are listening in, but as it's only us, and I don't think Frank here is a German spy . . . He's on the *Mashona*, a gunner. Pint, Frank? I think I can just run to it.'

'It's a big ship. The Jerries will be happy if they take that one out; no wonder Lottie is worried.' Frank looked at his nearly empty glass and smiled at Robert. 'Aye, I'll have another. The walk can wait, I'd rather sit and have a bit of company.'

'I'm just glad I have no family, nor a wife. I've only myself to worry about nowadays,' Robert said. 'I couldn't even think about any of my family being involved in the war. You must be worried about Bill, Flora. At least at his age they might not put him on the front line. Hopefully he'll get a cushy number and let the young ones risk their necks.' He watched as Flora pulled three more pints and smiled when she put them on the bar. Robert was a quiet, man, a little reclusive, one who kept himself to himself – unlike his friend Graham, who was outgoing and loved his music.

'I don't know why he felt he had to go, but there you go. He still thinks he's a young fella in his head. And with them enlisting men to the age of sixty-one, I couldn't hold him back.' Flora sighed as she took the money.

'He will be all right. He'll keep his head down, and all of us will make sure you're looked after.' Robert winked at the good-looking landlady, whom he had always admired. She was easy to talk to and much loved by her locals – even though the fellas always recognized Bill as the landlord, just because he was a man.

'Well, I hope you're right, Robert. And I hope that he will soon be back.' Flora watched the three men sitting together and discussing the war. It seemed as if they would be with her until closing time, and then she'd have to look over her account books before opening up again at six. At least May would be behind the bar to help when the dominoes match got under way. That would help the night run more smoothly.

Once the pub doors had closed for the afternoon, Flora sat in her small office beside the bar and kitchen. It had once been a broom cupboard, but Bill had put up shelves and installed a small table and chair, and now it was where she kept the pub's paperwork. In front of her were various unpaid bills, invoices, and a list of goods wanted – some of which she knew she would not be able to acquire, owing to shortages and rationing. She was going to have to find a way to keep the Vixen open, though, one way or another.

Bill had left at the worst of all times, just as rationing was starting to hit hard. A little pub in the Dales came a long way down the brewery's priority list, with ingredients for the beer and the petrol to deliver it in short supply.

Flora sat back in her chair and looked out through the open door of her office towards the window, with its view across the village. For the first time since she'd taken on the Vixen, the thought of giving the place up had crossed her mind as she sorted the pile of bills. She couldn't do it, not really – she loved the place too much.

But nor could she see how she was going to keep her head above water. It was only a small pub, and with half of the local men away at war, it was not making a profit.

Ever since childhood, when she'd walked through the village every morning on her way to the local school, Flora had dreamed of running the pub – of being like the woman behind the bar whom her father had always spoken of so fondly when he'd returned home happy after a pint or two. Perhaps he'd also appreciated the brief hour or two of freedom from her mother. She smiled now, remembering the friendly blonde landlady who had always made a fuss of her as she passed the doorway, always asked after her father. She had seemed very kind, despite Flora's mother dismissing her as no more than a common hussy. Flora wondered if she'd ever struggled to make her books balance.

She turned back to her little table and opened the order book, studying it in readiness for the brewery's weekly delivery. Times were desperate, but serving more food was out of the question. It was hard to find enough as it was, even though living in the countryside helped. The 'townies', as local people called those living in Leeds and Manchester, must be having an even tougher time of things; at least here in the village, a lot of people were nearly self-sufficient.

Glancing again at the window, she saw Bill's friend Jack standing outside. He seemed to be looking up towards her bedroom. She hoped he would keep away; she wouldn't be seeking him out for help in a hurry. He may have been Bill's friend, but she found his manners unacceptable and his language. He wouldn't be coming to see her hopefully, as he probably knew what she thought of him. She'd made it clear enough in past times when she had been curt with him.

She rose from her seat, climbed the ancient, creaking stairs to the landing and went into the bedroom, where she sat down on the edge of the mattress and gazed across at Bill's side of the bed. The room felt empty without him. His woollen dressing gown hung on the bedpost, and she lifted it to her face to breathe in his scent. How was she going to cope without him? Lord only knew, but cope she would.

The one good thing about his being away was that she didn't need to fear him losing his temper. Her mother had been right when she'd declared that one punch was one too many and told Flora she could do so much better than Bill. But Mary didn't understand how much his old injury dictated the rhythm of their lives together. Some days, Bill's pain got the better of him and made him short-tempered and edgy, but under it all, Flora knew that he loved her. He was jealous of anybody who gave her the eye, but it was only because his injury made him insecure.

Perhaps her mother was right that she would have been better off marrying Johnny Cowperthwaite. He was handsome, wealthy and he had always been kind to her. She also had slight feelings for him that she tried to bury in the past, but thoughts of him often returned a bit like Johnny when he thought the coast was clear of Bill. He would probably be showing his face once he heard that

Bill had gone to fight and she hoped that he would keep his feelings in check when he did.

'We've a good turnout tonight! Let's hope we can keep them all watered and fed,' Flora commented over her shoulder to May as she pulled a pint of the local brew.

'Half of them only come for the food. I bet some haven't even had their tea tonight,' May replied. She was arranging two platefuls of ham sandwiches on a tray along with sides of pickled onions. 'I'll tell them just two each, else they won't go round.' She lifted the tray high, balancing it carefully as she threaded her way between tables. The pub was crowded with local men in their shirtsleeves, smelling of carbolic soap and freshly shaven for the match. It was the highlight of their week.

'It'll have to be egg sandwiches next time, so they'd better make the most of what they get,' Flora called after her, handing the pint across the bar to a customer.

'A right good pork pie, a belly buster. That's what we want when we play doms,' the man told her as he paid.

'That's what I'd like to give you. You'll have to complain to Churchill and Hitler.'

He grinned, taking a quick drink from his pint before returning to his table. Everybody was in the same boat, but she heard plenty of complaints in the pub, especially as the night wore on and drink got the better of some of them.

'Never mind, lass, we know you're doing your best. You always make us welcome and the company is always good. You could serve us dandelion and burdock and some of us wouldn't complain,' Frank Capstick said as he looked up from the winning row of dominoes in his hand.

'That'd make Moaning Rawlinson happy. He'd leave you alone if nowt else, Flo.' Frank's dominoes partner winked at the landlady with more problems than most.

'Aye, you could put up with his excellent company instead of ours. You'd get no lip off him, just a list of who had died that day and how he'd told them up the Mains to keep their curtains closed. Just what you need while your fella's away!' Frank shouted across the room, and there was a general burst of laughter.

'You'll not be laughing if I do run out of beer. Anyway, it'll be cream soda I'll order in. Make you all look like proper men, drinking your pop with a straw,' Flora teased.

'Tha'd better not, else we'll be off into Settle for a pint,' Frank quickly replied.

'The day I run out of beer will be the day I close. So don't you fret, Frank – like you said this afternoon, if things do get bad, I can always start brewing my own.' Flora's comment was lost as Tom, who lived next door, shouted to her through the pub's open doors. He came red-faced and excited into the bar, pushing past the dominoes players.

'Flora, Flora, put your transistor on – listen to the news from London. Everybody, our lads and the Poles, they've gone and sunk the *Bismarck*! The bloody *Bismarck*! That serves the Jerries right for sinking the *Hood* – the bastards should have known we would get them back!'

There was a lull in the noise of the bar as they heard

him out, and then a cheer went up as the news sank in: the pride of the German fleet had been sunk.

'Go get the wireless, then! Let's be hearing the news! The dominoes can wait,' Frank said, and they all waited and watched as Flora brought in the heavy wooden radio and placed it on the bar. She switched it on, tuning in to the Home Service. The whole bar listened as the announcer's voice, suitably grave but with a note of optimism, confirmed that the mighty *Bismarck* had been destroyed earlier that morning, the twenty-seventh of May, three hundred miles from the port of Brest. There had been a terrifying sea battle involving British destroyers with air support from the RAF – HMS *Dorchester*, *Norfolk* and *Mashona* had taken part, along with others. They had not escaped totally without damage and would all be returning to port.

'The *Mashona*, Lottie Taylor's lad is on that'en. Let's hope that he's safe. He'll have some tale to tell when he comes home.' Frank Capstick got to his feet with his pint glass in his hand. 'A toast to our brave lads, at sea and in the air! We'll show these bloody Jerries!'

The room erupted in cheers as Flora switched off the radio and carried it back to her kitchen. Behind her, a chorus of voices launched into 'There'll Always Be An England', echoing around the walls of the seventeenth-century inn.

There would always be an England, she thought; but at what cost? The *Bismarck* might have sunk, but lives would have been lost on both sides, and that was nowt to be celebrated.

Chapter 3

It was market day, and Madge Capstick and Jenny Moon were walking up the steep incline of Belle Hill out of Giggleswick, heading for the adjoining town of Settle – a busy, thriving place full of shops stocking local produce. There was a good street market on Tuesdays and Saturdays along with seasonal fairs at Christmas and in autumn, when sheep, cattle and geese were sold. Settle was the central hub for locals to come and exchange news and gossip, catching up over a cup of tea.

'Did you hear the racket coming out of the Cunning Vixen last night? It'll always be like that now her husband has left. She won't give a damn how much noise is made or what time she closes,' Jenny complained as they paused to catch their breath after reaching the main road. She folded her arms, still holding onto her shopping basket and handbag, as they looked across at the white limestone outcrop of Castleberg Crag.

'Aye, Frank didn't come home until nearly one. What

a state he was in! It was two steps forward and three steps back. He fell climbing up the stairs to bed and swore at me when I told him to be quiet. I told him I'd not be putting up with him coming home many nights like that.' Madge, plump and rosy-cheeked, pulled a face at thin, tight-lipped Jenny. 'You don't know how lucky you are to be living on your own. If he's not in the pub, he's in his garden and brings back mud on his wellies all over my kitchen floor. I swear one day I'll show him the door.'

'You've been saying that since the day you got married forty-odd years ago. I think he knows he's safe,' Jenny replied. 'They can't help it, you know. Men are the weaker sex. That's why I never wed. You wouldn't get me putting up with snoring, drinking and moaning at everything. I'm content with my cat. She does what she wants, and I do what I want.' They moved on again, crossing the bridge that led out of the valley and into Settle. '. . . Oh, look at them ducklings. They'll get washed away in the first flood if their mother doesn't look after them.'

Jenny never saw the positive side of anything, and Madge knew it.

'To be honest, and to give Flora her due, it was dominoes night, and the fellas were celebrating the sinking of the *Bismarck*. Now, that is a thing to celebrate, taking out Germany's biggest destroyer, so I couldn't get that annoyed . . . Besides, Frank says she's struggling to get beer supplies. And we wouldn't want the pub to close,' Madge said, with an eye on Jenny's expression.

'A woman on her own in a pub is bad news. Fellas

will be going there for other things besides a pint. Especially with her; she's not exactly a shrinking violet,' Jenny snapped.

'She's a bonny woman. I often look at her and think that. She's keeping her age well,' Madge said quietly, not wanting to admit that she quite admired Flora Whitaker. Flora had the perfect figure, with long auburn hair and a complexion any woman would die for.

'It's war paint that keeps her looking young. I'd like to see what she really looks like first thing in the morning.' Jenny surveyed the busy market square, with its houses built of local stone. A three-storey building called The Shambles dominated the square, as it had ever since the eighteenth century. Local traders sold their wares in the shops and lived in small homes on the upper level.

'Eh up, the vegetable stall's here. Not that he'll have a lot on it – he never does nowadays. No fish man and no shoe stall; I don't know why we've bothered walking up into town.'

'Well, I need some meat from the butcher's, and there's already a queue. Frank will be upset if he doesn't get his weekly sausage. You get nowt, or hardly anything, with these ration coupons as it is,' Madge said, looking up the square past the Shambles.

'He'll get plenty of sausage if he goes to that Flora's. You'll have to watch him, Madge,' Jenny said, folding her arms even tighter.

'Jenny Moon, what a thing to say! Flora's not like that. And Frank is old enough to be her father.'

'I tell you, she's a woman on her own, and there's

many a good tune played on an old fiddle. So I'm told,' Jenny added quickly.

They joined a queue of local women outside the butchers. Several nodded their heads in recognition or wished them good morning.

'Remember that woman who ran the Cunning Vixen before?' Jenny went on. 'She took it over when Jonty Parkinson left. A blonde-haired woman. She was good-looking and all.'

'Was she called Margaret? Maureen? It was something along those lines.' They moved up the queue, Madge wishing that Jenny would change the subject.

'Maisy Walker. She had every man eating out of her hand and all their wives wishing she would go back to wherever she'd come from. She ran it more like a brothel, I'm sure. She didn't last long anyway, if I remember rightly. Everyone woke up one morning to find she'd done a moonlight flit.'

'Flora's not like that. She's a local lass. I always thought she would marry Johnny Cowperthwaite, until Bill set his cap at her.' They had reached the shop doorway. Madge stepped inside and spotted a few remaining sausages on the counter. She hoped there would be four left for her to buy when her turn came.

'She'd have been better farming up a fell than leading the menfolk astray in our village.' They watched the last piece of scrag end being chosen and wrapped for a customer, and Jenny sighed.

Madge had heard enough. 'Will you leave her be? She's all right, that lass. I don't know why you're so concerned anyway, Jenny. It's not like you have a fella, or want one.' She stepped forward with a smile for the young butcher's lad, passed him her ration coupon book and snapped up the last four sausages.

'Eh, I fancied one of them,' Jenny protested.

'Well, after all that's been said, I'm not sharing them with you. You'll have to make do with some of that cooked tongue. Yours has done enough clacking this morning.' Madge tucked the sausages safely into her basket. 'I'd shop more at our butcher's in Giggleswick, but they never have much on offer at the moment. Plenty of rabbits that the local lads have poached.' She looked at Jenny's disappointed face and sighed. 'I'll treat you to a drink of tea in the Naked Man after I've got some apples from the market. I don't suppose he'll have any oranges or bananas – I miss both so much since this war started.'

Jenny pointed to the piece of oxtail and waited for it to be wrapped. 'You cheeky devil, Madge. I'll make do with mutton. At least with living in the Dales, we don't go short of that. I'll get an onion and put it on the stovetop and it'll last me two or three days.' She looked at her friend. 'A cup of tea will be grand, and if you are paying, even better.'

'I'll pay, and then we will get back – Frank will be wanting his dinner, because he'd never think of making himself something to eat. He'd starve first.'

'You spoil that man of yours,' Jenny said as she tucked her meat into her basket. 'You get the tea, and I'll run to buy us a biscuit – that is, if they have any. Nobody has anything nowadays, except those who have connections. I bet that Flora is one of those sorts.'

'Jenny, not another word about Flora, else you'll be walking home on your own! She's only trying to make a living.'

Madge headed for the vegetable stall, with its attempt at a good show of fruit and vegetables. Potatoes, turnips and onions were in plentiful supply, but when it came to the fruit, only apples were available.

'Oh, there are only apples? Well, I'll take four and make do with them. They look sour an' all.'

'Best apples in Yorkshire, these are, missus. Not a bit sour.' The lad on the stall placed four apples into a bag and twisted the corners to seal it before passing it to her.

'I'll take your word for it, but I'll not be back for more if they are. Come on, Jenny, a tea; and let's watch the world go by looking out of the Naked Man's window. There's not much more to do at our age.'

'Aye, a warm-up. It might be the end of May, but that wind has a chill to it and I'm fair gasping.' Jenny put her arm through her best friend's as they passed various stalls and said good morning to the people they knew.

They entered a long, low-set whitewashed building with a stone carving of a naked man above the doorway, his private parts covered by a plaque engraved with the date of the building's construction. It had originally been a coaching inn, but now it was tea rooms and a popular spot with locals. The bell above the door jingled as Jenny and Madge went in, and they scanned the space looking for a free table as a waitress approached, dressed in black with a frilly white apron. She led them to a spot overlooking the square.

'Two teas, please. And have you any biscuits?' Madge looked up hopefully at the waitress.

'We only have oatcakes today. Or I could make you a toasted teacake?' The girl smiled apologetically. Everyone was missing the staples that had been so abundant before the war. 'Oh, and I'm afraid we have no sugar for your tea.'

'How about we share a teacake, Madge? Half each will just do before we walk home.' Madge nodded in agreement. 'A teacake it is, then. And it's a good job we're both sweet enough and don't need any sugar.' Jenny set her handbag down beside her chair and looked out of the window. 'What's that they're doing over on the Shambles? Looks as if they're putting up a banner.' She glared across at the balcony opposite, where three men on ladders were struggling to secure a large banner between the upper-storey living quarters and the shops below.

The two women peered out, reading the sign as it went up.

'Oh, my Lord,' Jenny said disapprovingly as the lettering became visible. 'That's all we need to look at while we try to forget the troubles of the world.'

Madge shook her head, smiling. The banner read, 'HELP PUT THE LID ON HITLER BY SAVING YOUR OLD METAL AND PAPER'. In one corner, a cartoon Hitler was being squashed by a dustbin lid.

'I've heard there's going to be a fundraiser for Settle to build their battleship destroyer. It'll be to help with that,' Madge said. 'We should help if we can – I know our knitting helps the soldiers, but we never think of those at sea. I hope Lottie Taylor's son is all right. He was in the thick of it yesterday when the *Bismarck* went down, I believe.'

The waitress arrived with their cups of tea and the toasted teacake, and Madge thanked her.

'Perhaps we should call by on our way home and ask,' Jenny suggested. She reached for the larger piece of teacake and put it on her plate.

'We could, but she'll not know anything yet that we don't know. It takes a while to get the news back home, and even then it's classified. We'd best not bother today. There's more worrying news closer to home. I hear that we have some Italian prisoners of war going to be staying at Whitefriars. As if we haven't enough round here, with the German POWs working at the quarry at Horton-in-Ribblesdale! It's only a few miles away.' Madge shook her head as she sipped her tea.

'More foreigners in Settle! Well, just as long as they don't come into Giggleswick – we are a civilized part of the world. That Flora Whitaker would be the first to make them welcome, I bet. Especially the Italians; although even I think they are handsome.'

'There may be hope for you yet, Jenny Moon. Sixty-one and single, but you never know. A lonely Italian, far from home . . .' Madge teased.

'Don't talk nonsense, Madge Capstick. I'll be old enough to be their mother.' Jenny blushed and, for once, went quiet as she sipped her tea.

'Talk of the devil – that's Flora just come out of the paper shop. See, now she's talking to the man on the veg stall. She's smiling, anyway; so she must not be missing her Bill that much,' Madge commented. They both turned their heads to watch as the young woman made her way across the market square.

'No, she'll not be missing him,' Jenny said. 'I tell you, if I know her, she'll make the most of him not being at home. And as for her mother – well, don't get me started.'

Madge looked across at her friend. If not for the fact that Jenny had a heart of gold beneath her hard face and gossipy manner, she would not have been sitting with her. As it was, she knew that if she ever had a crisis, Jenny would be the first to help – even if that was partly because she was so nosy and needed to know everything that happened in their part of the world.

'Frank, I'm home. And I have some sausages for supper tonight,' Madge called as she opened her front door.

Silence greeted her as she came through into the kitchen. She put the sausages away in the larder and then, placing the apples in the fruit bowl, she spotted a note in Frank's scrawling handwriting on the kitchen table.

Just gone round the pub to see Flora. Won't be long.

Madge shook her head. He'd better not be long, else there would be questions asked, that was for sure.

Chapter 4

Flora stood in her kitchen and leaned back against the stone sink, assessing the few heads of lettuce Frank had brought her. They were small but fresh. She would be able to use them in something, either a salad or perhaps mixed with egg – that would make a good light sandwich, she thought. She turned her head as May came down the stairs after cleaning her bedroom.

'May – this might have been a bit rash, but I've just walked up Settle and posted an advertisement in the newsagent's, Lambert's, to let out my double bedroom. I thought while Bill is away, I could take in a lodger, and I can make do up in the attic bedroom. I'm not fussy about where I sleep. It'll mean more work, but it will bring in more money at the same time. Plus, with a lodger comes his or her ration book, which will help.' Flora had thought about it all night, tossing and turning, wondering if she was doing the right thing. She needed money if she was to continue in the Cunning

Vixen, and this was just one of the ways she'd figured on doing so.

'Oh, you should've said – I'll go and dust and make up that spare bed. Will you be all right up there? It's only small, and it'll be freezing in winter . . .' May started to turn back up the stairs.

'No need to go this morning. It's nearly opening time, and I'll have to clear out our things from the wardrobe and drawers. Anyway, I don't suppose there will be any interest for a while. Settle and Giggleswick are not exactly thronged with visitors at the moment.' She crossed over to the table and sat down with a sigh. 'I just thought it would help cover the bills. The cost of beer keeps going up because the brewers are supporting the government with extra tax for the war, but that doesn't help me. Or my drinkers! One of the regulars came in the other day, plonked a sixpence on the counter and asked for a pint o' mild and an ounce of twist. Then he just looked down at the sixpence and said, "Lord, I'm being hopeful and living in the past. You'll need at least another three pence now that mild's five pence a pint." I even apologized to him! I felt like I was robbing him – but I had to get my money back. It's the duty payable on beer. It's filling the war chest, because they know folk want to drown their worries in wartime.'

'Oh, Flora. I wish I could help; you sound so worried. You work hard enough without having to leave the comfort of your bedroom. I'll go and see to it now, and don't worry, it'll only take ten minutes to sort it. You never know, you might find a lodger for this coming weekend.' May scooted back upstairs quickly and opened the door to the very top bedroom, directly under the roof. In summer it was lovely and warm, with the sun shining in through the skylight, but in winter the door was always closed as the cold air could be felt all through the pub if left open. It was no place for the landlady to sleep, May thought as she opened the bedding box at the foot of the bed and started to make up the bed. She dusted quickly round the room, knocking cobwebs away from the skylight window.

Downstairs, Flora went through to the bar and began setting things up as she listened to May moving furniture about. She didn't want to leave her bedroom, but if it would bring in more income, she'd have to do it. When and if Bill returned home for a brief spell, they could have the big bed if nobody was lodging; and if she did let the room out, then it went without saying Bill could have the single bed. She would sleep where she could. With all the young men away fighting, custom was low except for the ones who liked to discuss politics and the state of things as they drank their pint.

Someone knocked loudly on the pub's front door. Flora glanced at the clock – eleven forty-five. Somebody was eager for their midday pint.

'You're early; we're not open yet,' she called out. However, the knocking continued, even harder this time. Then a man's voice shouted her name.

'Mrs Flora Whitaker, kindly open the door. This is Richard Brown from the Home Office. I have come to inspect your premises after you failed to complete the form that was sent over a year ago. Open up now!'

Flora's stomach churned. What form was he on about? There had been so many new rules and regulations with the outbreak of war, she hadn't been able to keep up with them all.

'Coming, sir, right away!' Flora hurried over, patting her hair into place, and unlocked the door. She pulled it open to reveal a short, stout man wearing a bowler hat and carrying a briefcase.

'Well, at least you're keeping to the opening time. And, I hope, closing times,' he remarked, peering at her over the top of his spectacles.

'We are indeed. And as you can see, we have our windows taped in case of bombs and have everything else in place, I hope. Not that they're likely to be bombing in this area,' Flora added hastily.

'I'm afraid, Mrs Whitaker, we are not in control of whom Hitler chooses to bomb, and it is exactly that which I have come about. You have failed to reply to our letter detailing the necessary precautions in case of an air raid. It was sent in October 1939 – I think we have allowed you more than enough time to reply.' Mr Brown wore a self-satisfied expression as he passed Flora a copy of the letter.

Flora took it and scanned it quickly. She couldn't recall ever having seen it before. She took a deep breath and re-read the instructions more closely.

No more customers should be admitted into the pub when air-raid sirens sound.

Customers living or working within an easy distance should be advised to leave at once for their homes or places of business.

For the remaining customers, full use should be made of any suitable cellar accommodation.

Brown was peering around the interior of the small, homely pub. He puffed out his chest as Flora looked up at him. 'You will see that in light of your cellar perhaps not being suitable, we should have been asked to inspect.'

'But there was no reason for me to reply. I do have a suitable cellar for anybody who needs to shelter, not that it will hold many or that I'll ever need to use it. This is the Dales, not central London in the middle of the Blitz.' Flora shook her head. 'You're welcome to have a look down there.'

She led him behind the bar and lifted a large wooden hatch in the floor to show him the steps down into the cellar.

'No – I see that there is no need,' Richard Brown said as he looked at the steep, narrow stairs and thought better of inspecting them. 'However, there is another point you may need to address. Do you have separate accommodation for officers to drink away from the men? They really should not take their refreshments together.' He stood at the bar and gazed around him.

'We don't have many military men here, Mr Brown. And those we do see are local lads who'd want to mix with their mates on a visit home, no matter whether they're officers or not. But if they are that much up their own arses, they can sit and drink in the snug if that will keep your lot happy.' Flora was starting to lose patience with the jobsworth Home Office man. She pointed towards a small room at the very rear of the pub.

'Now, there's no need for you to take that attitude, Mrs Whitaker. I'm only doing my job.' Brown snapped his briefcase shut and tucked it under his arm as he made for the open pub door.

'Are you going now? Perhaps you could answer me this before you leave.' Flora followed him round the end of the bar. 'Why is it that Lord Woolton has agreed to supply over a thousand British restaurants with good, cheap meat, yet overlooked the supply to pubs? How are we supposed to make a living by offering our customers nothing but a pickled egg now and again? We don't get any preference or extra rations to help us cope with the way the price of beer is rocketing.' She restrained herself with an effort, although there was much more she would have liked to say.

'That is not my department, Mrs Whitaker, and nor is it my concern. Now, I must bid you good day – I have to be in Settle by twelve thirty.'

Flora stood in the doorway and watched as the bureaucrat made his way up Belle Hill. She swore under her breath. He really had no idea about the realities of life in a village pub.

'What was that about?' May asked as she came into the bar, noticing Flora's flushed cheeks.

'Just a fella from the ministry, trying to make life even harder for us publicans. It was all about nowt, really. He needn't have shown his ugly face.' Flora sighed. 'I don't know, May. With Bill gone, I'm almost tempted to sell up; but I love this place. I love the smell of the hops from the beer, the smell of tobacco and the banter between drinkers. I'd never admit that to my customers, though.' She opened the pub doors wide and stepped out to look down the winding village street. 'Eh up, it's starting to rain. I hope that Mr Brown gets sodden on his walk into Settle – it would serve him right, the busybody. There's my Bill going to fight for his country once more, and this fella will be getting paid twice as much for doing sweet Fanny Adams.'

'Don't you give in, Flora. Everybody loves having you run the Cunning Vixen. It wouldn't be the same without you, or Bill. If you do get a lodger, things will be better. I've cleaned the top bedroom and made the spare bed up. You never know – by the time you close, you could have someone living with you,' May said optimistically.

'I don't want anyone, May, but they would be a help. That reminds me, I'll need to put the details up on that noticeboard by the river. People often stop there; somebody might be interested.'

'I'll put it up for you when I go home. It's not far out of my way.' May took the card Flora had written out and read it. 'I hope you get somebody nice, else they could spoil your life with the Vixen only being small.'

'Well, hopefully they'll be at work most of the day. They can come down to the bar to eat and then go back to their room. I don't aim to share my small living room with them. I've put the rent as "to be discussed", so I'll have some room to negotiate. And at least it's summer, so they can go for a walk in the evening if they don't want to listen to the locals downstairs.' Flora had thought it all through. She had no intention of getting too friendly with any potential lodger. 'Besides, I may get someone who just needs a night or two and doesn't stay for any length of time. We'll just have to see who turns up.'

May nodded. She was thinking about how Flora's plan would change the daily routine at the Cunning Vixen. There would be a breakfast to make every morning, a bedroom to clean daily and an evening meal. She hoped Flora had thought about all of that. The Hart's Head on the old toll road that ran just above Giggleswick had plenty of rooms and staff, and most of its customers were passing travellers. It was a large place with an established reputation for taking in lodgers. The Cunning Vixen had never done that, so this was a whole new game for Flora.

'Right; I'll be on my way, then. I'll see you again in the morning. I take it you won't be needing me until Friday night as usual?' May said as she put the advertisement into her pocket. She picked up two drawing pins from the bar to secure it on the notice board.

'Yes, Friday night, if that's all right. It'll be quiet for the rest of the week until then. That will give me a chance to move things out of my bedroom. I might even close all day tomorrow – it's starting to be so quiet,' Flora replied. She saw one of her regulars coming in and knew automatically what he'd be asking for: a half of mild and a pickled egg. He would make both last at least an hour before wandering home.

'Things must be bad,' May replied, winking at Flora. 'He'll make you a fortune this afternoon.'

'Shh, cheeky. See you in the morning.' Flora smiled as

she went behind the bar and greeted her customer, asking if he'd like the usual as he fumbled in his pocket for his change.

It was raining lightly as May left the Cunning Vixen. She hadn't brought a coat, so she decided to go home before walking the few yards in the opposite direction to the noticeboard. She lived on Back Fold, a row of six little cottages near the church, and her father ran a carpenter's shop attached to their cottage. The buildings were old and in need of some renovation, but the place was home to May and her close-knit family. She ran the last few steps to the front door with her cardigan over her head to protect her hair. In the joinery doorway she could see her father sitting, carving wooden teeth for hay rakes. There would be a rush on them from local farmers as haytime approached.

'It's a wet'en, lass. You want to get yourself in and dry before you get a cold,' Harold Lambert said, glancing up at his daughter.

'It is, Father. I was supposed to put up this advertisement for Flora, but I'll do it later.' May stepped into his workshop and fished the card out of her pocket.

'Oh, aye, what's she advertising?' Harold asked as he deftly picked up smoothed, carved pegs of wood and hammered them into the rake head one by one.

'A room. She's letting out her bedroom and going to be sleeping in the small attic bedroom. I think times are hard for her,' May said, watching as her father assessed the finished rake before turning to add it to a pile of completed ones in a shadowy corner.

'Aye, she will be. It's to be hoped that Bill doesn't come back and play hell with her. He goes to war and she lets his bedroom out – now, that will give the local gossips something to talk about. They never leave her alone as it is.'

'I don't know why. If they knew her like I do, they'd know she's not got a bad bone in her body. She'll do anything for anybody.' May sighed as she stood in the joinery shop, which she loved. The smell of wood, and the soothing sounds of her father turning or sanding each item, had always been part of her life; and she loved her father. He was kind and forgiving and an easy-going man. Too easy-going, her mother often said, when he didn't chase bills that needed paying.

'Happen that's the trouble, lass. All the fellas round here go and share their worries with her, and their wives know they do. No woman ever likes a landlady. They know too many secrets, and they sell drink.' Harold smiled at his daughter. 'Come on, let's see what your mother's made for dinner. If it's bread and dripping again, I might have to say something.'

'You wouldn't dare, Father.' May grinned.

'Tha's right, I wouldn't bloody dare, it's more than my life's worth. Your mother's got a fair tongue on her when she lets rip. It's better to keep your head down and get on with what you're doing – and in my case, hide in the joinery.'

They walked into the low-set kitchen of number six, Back Fold. Betty Lambert was doing the ironing, and the place was warm and welcoming.

'I've had a busy morning, so you'll have to make do with what's on the table for your dinners,' Betty said sharply as she set the iron upright and began folding a crisp, sweet-smelling sheet. 'May, you brew up. There's bread and dripping and a bannock that I made when I baked on Friday. That should do you both, because there's not a lot of anything else.' She saw Harold and May exchange a grin.

'Well, I'm glad you two have got something to smile about, because I can't think of owt at the moment.' Betty shook her head. Her daughter and husband had always been close. Sometimes she thought they hardly needed her there.

'Thanks, Mother, that'll do just grand,' Harold said, winking at his daughter. It was better to keep his mouth closed than cause an upset. Bread and dripping it would have to be.

Chapter 5

'You can put the washing away after you've had your dinner and tidy the shed out, seeing it's raining. I'm sure I saw a mouse looking at me from behind one of your father's sacks of rubbish. I always said we needed a cat.' Betty folded the wooden ironing board and carried it back into the cupboard under the stairs.

'We don't need a cat, Mother. Next door has one. I'm forever chasing it off my garden, and it catches all my birds. I'll shoot the damn thing one day if it chases my pet robin.' Harold had waged war many a time with the striped tabby; it left deposits in his vegetable beds and was often seen with a mouthful of feathers. He hated cats.

'They keep the vermin down. I'll not have mice in the house,' Betty replied as she cleared the dirty pots off the table.

'We could always have a dog. I'd like a dog, it would be company.' May looked hopefully up at her mother, who put her hands to her hips and scowled.

'Oh, aye, and who would walk it? Your father's always working, you spend half your life at the Vixen, and I've enough on my hands. Besides, another few months and you'll be courting and have no time for anything.' Betty nodded firmly to her daughter. May had grown up into a good-looking young woman. If most of the village's young men weren't away fighting, they'd be knocking on the door; of that she was sure.

'That's a fine idea, Mam, but all the lads round here have gone to war. And I'm not looking at anyone from Giggleswick School – they're far too posh for me. Plus, a lot of them keep going to fight as well.' May pulled a face as she pushed her chair back, then scooped up her mother's ironing pile and carried it upstairs to put away.

'Aye, Mother, she does her best,' Harold said softly to his wife. 'You'd be lost without her, and hopefully a lad will come along. There's no need for her to rush into anything. She's still a baby.' He looked across at Betty. She had been so beautiful when they'd first married, but life was starting to carve its lines onto her face, and her temper had gradually worsened over the years. No matter how much work he did, it never seemed to be enough.

Betty sighed. 'I know Flora's a grand lass, despite what some folk think of her. But the Cunning Vixen is nothing but a drinking hole. If our May could get a job up at the Hart's Head on the Kendal road, maybe she'd come across somebody a bit more respectable.'

'Now, Mother, everybody is respectable that drinks in the Vixen. We're a village of decent people, although there's nobody in Giggleswick that isn't short of a bob or two. Some may be working class, but money isn't everything. You should remember that,' Harold replied, and immediately regretted it.

'Well, Harold Lambert, I don't see any fortune in this house. A rented two-bedroom cottage, and not enough money to keep the wolf from the door! My mother always said I should have married somebody better. I want our May to do well for herself and get a man that has brass, and works,' Betty spat.

'By, you're a hard woman, Betty. I work every day, and I easily give you enough brass to keep our family fed and shod.' Harold, for once, didn't hold back with his words. 'Perhaps I should have listened to my father. He said, "Look at her mother, and that's what she'll be like in twenty years." And by God, he was right, and the rest. Your mother was an old devil who never had enough money either. Our May will find somebody, but it won't be his money that takes her eye, that I'm sure about.' He pushed back his chair and stood up. 'I'm off next door to my joinery where I can get some peace. And make some money, no matter what you say.' He strode to the front door and slammed it behind him, making the cottage shake.

'Aye, bugger off to your joinery! You might as well live there!' Betty shouted after him. She sat down heavily at the table, shaking with temper and upset, and buried her face in a tea-towel as May came quietly down the stairs.

'Are you all right, Mam?' May asked cautiously. Rows were not unusual in the Lambert household. She didn't know why her parents kept together, she thought as she sat down next to her mother. Perhaps if there wasn't such a stigma against divorce, they would have parted; but they always showed a united front in public. All was apparently well in the joiner's household, even if their next-door neighbours knew differently.

'Oh, May. Sometimes I could honestly walk out and leave your father. He takes his time over everything, never worries about bills or how we are going to eat. He may be busy, but he never chases people for payment.' Betty sighed. 'The pile of hay rakes he's making will all be sold but not paid for, he'll let the farmers take them and then say, "Aye, pay me when you're ready," as if we can do without the money.'

'Oh, Mam. He's just kind-hearted and knows that some can't pay there and then. You're right, he could do with being a bit more businesslike. But we aren't that hard up, are we? We never seem to go without anything?' May asked.

'No; but we should be doing better than we are. I'd like a grander house, like Rose Cottage further up the village. A nice settee, and chairs, and just a treat occasionally. Your father thinks he's treated me if he buys three kippers from off Settle market. He has no idea.' Betty looked across at her daughter and tried to smile. 'That's why I want so much more for you. I don't want you to waste your life as a cleaner in the village pub – I want you to have a better life, to be properly looked after and cared for.' She reached for May's hand.

'I'm happy doing what I'm doing, Mam. I don't want

a man yet. And as for working at the Hart's Head – I'd rather work for Flora. She's more like a friend to me than an employer.' May paused for a moment, thinking. 'What if I looked after Father's accounts? I could send his bills out for him. I know he hates paperwork, and I don't mind doing it. I've heard him moaning when he has to tackle it. If I took that over, he'd get his payments in quicker.' She looked out of the window. It had stopped raining, so she would go and put up Flora's advertisement and speak to her father before tackling the outside shed.

'You, do the accounts? Even if I don't touch them, he won't let me near them!' Betty half laughed. 'It would mean I'd know how much he makes, and he wouldn't have that.'

'Then that's all the more reason for me to take them on. I've got time between my shifts at the Vixen. I'd enjoy it – I'd be part of the family firm then, even though I'm not a lad.' May got up from the table. 'I've got to go put up a card for Flora on the noticeboard. I'll ask him on my way back, and then I'll tidy the shed for you. Anything to spare us some rows between the two of you.'

Betty watched her daughter walk to the cottage door. 'I'm sorry, May. I do love your father, and we only want the best for you . . . I worry so.'

'Well, stop it! We are not destitute, and when I want a man, I'll find one.'

May stepped out into the sunshine, closing the door behind her. The fresh smell of recent rain and the warmth of the sun felt good as she headed up the road towards the noticeboard beside Tems Beck. Once she'd pinned up

Flora's advertisement, she paused on the old bridge made of huge sheets of slate and looked down at the water-crowfoot that was just starting to bloom in the gently flowing stream.

The village was beautiful. She loved it, and she knew everybody who lived there. Giggleswick School, along with its houses and the copper-domed chapel high on the hill, had brought it fame, but the village itself was like any other in the Dales: cottages made from local stone along a main street, a few shops and businesses, a primary school for the local children. And an ancient Norman church – St Alkelda's. The village got its name from the old Norse name for a local farm, Ghigel, and *wick*, which meant village. A schoolteacher had told May that when she was very young, and she had never forgotten. To May, it was home, and she would never want to leave it – not even if a millionaire were to enter into her life. Unlike her mother, she liked the simple life. She could sympathize with her father.

She sighed and could have cried quite easily if it hadn't been for a group of young Giggleswick schoolboys passing nearby with their master. Her mother and father were always arguing, and to be honest, they were each as bad as the other when it came to being stubborn-headed. She breathed in and watched the group wend their way up towards the long Victorian building of Cattrall Hall, returning to their schooling. They were mostly privileged children from wealthy families, although some were local children who were exceptionally bright. Their parents were happy to pay for an education, whereas May had just attended the village primary school. But that made no difference to her, she thought as she turned homewards; she was bright enough. It was time to tackle her father over his accounts.

'It's a bit happier now, May,' Harold greeted her. 'I'm just going up to repair a window in Settle. You can tell that mother of yours I'll be back about six. That might give her time to cool her head.' He picked up his bag of tools.

'I'll tell her. But first, can I have a word with you, Father?' May had never dared talk to either of her parents about their problems, and she felt quite awkward as she plucked up the courage to continue. 'You know Mam only gets annoyed because she thinks you don't watch your accounts, or chase people when they owe you money . . .' She watched as her father turned back from the doorway to face her, setting the hessian workbag down again.

'She'll never be happy, lass. She always wants more than I can give her. Besides, it isn't right that I chase my customers for payment. Some of them are a lot worse off than us.' He sighed. 'Anyway, paperwork isn't my favourite. I send out what I can once a month, and we're not going that short.'

'Well, I thought I could help you both, if you'll let me. I don't mind, and I don't work full time at the pub. What if I were to sort out your invoices once a week? On a Monday, when my mother's doing the washing – and then she'll feel we're both working as hard as she is. She hates washing day, and to be honest, so do I. I'm always in her bad books when I come home from the Vixen.' May looked at her father hopefully. 'I could do them in your joinery, out of Mam's way.'

'Nay, they're complicated. You wouldn't be able to manage.' Harold shook his head. 'But I can see why you'd want to keep out of her way.'

'I'd be all right, Father. I was always good at sums,' May persisted. It would be to everyone's advantage if her father would only agree. 'At least, I can give it a try, and then Mam will think we are keeping on top of things.'

'I'll think about it. Now, you go and get that shed tidied for your mother, or else we'll both be in trouble. There's some rhubarb behind the shed, nearly ready. That would be grand stewed with a bit of custard tonight, but I daren't ask her.'

'I'll pull some and put it on to cook and cool for your tea. It won't want hardly any sugar, with it being new.' May smiled.

'Bloody hell, don't pinch her sugar, else we'll be shot at dawn,' Harold joked. He picked up the tools again and went off, whistling, down the village.

May watched him go. Doing the books and sending the bills out might just work – and at least it would get her mother off his back.

By Friday evening, the charged atmosphere at the Lamberts' cottage had dissipated. May left her parents in a more relaxed mood as she stepped out of the cottage on her way to help Flora behind the bar at the Cunning Vixen. Her father was reading the *Craven Herald and*

Pioneer, and her mother was embroidering a new tablecloth. Pulling the door closed behind her, May heard Harold exclaim in surprise at something in the 'hatches and despatches', as he called them; but she carried on to her work, not thinking any more about it until she reached the pub.

As Flora greeted her, May saw with surprise that she had been crying. 'Oh, May – it's going to be a sad night tonight. Folks are either going to drown their sorrows or go back to their other halves, thankful to be safe here in Giggleswick and not on the front line.' Flora was moving round the tables, setting out drinks coasters.

'Why? What's gone on?' May asked as she went behind the bar to put her small handbag away.

'Have you not seen the paper? Lottie Taylor's son, Richard, has been killed in action. He was on the *Mashona*, and it was bombed and sunk off the coast of Ireland. Oh, poor Lottie; I thought I hadn't seen her in the village this week. I must go and visit her in the morning.' Flora leaned against the bar for a moment and sighed.

'I went to school with Richard,' May said, shocked. 'He was in the class above me. He must only have been nineteen. He was such a nice lad, never had a bad word for anyone, unlike half the lads at school. Oh, the poor soul. His poor mother.' She dropped her head, thinking about the blond, rosy-cheeked lad who had always been kind to her. Before he joined the navy, she had nearly agreed to walk out with him. 'Poor Richard. He was a good lad.'

Frank Capstick heard her words as he entered the bar. 'Aye, he was a good lad. Those bloody Jerries were paying us back for sinking the *Bismarck*. Our lads were on their way back home to drydock after being damaged in the battle – they were sitting ducks. Bloody bastards. They couldn't even fight back.' Frank threw his cap down on a nearby table, marking where he intended to sit out the night. 'A pint, please, Flora. I might down a few more an' all by the time the night's out.'

'I don't think you'll be on your own, Frank. When one of us is kicked in this village, we all limp. Lottie will be in a right state. She's not long buried her husband after losing him in that accident at Horton Quarry, and now Richard.' Flora handed Frank's pint across the bar and waved away his money. 'Payment for the lettuce.'

'Oh, thanks, Flora. You'll get enough out of me tonight, and I bet you'll have a full house. Here's where we can all come to discuss things and have a moan. My Madge is with Lottie now. She thought she would try and bring her some comfort. It's the least we can do; she's a good woman. To make it even worse, she'll have heard that there are German prisoners of war doing her Larry's job now. You couldn't make it up. I hope they work the buggers to death.' Frank sounded bitter. Usually he hardly had a bad word to say about anyone, but tonight, as he sat down in the corner where he'd set his cap, anyone who knew him could see he wasn't in the best of moods. His face was dark with anger.

As more customers trickled steadily in, both the main room and the tap room filled up with debate over the war and angry words about the sinking of the *Mashona*. The war felt more personal with every loss of a local lad; Richard was not the first, but the outrage at losing him was fresh. The bar was thick with tobacco smoke and the smell of beer and whisky, and the temperature rose as the main door was closed with the coming of night. Flora pulled the blackout blinds tight before George Rawlinson could show his face and tell her how to run her business. The night was taken up with argument and discussion over how the government was handling things and where they were going wrong. Beer drinkers moved on to whisky, and by the time Flora shouted, 'Time, gentlemen, please,' there were a few regulars very much the worse for wear. At last they began to file out and head home, swearing and muttering, to their vexed wives.

'Any chance of a lock-in, just for an extra hour?' Graham Windle asked Flora, waving an almost-empty whisky glass.

'Now, Graham, what do you think? You should know better. Besides, PC Whinray will be doing the rounds about now, and it'd be just my luck to get caught. I can't afford to lose my licence.' Flora shook her head firmly, but she wished she could stay open; she was making good money. As Graham quickly drained his glass, all eyes turned to the main entrance, where an arm dressed in a blue uniform appeared.

'Evening, all. Just doing my rounds. Had a good night, have we, Flora? Looks like you've had a full house, and I've met a lot wandering their way home.'

'Yes, we've had a good night, thanks. May and I have been run off our feet. I've just shouted last orders.' She watched as Trevor Whinray took off his helmet and put it down on the nearest table, looking round at the familiar faces of her regulars.

'Did I hear somebody asking for a lock-in? Now, you should know better than that when I'm on my beat.' He grinned. 'Luckily for you, I've just finished my shift, and I'm bloody dying for a pint. It's been a right bad week so far, so I suggest we all have an odd'en before we go home.' Trevor glanced once more at the customers, who lifted their glasses to him and quietly cheered. Then he added, 'Just as long as George bloody Rawlinson doesn't find us. He's the biggest hypocrite I know. At least I know what you lot get up to. He's just plain sneaky. Now, what's everybody having? And fill 'em up, you two lasses. I've looked forward to this all day.'

Flora glanced at May. 'It's right, May – PC Whinray won't mind if you want to get home. I can serve until everybody's finished.' She glanced back at the copper for confirmation.

'Aye, you get off, May, so your father and mother won't worry. Not that you've far to go, but you're best at home.' Trevor set his freshly drawn pint down on the bar. 'In fact, I'll see you back. It's dark out there, and it's only a few yards. Come on, grab your bag and gas mask.'

May hesitated.

'Go on, you'll not get a better offer than that. Escorted to your door by our man in blue.' Flora winked reassuringly.

'All right, then. I wouldn't want my parents to think I'd been in trouble,' May said quietly.

'They won't even know I've seen you home if you don't tell them,' Trevor said. He waited for her at the door, and the drinkers watched as the two of them walked out into the night.

'Perhaps he's come for more than a late-night pint,' Robert Pitcher commented. 'Happen he's come a-courting. Now, is that going to be a good thing or a bad thing, if he's never going to be away from here?' He drank his pint back.

'Only time will tell, Robert, but I'd rather have him on our side than against us. He's eager for promotion, that one. And he knows everything about everybody.' Flora leaned on the bar. She was wondering the same as Robert. 'I'll just serve you with one more, and then that'll be that. You can never trust a copper.'

'Oh, bugger. I hope he doesn't know all we get up to, else we'll all be in the clink,' Robert said quietly, retreating into his corner. Trevor came back in and stood at the bar, making a note of all the faces drinking there. They were all locals, and he knew they were drowning their sorrows. If there was a death in the village, it hit hard; especially a young lad who'd been fighting for his country.

'Did you see May home safely?' Flora asked, trying not to show her discomfort at having a copper standing at her bar.

'I did. She's a grand lass. I didn't realize she was only eighteen; she looks older. Has she got a fella in tow?'

Trevor took a long sip, studying Flora's face. He noted the full whisky bottles behind her, barely visible at the far end of the bar in the darkness of some oak shelves.

'No, she's not courting. Nobody has caught her eye yet. She's a good lass, and bright – she needs to find somebody decent,' Flora replied. 'Thanks for letting everybody have an extra pint. Folk need it tonight, what with the bad news in the village. But I don't usually serve after time,' she added quietly.

She hoped everybody would drink up promptly and go home; she needed to get rid of Trevor Whinray. She stole another glance at the tall, dark-haired man with his darting eyes. She didn't like him, and it wasn't just that he was a copper. She didn't trust him as a person.

Trevor caught her eye with a knowing expression, and Flora realized instantly that he knew something different.

'Yes, she seems a pleasant lass. I'll have to come by more often. A good pint, a bonny lass and local talk – couldn't be better.' Trevor grinned as he noticed all the regulars swigging back what was left in their glasses. They didn't want to get Flora into his bad books – or let the local bobby into their conversation. 'Night, all. Take care out there,' he said, watching the pub gradually empty as the clock struck twelve.

'The witching hour. I'd better get back myself. Evening, Flora, and thanks for the pint. I don't think I paid you for it. I was in too much of a hurry to see the young lady home.'

'It's on the house, PC Whinray. My thanks to you for looking after us all.' Flora smiled, and underneath her smile she was glad that he was going. There were too many secrets to be heard across the bar, and he probably knew it. She hoped he would not become a regular in her pub.

Chapter 6

It had been after one o'clock by the time Flora finally got to bed. The following morning, she yawned and stretched over her brew at the kitchen table, still tired after tossing and turning in the attic for most of the night. She hoped tonight's customers wouldn't expect her to keep the same hours. One evening of everyone sharing their grief and anger was enough, especially with the local bobby having joined in.

Trevor Whinray was a right enough bloke, but nobody ever felt comfortable with a copper standing next to them – least of all Flora, who had one or two illegal dealings going on under everybody's noses. The most significant of these was the whisky everyone turned to when they needed to drown their sorrows. She acquired that through the local milkman, whose brother worked at Liverpool Docks and helped himself to the occasional crate when it came in. Why pay top price when she could buy it on the black market? It made sense, and if she didn't buy it, somebody else would. She might as well save some brass. It was the same when it came to tea, sugar, or whatever else he thought she would buy.

She hoped Robert had been wrong about Trevor having romance on his mind. He'd never be away from her pub if he'd decided to set his sights on May. She looked up at the kitchen clock. May would be in shortly to clean the bar, and she'd ask her what she thought. Then, while May was cleaning, Flora would walk through the village to visit Lottie Taylor and pay her respects. It was the least she could do.

Flora yawned and closed her eyes, wishing she could go back to bed for an hour; not that her bed in the attic room was very comfortable. The only good thing about it was that while she was lying there, she could see the stars through the skylight. She was dreading winter if she did find a lodger for her main room, although there'd been nobody showing interest as of yet.

'Caught you yawning! What time did you throw them all out, then?' May bustled into the kitchen through the open door. She was humming to herself as she sat down next to Flora and spotted the teapot filled with tea. She hoped Flora would pour her a cuppa, seeing it was in short supply at home.

'Not long after Trevor Whinray came back in from seeing you home. He took his time. Had a lot to say for himself, did he? Or did you help him catch a criminal or two on your few hundred yards back home?' Flora smiled as May blushed.

'No, we just sat on the bench next to the church and

talked. It was a warm night, and although he's a copper, he's quite good company. I've never really looked at him or talked to him before,' May said quietly. 'He couldn't have been that long. The bells were ringing eleven thirty as I got home.'

'He might have said goodbye to you then, but he didn't leave here until twelve along with the others, and then I had to have a quick tidy. Still, I'm not complaining; I made some money last night. It'll keep the wolf from the door for another week.' Flora smiled at May. 'Pour yourself a brew. I'm going to see Lottie Taylor while you clean. The poor woman – I would have gone to see her sooner if I'd known. I wonder how she'd feel about me setting up a charity box at the end of the bar in memory of Richard. She'll not have a lot of money, and it might be a way for my regulars to feel that they are helping; but I don't want to offend her. Perhaps I won't. People in Giggleswick are good, and they'll gather round and look after her.'

May reached for a teacup from the dresser and poured herself a cuppa, glancing up at Flora across the table.

'I'm sure she would appreciate every penny. Trevor says they haven't found Richard's body, which makes it worse; he must have gone down with the ship. He had called in to see her yesterday evening before he came in to us. That's why he needed a drink,' May replied. She took a long sip. The supply of tea never seemed to be an issue with Flora, but she wasn't going to ask why.

'Trevor, is it? You must have got on well last night. When you first walked out together, you looked as if you thought he might arrest you.' Flora pushed her chair back and got up to put her cup and plate in the sink. 'Will you be seeing him again?'

'Oh, I don't know about that – I think he only needed someone to talk to. He might be a copper, but he's still human,' said May.

'Aye; don't you forget that he is a copper. If you do walk out with him again, remember, what goes on in the Vixen stays in the Vixen. I don't want him snooping about my pub at all times of day and night. It puts the drinkers off.' Flora sighed. 'Now, I'd best be going – I won't be long. I'll be back in an hour.'

May watched her leave. She knew Flora didn't much like the idea of her talking with PC Whinray. However, it had only been a talk with a man she hadn't even looked at before; but she'd found him interesting. She hoped he would ask her to walk with him again.

Flora took the same route as she did to her mother's, heading towards Tems Street. There were two adjacent rows of cottages over that way: her mother lived in the older row, and Lottie Taylor was in the Victorian-built one just in front. There was only a pathway between them, and Flora thought her mother must have been among the first to hear about Richard's death; in fact, she was surprised Mary hadn't called into the pub to tell her about it. But that was just Mary – she never gossiped. She never thought of telling anybody anything if it did not suit her to do so.

Flora followed the stream until she reached the first

house in the row. The path ran directly in front of them, so you could see straight into the main living rooms, and Flora waved as she saw movement inside before she knocked on the front door. She didn't know exactly what she would say to Lottie. What could you say to someone who had just lost their only son? She waited as footsteps approached the door from inside and it opened.

'Oh, Lottie – I just thought I'd come and see if you're all right,' Flora blurted out before realizing that it was local gossip Jenny Moon standing in Lottie's doorway.

'Of course she's not all right. That's why I'm here. Somebody has to look after her,' Jenny replied with venom in her words.

'I know. That was a bit clumsy of me,' Flora acknowledged, but she glared at Jenny.

'Oh, Flora – it's so good of you to come round. Please do come in. Jenny, let Flora in, I'd like to talk to her,' Lottie Taylor said, coming up behind Jenny's shoulder. She managed a smile at Flora.

'I didn't know if you would be up to visitors or not, but when I heard the news, I had to come.' Flora stepped across the threshold and into a cosy front room dominated by an oak sideboard. On it stood a photograph of Richard in a silver frame.

'You can't stop the world from turning, Flora. But now I've lost my lad, I can't see the point of being on it.' Lottie sighed and wiped tears from her eyes.

'Now look what you've done. You've started her crying again,' Jenny Moon said sharply.

'It's all right, Jenny, I can't stop myself, but hadn't you

best be getting back home? I'm all right, I've got Flora for company for now, and then I could do with some time to myself.' Lottie looked at Jenny, who had been standing on her doorstep since first thing. No matter how low she was feeling, there was only so much of Jenny's company she needed.

'Are you sure? I can stop a while longer, even though you have company,' Jenny folded her arms and glared at Flora again.

'No, you're all right, Jenny, thank you. I don't know what I'd have done without you this morning. You made me breakfast and were a real comfort. But now, once Flora goes home, I'll try and have a nap. I'm not sleeping that well.' Lottie nodded at Flora and opened the door for Jenny to leave.

'As long as you're all right,' Jenny replied, making her way out. 'I'll be back tomorrow, and you know where I am if you need anything.'

'Yes, Jenny, thank you again. You have already done enough.' Lottie closed the door behind her, and Flora watched as the woman passed the window. 'Has she gone? I shouldn't be so ungrateful, but Jenny Moon is the last person you tell your worries to and cry your heart out with. She will have told half the village and added more to my worries every time she opens her mouth.' Lottie sighed and then sat down heavily in her armchair. 'It's good to see you, Flora, you did right to come around. Some don't know what to say to me, and then there's the Jennys of the world that need every detail.'

'Well, to be honest, I don't know what to say to you, Lottie. You must be broken-hearted. I don't know how you are coping.' Flora reached for Lottie's hand as she sat down across from her.

'It's the fact that I may never get his body back – that I can't bring him home, Flora. I hate the idea of him being down at the bottom of the Irish Sea with his shipmates. I keep looking at his photograph, so proud in his naval uniform. Little did he know it would be the death of him. All those lads that have died, all because of a madman who wants to rule the world. But why *my* lad, Flora?' Lottie's voice cracked into a sob, and Flora knelt beside her and held her tight. 'He should be here, in quiet Giggleswick . . . He should have got a job with a local builder, or a joiner, instead of going to sea.'

'Shhh . . . shhh,' Flora soothed her. 'He was doing what he wanted to do. I know that doesn't ease your pain, but we're all so proud of him. And grateful to him; and to you.' She wrapped her arms around Lottie and gazed across at the photo of the youthful sailor who was never to come home. Just how Lottie was going to live with her loss, she didn't know, but she knew one thing: this cottage in Giggleswick wasn't the only one in mourning. All over Europe, mothers were crying for their lost sons and wives for their husbands. Flora only hoped she wouldn't be one of them herself when Bill left the country to fight. '. . . We are all here for you, my love. If there's anything I can do, you just tell me.'

'I will, Flora. You're a good friend.' Lottie blew her nose and looked up at the woman Jenny had been calling fit to burn. Jenny never had a good word to say for anybody who didn't tow her line, but nine times out of ten she was wrong. Lottie drew a deep breath. 'If they do find my lad and bring him home, can I ask you to help arrange a bite to eat in his memory and a drink to his name? I know he used to sneak in and you'd serve him, even though he was that bit too young. But I also know that you served him just the one before sending him home.'

'Of course, Lottie, and I don't want a penny for it. It will be my privilege and my way of thanking your lad. Now, is there anything I can do for you just now? Anything at all?' Flora sat back down, but she kept hold of Lottie's hand.

'No, I'll be all right. I'm going to lie down on my bed and try to close my eyes and not think of my lad in that cold ocean. It is all I can think of.' Lottie breathed in deeply again and sighed. 'How's that husband of yours? I was surprised when he went and enlisted again. What about his back? He's always suffered from it – shouldn't he have stopped at home, seeing he'd already done his bit in the last war?'

'He never let on about it when he went to put his name down. They must not have checked his service records – or they're that desperate for men. When I get a moment to myself tomorrow, I'll write and see how he's getting on. I still can't quite forgive him for leaving me running the pub, but he's a patriotic soul, and there was no chance he was going to be happy just serving in the Home Guard.'

'You be proud of him, Flora, and God willing, he will

be safe wherever he goes. My late husband was in the last war, but mustard gas damaged his lungs. Then when he went back to work in the quarry – well, it just killed him. We women with husbands and families have to bear the worries of the world, you know. The likes of Jenny Moon know nothing; they just live for themselves. But I shouldn't speak ill of her. She means well.'

'She doesn't like me, of that I'm sure, and yet I've never done anything to harm her. She doesn't really know me at all.' Flora sighed. 'Has my mother been in to see you? I'm surprised she didn't come round to tell me your news. I heard it in the pub.'

'Your mother hasn't been in my house since the day your father died. I don't know why. We had a difference of opinion over something, and she's not been back since. She keeps herself to herself, your mother, she's always busy in her garden.'

'Ah, well; she doesn't come to see me very much. She's never quite forgiven me for marrying Bill and taking on the Cunning Vixen. Although, as you say, we haven't fallen out either, just have our own lives to live.' Flora smiled. 'Now, are you really sure I can't do anything else to help while I'm here?'

'No, love, there's nothing anybody can do for me at the moment. Like I say, I'm going to close my eyes for an hour or two, to try and find a bit of peace. I can't bring him back no matter how much I cry.' Lottie wiped her eyes. 'You look after Bill; make sure you're there for him, and keep the Cunning Vixen running. It's needed in times like these.'

'I will. Times are hard, but it gives people a place to share their worries. That's my contribution – keeping everyone's spirits high, in more than one way. I'll write to Bill; he should be coming home for a short leave once he's done his training. I bet he's regretting going now and realizing he should have stayed at home.' Flora leaned forward and kissed Lottie on the cheek. 'Don't get up. Stay in your chair; I'll see myself out.' She patted Lottie's hand. The poor soul was only in her early fifties, but she looked to have aged dramatically overnight. Flora caught her own reflection in Lottie's sideboard mirror. She herself was in her thirties now, and she hoped she'd keep her looks a bit longer.

'Thank you, Flora. You'll not forget about organizing that tea, will you, if they bring my lad home? It would mean a lot to me.' Lottie closed her eyes.

'I'll not forget, Lottie. Either way, if they can return his body or even if not, we will celebrate his life. It'll be my pleasure to do that.' Flora found herself fighting back tears. She remembered serving young Richard a half over the bar before he was quite old enough, and then sending him off home once he'd finished it. If only she could go back to that moment and urge him not to be in such a rush to grow up, not to join the navy and see the world.

Saturday night was busy, the pub filled again with all her usual locals, but many were more subdued now. The blow of a young lad dying in a war that nobody wanted had hit home. There was no fighting talk, just a low, steady murmur of conversation from every corner of the bar. When Flora called time, the place was nearly empty.

'Well, your police officer friend didn't appear, May,' Flora said as they washed up the glasses and emptied spittoons and ashtrays.

'I didn't think he would. He was only down here because of what happened to Richard and having to visit his mother. As I said, I think he just needed somebody to talk to, and he settled on me.' May collected the beer mats and stacked them behind the bar, ready for Monday morning. 'I'm glad it's Sunday in the morning – although there's never any peace, is there, when the bells at St Alkelda's start chiming to bring people into church? Then again, sometimes I like it. It gives you a good feeling. Mam goes to church, and I keep an eye on whatever's in the oven until she gets back.'

'This will be my first Sunday on my own here, so I'm going to have a lie-in and then write to Bill. He's been gone almost a week, and I've not heard a word from him. He's not the most regular letter-writer, and nor am I, but I do miss him; and listening to Lottie this morning made me think about how it would feel if anything happened. You tend to take one another for granted until something like this comes along.' Flora looked thoughtfully at her young barmaid and friend. 'You know, you could do worse than Trevor Whinray, May. I just don't want him hanging round the pub like a bad smell.'

May laughed. 'Well, like you say, he's not shown his face tonight, so I don't think you need to worry about that. Dad wasn't keen when he heard who had walked me home, either. He's a bit like you, never trusts a copper, even though he's done nothing illegal in his life.' She sighed. 'Right – I'll see you Monday morning and will clean the brasses as always. That's a job that comes round too fast for my liking.'

'I know it does; the times I have to chase you to do them! You get home and enjoy your Sunday. A day of peace for us, but not for those who are fighting or being bombed. We're lucky to live where we do.'

'Yes – take care. See you soon.' May pushed aside the heavy blackout curtain from the front door and let herself out, hurrying the few yards across to her home and the comfort of her bed.

Flora looked one last time around the bar before turning off the lights and going through to the kitchen, where she made herself a cup of tea before going to bed. The pub was a lonely place when she was on her own. She could hear the wooden beams creaking with age, and the walls all but spoke to her of drinkers and visitors from the inn's past as she climbed the ancient stairs to her attic room. Perhaps next week she would have a lodger in the double room; that would at least give her company, she thought as she undressed and gazed up at the starlit night through the window. Would it be a good thing or a bad one? Still unsure about this, she closed her eyes, and sleep came quickly over her.

Chapter 7

Flora stumbled downstairs. She was tired and thankful that it was Sunday, the only day of the week she had to herself. Usually, when Bill was at home, they would have a walk around the outlying countryside if the weather was fine; if not, she looked through the pub bills, although Bill always chastised her for doing business on a Sunday. His Methodist upbringing still had its say, even though he was running a pub – never mind that drinking had been considered one of the worst sins.

She smiled at the thought of him as she filled the kettle. She would write him a letter and take a short walk to post it, then come home and go over the week's accounts. She poured her tea, buttered a slice of bread and covered it with marmalade that her mother had made. It was sunny, so she decided to sit outside her back door and enjoy the peace of the small village on a sleepy Sunday morning.

They were so lucky that it was peaceful; that the rest

of the world had never heard of the little village of Giggleswick. People in towns and cities would be waking up to the destruction of German bombing raids, but Giggleswick was in its own backwater and almost silent until the church clock chimed on the hour to summon the congregation. The sun was warm, and the red climbing rose around the kitchen door was starting to develop buds, she noticed. She took a leisurely bite of her bread and marmalade and closed her eyes.

'I thought I'd find you out here. Is that all you're having for your breakfast? You need some porridge, my girl. A slice of bread is not enough.' Flora's mother made her way through the backyard gate and sat down next to her daughter, setting a basket down by her feet. 'I knew you'd not be looking after yourself. You look after everybody else, but not yourself. I've brought you your supper for tonight. It's only a vegetable stew with a bit of bacon thrown in, but it's better than nowt. Which is what I suspect you would be eating otherwise, if I know you.' Mary looked at her daughter. Her skin was pale, but her hair was a fiery auburn that hung down in curls around her face. She was a bonny woman but didn't spend a lot of time on herself – although, to be fair, she didn't need to. She had a natural beauty about her.

'Oh, Mam, I'm all right. Stop fussing. But I won't say no to a free supper. I'm going to write to Bill, go for a walk and then spend the rest of the day looking at my accounts and seeing to the bills.' Flora put a hand up to shade her eyes from the sun and looked at her mother. 'What about you? Have you called in to see Lottie Taylor yet? You must have heard that her Richard has been lost at sea.'

'Aye, I heard, and I feel sorry for her. She didn't deserve that. She's going to struggle now, without a son or a husband. Happen she'll realize now that you have to make a life for yourself when you're left on your own,' Mary said sharply, her gaze directed down the length of the yard.

Flora turned to her mother in surprise. 'And what does that mean? You've never been left on your own; you've always had me, even when Father died. I know I moved to Skipton for a year, but I came back to rent here and be next to you.'

'The less said about it, the better; but Lottie wasn't kind after your father died. I heard that she told folk I'd nagged him to death, and that you couldn't get away fast enough from home. Not that she had a good word for your father while he was alive. That was before her husband died, so she's regretted saying it since. But I'll not forget, and that's why I don't bother with her.' Mary sighed. 'Folk shouldn't say anything about other folk. They don't know what goes on behind closed doors.'

'Oh, Mam. You used to be such good friends – she wouldn't have meant what she said. Besides, I only went to Skipton because I got that job at the Cock and Bottle. If I hadn't learned bar work then and saved, I wouldn't have been able to buy here. She'll know that now.' Flora drew a deep breath and let it out. 'I called in to see her yesterday morning, and I think she was glad I did. Jenny Moon was there, and it seemed as if Lottie had had enough of her company.'

'Aye; that's another one. Gossiping with nothing else to do. Birds of a feather. I keep myself busy in my garden and don't bother with anyone, apart from old Minnie next door. Even she comes out with a load of rubbish sometimes, but I bite my lip.' Mary paused, then said, 'Is she all right? Heartbroken, I bet. She lived for her Richard.'

'Yes; she's not good, bless her. They've not found his body yet, so she can't bury him,' Flora said quietly. 'I'm sure she would appreciate seeing you, Mam. Call in on your way home, won't you? You pass her window.'

'I'll see. I'm slow to forgive, but as you say, perhaps now it's time to put that behind me.' Mary patted her daughter's hand. 'Make sure you get that stew inside you tonight and have an hour or two to yourself. The bills can wait until tomorrow, when May is here.' She stood up. 'Right, I'll go and spend the day in my garden.'

'Thanks, Mam, you are good to me.' Flora stood up, took the stew from her and smiled. 'I'll look forward to this tonight. It always tastes so much better when you don't have to cook it yourself.'

'Aye, well, make sure you eat it all. Else you'll be sliding down a drain, you're that thin.' Mary smiled back. She might no longer have a young daughter, but she still looked after her.

Flora watched her mother go and then went into the kitchen, where she pulled a writing pad and envelopes out of the dresser drawer. It was time to write to Bill. She would tell him how much she missed him, but also reassure him that life was just as usual in Giggleswick and he didn't need to worry about home. He had enough worries on his plate going to fight Hitler.

She sat down and stared at the writing paper. She wouldn't tell him everything. Just what he needed to know, she thought as she put pen to paper.

The Cunning Vixen, Giggleswick

My dear Bill,

These last few days have gone so fast since you left me. I miss you so much, and I'm hoping that you are not having it too hard in your training. The pub has been holding its own, and May and I have been kept busy.

You will smile at this, but I think May has found herself a boyfriend in our local bobby, Trevor Whinray. He walked her home the other evening. He hasn't shown his face again, but no doubt he will, as I think they got on quite well.

We have had a bit of bad news in the village. Young Richard Taylor has been lost at sea when his ship, the Mashona, *went down off the coast of Ireland. I've just had my mam here bringing me some stew for my supper, and I tried to persuade her to visit Lottie. I know they fell out years ago, but I thought it was worth trying to get them reconciled.*

Business has been steady. An annoying little man came from the ministry and tried to tell me what to do. I soon sent him on his way.

Is the food good with you? Do you need anything sent? And I hope you've got a good sergeant major. I still wish you had stayed home, but I know you felt it was your duty to enlist. Have you had any orders yet, or do you know when and where you're to be posted? Will you get a few days' leave to return to me for a while?

I miss you, my love; it seems strange without you by my side. There isn't a minute of the day that I don't wish you were here. The main thing is that you take care of yourself, keep your head down and return to me when this war is over.

I love and miss you. Stay safe.

Flora

Flora read through her letter, and a tear dropped on the last line as she folded it and placed it into the envelope. She and Bill had had their ups and downs like any other couple, but now that they were apart, she realized just how much she loved him. She wasn't going to tell him that she was letting their bedroom out to a guest; it would only worry him, and besides, there was nothing to tell, as no one had shown any interest yet. She had to reassure him that she was coping, not give him new things to worry about. He was doing his bit for the war, and she had to do the same.

Closing the door, she left the problems of the pub behind her and walked across the road to put her letter in the post box outside the small post office, its windows criss-crossed with blast tape in case of a stray bomb hitting the village. Although that was highly unlikely, everyone had followed orders. The tape made it difficult to read any of the notices about events posted in the window; you had to squint to see what was going on at the Women's Institute or the Mothers' Union.

Flora kissed the back of the envelope and dropped it into the post box. Never had she missed Bill so much, she thought as she wound her way up the hill; past the grand grounds of the private school, up Craven Bank towards the highest point of the village, where the spectacular Gothic Giggleswick Chapel stood. Its copper-green dome reached into the sky, swallows and swifts darting around it.

She took a seat on a bench outside the chapel and gazed down on the village where she lived. Across the valley stood Castleberg Scar, looming over Settle; the river Ribble parted the town from the village, flowing between them and out to the sea at Preston. To her left, she could just see the distant outline of Pendle Hill and into Lancashire, and just below where she sat was the old workhouse that had formerly housed the parish poor. Now it was partly a 'hospital for those of slow learning', as her mother tactfully called it. There but for the love of God go I, Flora thought as she looked down at the drab building. Then she closed her eyes and let herself enjoy the warmth of the midday sun.

Her thoughts wandered back to when she was a young woman; specifically, to the summer of 1929, when Giggleswick had been absolutely packed with more than a thousand visitors who'd come to view a total eclipse of the sun. The village was perfectly placed for observing this event, and the hillside and surrounding fields had been crowded with astronomers and their telescopes and spectroscopes. Some locals had complained, but not the shopkeepers or innkeepers – they'd been happy to make some extra money while they could. How she wished something like that would happen now! Just to give her business a boost and ease her worries . . .

She opened her eyes and looked up into the bright blue sky, hearing the sound of a solitary Spitfire high overhead. Hopefully there was no German plane nearby to intercept it. The war was impacting everybody, everywhere. There was no way of escaping it, she reflected as she stood up and decided to go home. No matter what her mother said, she would tackle the accounts and orders next. Sunday was quiet, and that was how she liked it while she studied the incomings and outgoings of the pub.

At home, she unlocked the back door and stepped into the empty kitchen. She missed Bill so much. The pub was no home without him; there was no reason for her to be there, she thought as she walked into her cramped little office and sat down at her tiny desk to tackle the job at hand.

It was nearly six o'clock when she lifted her head, hearing a quiet knock on the back door. She looked up, pulling the net curtain away from the window to see who it could be at this time; then she dropped everything and quickly made her way to the back door.

'Now, then, Flora, I didn't want to come while you

were open. You never know who's seeing and saying what.' Ted Mathews, the milkman, stood on the back step. He had two bottles of milk in his hands. He nodded towards his horse and cart, speaking in a low voice. 'My brother's got a new delivery. Do you want someone to drop it off later, when it's dark? I've brought these so if anybody's seen me here, you've just run out of milk like you sometimes do on a Sunday.'

Flora glanced around. Nobody was watching them. 'Aye, I'll take as much whisky as you've got. Has he anything else?'

'There's some brandy, John Player fags, sugar and some lemons, if you've any use for them. I can't let you have much sugar, though. I promised it to the sweet shop if I could get my hands on some.' He winked.

'I'll have whatever you can spare. Cash, is it?' Flora took the milk from him with a smile.

'Aye, cash and no questions asked. I'll come back just before midnight. That nosy bloody copper should've finished his shift by then.' Ted sighed. 'He gets everywhere at the moment.'

'He's down here more than he used to be. I think he's keen on courting May, but he isn't getting on with it very fast.' Flora frowned at the thought. It was risky dealing with the black market; she could lose her licence over it, and even go to prison.

'She doesn't know anything, does she? She isn't likely to say anything?' Ted asked anxiously.

'She knows nothing, and that is the way it's going to stay. I wouldn't want her caught up in our dealings. What you bring will be put away by the time she comes in tomorrow morning, and she'll not know any different than that I've bought it through the usual channels.' Flora spoke quietly but firmly, hoping to reassure Ted. He was too good to lose as a supplier.

'That's all right, then. Less folk know the better,' he murmured, turning to go down the garden path.

'Thanks for rescuing me with these two pints, Ted,' Flora called after him as she saw Jenny Moon walk past her yard wall and glance towards them.

'Aye, no problem, Flora. You can't make a rice pudding without milk, and I was passing your way anyway.' Ted winked and tipped his cap to Jenny as he walked over to his horse and cart. She had to be the last one to suspect anything, else it would be all round the village in a flash.

'Special delivery, is it, Ted? I didn't think you delivered on a Sunday,' Jenny said, glaring at Flora as she closed her back door.

'Aye, she wanted to make a rice pudding in the oven overnight for some visitors coming tomorrow, and I was passing anyway.' Ted climbed up onto his cart. 'It's going to rain, Jenny. You'd better get yourself home.' He clicked his teeth, urging the horse forward. He had no time for the likes of Jenny Moon.

That evening, Flora busied herself clearing the drawers in the double bedroom. She folded Bill's clothes lovingly and held them close to her, especially his big woolly jumper that he wore most winters. His smell was still on it, and she kissed it as she placed it into the bedding box for safekeeping on the landing. She felt strangely guilty, as if she were folding her husband's life away – as if he were no longer alive, just like young Richard.

Was she tempting fate by letting out their bedroom and putting away Bill's clothes? She hoped not. It was purely out of necessity, she told herself as she wiped a tear away and closed the lid on the box.

'I've brought this bloody weather on myself,' Ted growled as he passed Flora a crate of bottles from underneath the tarpaulin on his cart. Rain ran down his back. 'I should never have said owt to that bloody Jenny Moon. I'm sure she's a witch.'

'I'd rather it was weather like this,' Flora said, pulling her hood up over her head. 'There's nobody about to see us.'

'Aye, I suppose you're right. The things we do to keep body and soul together. Here, just the fags now, there's a thousand. Be careful who you sell them to.' Ted pulled the tarpaulin back into place. 'Have you got payment for it all? Price as we agreed, and cheap at half the price.' He sniggered as Flora ran back from putting the cigarettes down in the dark kitchen and passed him a wad of money.

'Yes, you'll find it's all there. Thank your brother again. And you call in for a pint on the house tomorrow night.' Flora was keen to get out of the pouring rain and back into her kitchen, closing the door to shut out prying eyes.

'Aye, I will. It'll be another fortnight before I have another lot. That'll be if he manages to put anything aside. He says everybody's at it on the docks.' Ted saw that Flora was getting soaked. 'Go on, get yourself in. I'll see you tomorrow. I'll be round for a bowl of that rice pudding,' he joked, tapping her fondly on the arm. 'Rice pudding – I hate bloody rice pudding. I could've said macaroni, ten times better.'

Flora hung up her dripping coat behind the kitchen door and made sure all the blinds were closed before she switched the lights on. Thank God for Ted Mathew's brother. The whisky and fags would keep the pub in profit for a while longer, not to mention the precious sugar. Hopefully there would be some tea in the next haul. She was starting to run short of that, and May always had at least two brews each day she came.

She opened the cellar door and carried the crate of whisky downstairs, then hid the cigarettes in a cupboard under the bar. Those local drinkers that she trusted would know how to ask for extra cigs at special prices and would keep it to themselves. Outsiders were not to be trusted, and May just thought they were her normal supply. Sometimes that lass couldn't see what was going on under her own nose – and thank heaven for that, Flora thought. Especially if PC Trevor Whinray was going to be courting her.

Chapter 8

Jenny Moon opened her front door and peered out. It was pouring down, but she wasn't going to miss going round to Madge Capstick's for the afternoon knitting group and a catch-up on gossip. She looked back at her tabby cat asleep on the window seat, curled up warm and happy on a cushion, and wondered if the creature had got it right. Or was it she who had got it wrong? She tied a plastic rain-cover over her permed hair and stepped out with her knitting bag in hand.

It was a grey summer's day as she made her way down Belle Hill, past the sweet shop and post office, whose doors were closed due to the wet weather and the fact that an easing spout had burst and water was splashing up at the windows. The houses had turned to dull grey as the rain seeped into the local stone of which they were all built. It felt dreary compared to the previous day, when the sun had shone and the village had looked like a perfect chocolate-box setting.

Jenny glanced up the walkway towards the Cunning Vixen and muttered to herself under her breath, 'Aye, her door's always open. I should have known,' as she saw the pub's doors standing wide open and heard the sound of men's voices from within. She shook her head and, despite the bad weather, stopped and checked the notice-board just in case she had missed any village news. She hadn't looked at it for a day or two. With rain running down her head covering, she read about a vicarage tea party later in the month and a primary school jumble sale in aid of school funds and the army cadets. But then she spotted it:

Room to let. Double bedroom for single occupancy or a married couple. Rent by negotiation, and meals are available upon request. Please ask for Flora Whitaker at the Cunning Vixen.

The common floozy! No sooner had her husband gone to war than she was advertising his room to let.

Because there was no doubt in Jenny's mind that Flora was after a man to lodge with her. It was a fact that you never saw her with any woman except that young May Lambert, and she'd looked as if she was starting to get loose ways too the last time Jenny had seen her, with bright red lipstick on and a low-cut blouse. Flora Whitaker was a bad influence on the village. If she hadn't snapped it up, the Cunning Vixen could have been made into a genteel tea room where respectable village people could meet. She should never have been allowed to buy it.

Jenny clutched her knitting bag as she marched down the road, past the swollen stream to Madge Capstick's, stopping herself just in time from walking straight into her friend's house. That was what she usually did if the front door was open and the weather fine; but today it was wet, and Frank might be at home. He was a stickler for manners. She'd seen him giving her a dirty look when she'd just opened the door and shouted 'Coo-ee', like good friends do; and then Madge had commented about knocking on the door before she came in. It wasn't as if they'd be up to anything, not at their ages anyway, thought Jenny as she stood on the doorstep and then stepped to one side to look through the front room window.

She saw Madge coming to the door after getting up from her seat beside her next-door neighbour, Sally, and stepped back quickly to meet her.

'Jenny, oh, it's a wet day! There are only three of us here. Come on in, don't stand on ceremony; Frank is out in the garden in his shed, the best place for him. He would only moan if he had to sit with us.' Madge opened the white-painted door and held her hand out for Jenny's mackintosh and head covering. 'I didn't think you'd be joining us, as you have to walk down the street. Sally just ran round from next door, and Brenda, as you know, is only across the road, so they just had to run between the drops. And of course, poor Lottie doesn't feel like coming after her terrible news. It has been a blow to everyone, the death of young Richard at sea. It's a pity none of us has the telephone installed, we could all catch up that way.'

'Rose Cottage got it the other week – I noticed it being put in. But the fella that lives there has enough money; he can afford it, not like us,' Sally piped up, lifting her head to look at Jenny. 'He's in business, something to do with making jungle clothing at his factory in Bradford. He'll be making a fortune if the government's taken him over. No wonder he's getting the phone in.'

'I hear his wife is part German. It's a wonder she hasn't been taken into an internment camp; I suppose money talks. And you can't tell. She speaks just as gooder English as we,' Brenda said as she cast on an extra line of stitches, not blinking an eye at her own grammar.

'Do we have internment camps here for women?' Jenny asked. 'I know some Italians are coming to the big house at Whitefriars to work on the farms. They can't let the rooms out at that place. Nobody's interested in visiting Settle now the war's on. Mind, it's in a terrible state; I wouldn't want to stay there.'

Madge settled back into her chair and watched as Jenny took her knitting out of her bag. She'd been knitting the same scarf for a few weeks now. If her stitches were as fast as her tongue, Madge thought, she'd have finished it nine times over.

'Whitefriars isn't in a bad state, Jenny. It's quite respectable, even though they aren't overrun with visitors. I called in there with some flyers for the church, and it looked lovely. Clean, with beautiful well-kept gardens . . . You must be getting your houses mixed up.'

Jenny was bursting to share her news. 'Mind you, it's not the only place letting out rooms. Have you seen that

Flora Whitaker's letting her main bedroom out? No sooner has her fella gone to war than she wants somebody else in her bed. I bet her husband won't be suited. A stranger in his home? And there's not that much room in the living quarters. I know that pub like the back of my hand from when I used to clean there in my younger days.'

'I never knew you did the cleaning there, Jenny. That must have been a long time ago? I've only known you work in that grocer's shop they used to have round the corner, and that was a good while ago too.'

'It was my first job after leaving school. It was a respectable place then – gentlemen enjoyed a drink there. Not like it is now,' Jenny quickly said, starting to knit.

'Here, my Frank likes a pint there, and so does Sally's husband. It's still respectable. It's just that you have a gripe with Flora. The lass does her best.'

'She's always got men around her. Drink, gambling and men. She brings the village down. Before you know it, she'll be encouraging the Italians that are coming, and then you'll soon be complaining . . . I just don't like her.' Jenny paused to take a breath. 'She can even get some milk delivered on a Sunday from Ted Mathews. He was there with two pints in his hand yesterday afternoon. He wouldn't deliver to any of us on a Sunday!'

'I wouldn't mind a delivery from Ted Mathews on a Sunday, but I think his wife and my old man might have something to say about it,' Brenda laughed, blushing. Even though Brenda was in her mid-sixties, she still wore lipstick and permed her hair regularly. She had often gazed at the tall, blond milkman, whose muscles could be seen under his checked shirts.

'Two pints of cream with a cherry on top, and a hot buttered crumpet to finish his visit off. That would do me, he needn't do anything else,' Sally said. 'He does nowt for me, far too mouthy. And that Scouse accent grates on me.'

'I don't know why I bother with you lot. All you think about are men. And you're all past it, anyway,' Jenny tutted.

'Speak for yourself! Not all of us are going back to our maker with a note on us saying "This one is returned still sealed." You could do with getting to know a fella, Jenny; it would stop you from moaning.' Madge nudged her friend's arm and giggled.

'You are just vulgar, Madge Capstick. I don't know why I put up with you.' Jenny sat back and looked round at the knitting group. It was true she was the only one who didn't have a man in her life, but that didn't mean she hadn't in the past. 'And now look what you've made me do – I've dropped a stitch,' she added, looking daggers at Madge.

'Enough, ladies. No wonder my Frank never shows his face when you're all here. He wouldn't know where to look. Now, I'll put the kettle on, and we will have a brew. Next week, if you're all here, may I ask somebody else to supply the tea? It's just that we use the leaves at least three times nowadays because it is so scarce.'

'We're all doing the same thing. I don't think it was ever as hard as this in the last war. But then again, I wasn't that old,' Brenda said quietly; and everybody looked at one another and thought it better not to comment.

It was well after dinnertime when May went into her father's workshop after her Monday morning shift at the Cunning Vixen. Her mother was moaning because the kitchen was full of wet washing, and with no sign of a break in the weather, it would probably be dripping there for a while.

'Mam, I'm going to make a start on Father's books,' May called through as she stood in the doorway. 'He's not in, but at least I can look through them and sort the invoices and bills into two piles.'

'Where's he gone trailing off to? He'd better be doing a job instead of sitting and talking to his cronies. Or even worse, in that pub that you both seem fond of.' Betty wiped her hands on her pinny and looked at her daughter. 'Will you be all right? Or had you better leave well alone until he returns? I don't know what he keeps where, or what belongs with what in that hiding hole of his.'

'Well, I can't make it any worse than it already is. I'll just sort it into two piles and order it by date. It'll be a start. He's away to fit a lock up at the big school, at least I think that's what he said.'

May wasn't going to tell her mother that on his way back from the school, Harold would be visiting Frank Capstick in his garden shed to sample his home-made parsnip wine. No doubt she would discover that when he returned home a little too happy from just fitting a lock.

'Well, don't throw out anything important. Lord knows what he'll have in those drawers – I haven't dared tackle them in all the time I've been married to him. He wouldn't let me even if I offered.' Betty was ever so slightly envious of the close relationship between Harold and May. She felt as if she had lost his special love for her over the years; but he was always loyal to her, and to May.

'I'll sort him out, don't worry. His bills will run like clockwork by the time I've finished in there.'

May closed the cottage door behind her and darted through the rain to the joinery workshop next door. She switched on the makeshift light – a bare bulb hanging on a piece of twisted cable, plugged into the building's only electric socket – and paused to look around her father's workshop.

She loved the fragrant wood shavings everywhere and the half-completed projects covering every surface – the window frames being repaired, the traditional farm tools her father made with such skill. No wonder he spent most of his life in here. Making her way to the back of the workshop, she sat down at his office table. Unlike the rest of the space, which had a system of its own, this area was in total disarray. Bills and invoices protruded from the desk drawers, and the accounts book she found in the top drawer had not been updated for at least six months. No wonder there was no money coming into the family coffers – her father was far behind with his accounts and billing.

May sighed and decided to start by sorting things into piles. Invoices; bills; work done but not yet invoiced; tax bills; and a final pile for anything she didn't know where to place. It was going to take a while, and then she would have to sit down with her father to make sure everything she'd done was right and find out who needed to be sent what.

Once that was done, though, it would just be a matter of filing – a concept he didn't seem to know about, she thought to herself as she picked up an unpaid invoice from eighteen months earlier. She used it to start the pile of unpaid invoices, marking it as urgent.

'I thought I saw the light on in here. It's needed on a gloomy day like today,' said a voice from behind her, making her start. She twisted round in the rickety chair to see Trevor Whinray in the open workshop doorway, silhouetted against the natural light outside with his bulky police cape and helmet. 'I was hoping for a minute with your father – just to see how things are and get out of the rain for a while?'

'I'm afraid you've got me instead,' May smiled. 'I'm trying to make sense of these accounts, but it looks as if my father has no system when it comes to his invoices and bills. It's a wonder he's kept the business going as long as he has.'

'It's probably *why* he's kept it going as long as he has. Everybody speaks well of him around here, and nobody likes somebody who puts money before friendship.' Trevor took his helmet off and put it on the workbench.

'You tell my mam that. She's going mad at him for

not sending his invoices out on time. That's why I'm in here today; I thought I would try and help, but honestly, I need my father to talk me through half of these.' May got out of the chair and came to join Trevor nearer the front of the workshop, leaning against her father's workbench. 'Another wet, crime-filled day in Giggleswick and Settle is it for you, then? Have there been any bank robberies or wild police chases?' she teased.

'No, not a lot. Mrs Finnegan's cat has gone missing, and I had to clip a young lad's ear in the sweet shop – he was giving lip when he should have known better – but that's about my lot for today. Although there's always something going on, and we're always on the lookout for illegal contraband. And, of course, German spies. You could be hiding one in here, for all I know!' Trevor grinned.

'Well, feel free to have a nosy, but I think you'll be disappointed. A few spiders and next door's cat, perhaps, but no spies.' Gazing up at Trevor, May felt her heart skip. Everyone else kept him at a distance, but he was all right; quite good-looking as well, once you took notice of him properly. And he looked at her in a way nobody else had ever done.

'I don't suppose you'd like to join me at the dance they're having at the Victoria Hall in Settle? It's to raise funds for a battleship, and I thought of going, but it's not much fun on your own. For once, I've got a Saturday night off.' Trevor glanced down at his feet, looking as if he didn't expect May to say yes. Nobody wanted to date a copper.

May felt her heart beating faster. She very much wanted to go to the dance, but her mother and father would have something to say about it, and she was usually at work on Saturday evenings. 'Oh – I saw it being advertised, but like you, I had nobody to go with. And I should be working. But I could ask Flora at the Cunning Vixen if I can have the night off. She might not give it to me, though, now she's on her own with Bill joining up. It means she's always busy.'

'I can sort that one for you.' Trevor glanced slyly at May. 'Tell her from me that I know about the extra milk deliveries, and that I can turn a blind eye for a while.'

'I don't know what you mean.' May looked puzzled.

'She'll know. And you'll get your night off, so that's all that counts.' Trevor winked at her. 'I keep my eyes peeled and, sometimes, my mouth closed; let's put it that way.'

May looked at him curiously. 'I still don't know what you're on about, but if it gets me the night off . . . I'll just ask her first. If she says no, then I'll tell her that from you.' She smiled.

'It's best you don't know, but Flora needn't worry. There's a lot worse than her around and about.' Trevor realized that May really was innocent of Flora's wheeling and dealing with the local black market. However, he could still use his knowledge to get what he wanted and wait to catch the main culprit in the act.

Everyone had to make a living in these hard times. Sometimes it paid a copper to keep his mouth shut, just to rub along with the locals; but he knew the Merseyside police were interested in who was supplying black market goods. For now, he'd just keep watch – keep it under his bobby's helmet until he could use the information to his advantage.

'Now, I'd better get back out there. Rain or no rain, I should be walking my patch. I'll try to come down for a pint in the Vixen on Friday night and see you then to confirm.'

Both of them went quiet as they heard the front door of the cottage slam, and a moment later May's mother appeared in the doorway.

'Oh – is everything all right, officer? Harold isn't here at the moment.' Betty was taken aback to find the local bobby standing in her husband's workshop.

'Nothing wrong at all, Mrs Lambert. I'm just taking a minute from out of the rain and having a natter with May. Don't you worry, I was about to go on my way.' Trevor gave May a smile and picked up his helmet.

'You don't have to go. I only came through to see how May was doing and ask if she needed any help,' Betty said, taking note of her daughter's flushed cheeks.

'I'm fine, thanks, Mam. PC Whinray gave me a welcome break from Father's finances. They're going to take a while to sort out, but I'll get there.' May took a deep breath and smiled at Trevor as he turned to go.

'Afternoon, ladies – I'll leave you to your business and go and dodge the rain as best I can.' He fastened the helmet and touched the edge to them both, giving May a last knowing glance before he stepped out into the rain.

'Had he been here long, May? What was he after? He must have been after something?' Betty folded her arms as they both stood in the doorway, watching Trevor disappear towards the village.

'He was, Mam; he came to ask me to the dance at the Victoria Hall in Settle. I can go, can't I? It's for a good cause. And I'll be safe enough with him.' May caught the surprise on her mother's face.

'He's asked you to a dance? But you don't even know each other,' Betty exclaimed.

'We met after he was along this way to tell Mrs Taylor about Richard being lost at sea,' May said. 'He saw me home after closing time at the pub, and we had a chat on that bench outside the church. I think he just needed somebody to talk to.' She bowed her head.

'You never thought of telling me or your father this before now? I'd have asked him in for a brew if I'd known. He'd be a good catch for you, May. Your father might not be so suited, but I'm all right with him calling.' Betty grinned.

'Mam, he's just asked me to a dance. I'm not about to marry him.' May rolled her eyes. 'Besides, like you say, he's a copper. Everyone knows you have to be wary of what you say to them.'

'Only if you're doing something wrong, so you should be all right,' Betty replied. She turned to look round the workshop, taking in the disarray on the desk at the back.

'Well, I'm not – but Flora at the pub must be. He's got something on her, the way he's talking. Something about the milkman? I can't see her having an affair with the milkman; she loves Bill too much. And Norma, the milkie's wife, would kill him if he so much as looked at another woman.' May returned to her seat at the desk, feeling warm and excited about being asked to the dance.

'Nothing would surprise me about that Flora. There were always rumours about her father and various women. It's no wonder her mother keeps herself to herself; I would, too.' Betty sighed. 'Happen that's what your father's up to, seeing he's not come home yet. But then again, I couldn't be that lucky for another woman to want him.'

'Mam. You'd be lost without him and you know it,' May said, watching as her mother wandered out of the workshop and back to the cottage. It was true, she thought: her mam and father would be lost without each other. They might have their rows, but she knew they loved one another, no matter what.

Chapter 9

'Flora, could I have next Saturday night off, please?' May had chosen her time well, she thought as she pulled her coat on after Tuesday morning's cleaning. 'I wouldn't ask, but Trevor Whinray has asked me to the dance at Victoria Hall, and I would really like to go.'

'So he's still sneaking around here, is he? When did you see him? He's never shown his face in here until lately. You're going to leave me short-handed – Friday, perhaps, but Saturday is always busy. I really could do with you here.' Flora sounded agitated as she replied. She was washing her hands after peeling some boiled eggs to be pickled in vinegar and sold behind the bar.

'He was passing Father's workshop when I was in there yesterday afternoon, and he came in to ask me to join him. He's coming down here on Friday evening after his shift to find out if you've agreed.' May wondered if she dared say the message that Trevor had told her to pass on.

'Bloody hell, May. Of all the fellas you decide to court, you choose the local bobby! Then again, there aren't many to choose from at the moment, so I can't blame you. Have you really set your heart on going to this dance? It's a fundraiser, you know, so you'll have to buy raffle tickets and bid for things in an auction. It'll only be the great and the good in there.' Flora was hoping to put May off; she had no idea who would be there, not really. But the last thing she needed was for May and Trevor to start seriously courting.

'Well, I'll just let him pay for everything. He's probably only going because he's the local bobby. He'll have to show his face, especially as it's for such a worthy cause.' May hesitated. 'Flora, I don't know what he means by this, but he says that he knows about your extra milk deliveries, and he's turning a blind eye. He didn't explain to me, but he smirked when he said it.'

'I don't know what he means either, but he thinks he does,' Flora said, trying to conceal her shock. 'I suppose I could always let you have this Saturday off. If there's a dance at the Victoria Hall, it'll probably be quieter anyway. At least, I hope that it is.' Flora couldn't quite look May in the eye, just in case she did know what Trevor meant.

'Oh, thanks, Flora. I'll make it up to you, I promise – especially if you get a lodger. You'll need more help then.' May stood on tiptoe and kissed Flora on the cheek. 'Right, I'll get back home – see what a mess my dad's made this morning and if my mam's still talking to him. He's in a right state, but I'll get there and money will soon be flowing in. That will keep Mam happier.' May picked up her gas mask and left the pub.

As she headed home, she wondered to herself – were Flora and the local milkman more than friends? She had never actually seen him there other than having a pint or two; and besides, he wasn't that good-looking. No, it would be something else. Everyone knew that Flora loved Bill. But then, why did Trevor say it? Whatever it was, it had worked to make Flora change her mind quickly.

Flora was far from happy that the local bobby knew about her scam with the milkman – and not only that, but he was going to be a regular drinker now that he and May were courting. There was only one thing to do: keep him sweet and take even more care with her deliveries. It was just one more thing to add to her worries.

She glanced discreetly over at Trevor, who was standing at the end of the bar and flirting with May. It was Friday evening, and he'd walked into the pub around ten thirty. She knew he was watching her every move as she picked up the bell on the bar and rang time. He was going to be a problem, she thought, as all her locals turned to her, knowing she had no choice but to send them all home. That night when he'd needed a late drink had been a one-off, and she wasn't going to give him anything else to hold over her. She trusted him even less now than before; apart from anything else, Trevor was after promotion, and everyone knew it. The sergeant at Settle was coming up for retirement soon and Trevor was expected to fill his shoes.

‘Come on, lads, drink up! Haven’t you got homes to go to?’ Flora shouted as the clock behind the bar chimed eleven.

‘I could’ve sunk another pint, Flora. I’ve had a busy day today, been helping in the churchyard,’ Frank Capstick protested, although he knew the reason time was being called. He passed his empty glass over the bar to her.

‘Aye, I know, and I could do with your brass.’ Flora gave another sideways glance at Trevor, knowing Frank would understand.

‘Let’s hope it’s not a regular occurrence, but he’ll be a good catch for May,’ Frank whispered. Then he shouted, ‘Night, everyone,’ as he left the pub with everyone sipping their last dregs.

Flora watched as Trevor sidled his way up the bar towards her.

‘Closing bang on time tonight, eh?’ He smiled. ‘I’m glad that you’ve let May have tomorrow night off. I didn’t want to have to say anything on her behalf.’ He finished his drink.

‘It’s no problem, as long as it doesn’t become a habit. The dance you’re going to deserves supporting, so I hope she enjoys herself.’ Flora didn’t want to make eye contact with Trevor; she wasn’t good at hiding her emotions.

‘Yes, well, you’ve got to give a little something back. Some folk just take all the time. Not that I blame them – times are hard.’ Trevor looked steadily at Flora. ‘She’ll have a good night, and it’ll do me good to have a night off from my beat. My one Saturday off in the month doesn’t come round fast enough for me.’

'No, I'm sure, but it is my busiest night,' Flora replied, wondering why he was telling her his shift pattern.

'PC Bob Mason never can be bothered to walk this far out of Settle when he's doing my beat. I keep telling him, owt could be happening here on a Saturday and Wednesday when he stands in for me. After all, there are some big lawbreakers in Giggleswick; it's the capital of North Yorkshire crime, if you ask me. He'll never catch them, though.' Trevor grinned and winked at Flora.

'Then we had better be on the lookout for wrongdoers on those nights. But as you say, not a lot happens in our village. And if it does, it's only to keep the wolf from the door.' Flora felt her cheeks burning.

'Aye, that's what I think. As long as folk are careful.' Trevor smiled. 'Thanks again for letting May have the night off. I'll make sure she has a good evening.'

'You make sure that you do. And thank you for your custom. There'll be a free pint next time you come in.' Flora glanced up at Trevor and smiled.

'Now, that could appear to be bribery, and we can't have that; so no, I'd better not accept. But thank you.' Trevor winked again, then went to sit by the door and wait for May to finish for the night.

'Everything all right, Flora? I saw Trevor was talking to you. I hope he was thanking you for giving me the night off.' May came to the bar with her hands full of beer glasses.

'Yes, we got on just fine; we both know where we stand now. I've no problem with you courting him. He's a better sort than I thought he was. Now, go on – I'll finish off, don't keep him waiting for you. I'll see you in the morning.'

Flora would have to talk to Ted the milkman and see if his deliveries could be made on a Wednesday from now on. She was thankful for the tip-off, if that was what it had been. Perhaps Trevor Whinray wasn't as hard-hearted as people made him out to be. He seemed all right to her, anyway.

'How do I look, Mam? It's the best I can do with the clothes I've got.' May stood in front of her parents, trying not to feel nervous.

'You look lovely – stunning, love.' Betty stood back and took in the sight of her daughter in a bright blue summer dress with a simple necklace of artificial pearls round her neck and a pair of white sandals; a sensible choice, seeing that she had to walk the mile into Settle from Giggleswick and return when her feet would no doubt be aching.

'Tha'd look better without that bright red lipstick; there's no need for it. You are bonny enough without that on your lips,' Harold commented, looking up from his paper.

'Shush, Harold – all the young ones are wearing it nowadays. It's the new thing from America.' Betty jumped to her daughter's defence. She knew May was nervous enough without her appearance being questioned. 'You look lovely, pet. Take no notice.'

'Do you think so? I can change it to pink, but I thought it went so well for this evening. I don't want to seem out of place. Trevor says all the good and grand will be there, that we've got to look the part. He says you don't have to worry if he knocks on your door in his full uniform, but it might get the neighbours talking if they don't know that he's invited me out.' May reached for her matching white handbag and her gas mask, checking inside to make sure she had a handkerchief, compact and her beloved red lipstick.

'I don't think there's any chance of the neighbours not knowing he's asked you to this dance,' Harold said drily. 'Folk have been nodding at me all week and wanting to know if it's true you're courting the local copper. I bet Flora at the pub is not suited. She'll know that you can never trust them.' Harold had never forgiven the previous sergeant at Settle for fining him after he'd poached a salmon out of the Ribble, back when May was still in her cot and times were hard.

'She didn't like it at first, but she seems all right with it. She was happy enough to give me the night off, anyway,' May replied. She'd thought her father would be pleased with her choice of suitor, but he'd done nothing but complain since her mother had told him.

'She perhaps had no choice. He probably has something on her, knowing him,' Harold growled.

'What do you mean?' May asked, and then felt her stomach flip as they heard a polite knock.

'Be quiet, you two; he's here. Father, hold your noise and wish May a good night with her young man,' Betty said quickly, hurrying to answer the door.

'Aye, have a good night. Just don't tell him owt, else

he'll make a note of it,' Harold replied. He hid behind his newspaper as if hoping it would keep Trevor at bay.

'Good evening, Mr and Mrs Lambert – May.' Trevor stepped into the front room of the cottage and glanced around him. He was smartly dressed in his police uniform, but without his helmet. 'I hope I still have your permission to take May to the dance at the Victoria Hall? I will, of course, escort her there and back.' He waited as the newspaper was lowered, and Harold fixed him with a look that would put any prospective suitor off his stride.

'Aye, well, it's all been settled, lad, without me having a say. The women seem to rule this house. You bring her back before twelve, and no how's your father. Else you'll have to answer to me, whether you are a copper or not.' Harold raised his paper again, cutting them off before anybody had a chance to reply.

May's face flushed bright red as she gripped her handbag and looked pleadingly at her mother.

'It's grand with both of us,' Betty assured them. 'Now, on you go, and have a lovely night. Enjoy yourselves. Back just after twelve, mind, because I'll not sleep until you're home.' She smiled at them both as Trevor offered May his arm and they stepped out into the early evening sunshine.

'Don't they make a handsome couple? She's done well for herself, has our May, if she keeps him on her arm,' Betty said, watching from the doorway as they walked up through the village and out of sight.

'He might have brass and a good job, but I reckon nowt of him,' Harold mumbled from behind the paper.

'Just try and be happy for her and stop your moaning. Or go into your work shed and give me some peace.'

'Even that's been taken over nowadays. I can't find a bloody thing in my desk, and there's a pile of bills that she says I've to post on Monday,' Harold moaned.

'Aye, she's doing well, is our lass. I hope she has a good night.' Betty settled down with her magazine to read. May had her head screwed on, and it looked as if she would make her way in the world.

'I don't think your father is that keen on me taking you out tonight. He wasn't very talkative,' Trevor said, linking his arm through May's as they crossed the river bridge into Settle.

'He doesn't have a lot to say at the best of times, my father – unlike my mother. She's quite happy for us to be going to the dance,' May replied, smiling up at her good-looking officer.

'Well, you look very beautiful tonight, and it will be a pleasure to spend the evening with you. I think there will be a lot of people there. The Beresford Band is playing, and they have a good following. I must admit, I'm not the best dancer, but we'll give it a go. And of course the parish council for Settle and Craven is starting their battleship fundraiser, so I believe there's to be a raffle.' Trevor glanced at May. She did look very attractive. He had seen her a time or two in the past but had never had an opportunity to approach her. She'd been just the medicine he had needed after his visit to Lottie Taylor's to break the news about her son. Now that they'd met, he had no intentions of losing her just yet.

'I can't wait. I hope I don't look out of place – I must have changed my mind about what to wear at least ten times. Not that I have many clothes anyway, but you mix and match nowadays.' May caught her breath as they turned down by the side of Shepherd and Walker's, the chemist for Settle, and approached the Victoria Hall. It was a square, well-built building with a foyer, dance floor and upstairs seating area, frequently used for local community events. People were standing outside dressed in their finest, and the Union flags around the entrance fluttered brightly in the sharp evening light. From inside the hall, they could hear a dance band warming up for the night's performance.

May felt butterflies in her stomach as they approached the mayor of the town council and Trevor held his hand out to be shaken. Her father was just a village joiner; she wasn't used to mixing with society at this level.

'Good evening, PC Whinray. It's good to see you attending our first event in aid of Craven sponsoring and buying its very own battleship.' The mayor shook Trevor's hand and then turned to May, smiling. 'I don't think I know you, my dear. Are you Trevor's wife or intended?' He shook her hand warmly.

'No, we're just friends, sir, and Trevor was kind enough to ask me along tonight.' May's legs felt like jelly as she replied. The mayor and his wife both wore important-looking chains of office around their necks.

'Very good. I must say, Trevor, you've got an eye for

a bonny lass, but have you got deep pockets? We're after some of your brass tonight.' The mayor chuckled, then lost interest in the young couple as someone more important approached to greet him.

'I'm sure I'll place a bid or two,' Trevor replied politely as he ushered May up the steps and into the foyer. Inside, the walls were covered in posters encouraging saving, sewing and making do in aid of the war effort. Passing through the main doors, the couple were greeted by two attendants who checked their tickets. Trevor gestured for May to step into the hall ahead of him.

May gasped as she entered, taking in the immaculate wooden floor and the huge Victorian stage, where the band was already assembled. She glanced back at Trevor. 'I've never been in here before. We usually go to the parish room at Giggleswick to attend anything they hold there . . . I didn't realize this was so grand.' The stage had heavy velvet curtains at either side and a painted backdrop depicting an old-fashioned scene of town life. Although it was still light outside, everything was brightly illuminated. 'It's beautiful,' May sighed.

'It's one of the oldest music halls in the world. We are indeed lucky.' They found a table at one side of the space and Trevor pulled out a chair for her. 'Busy, isn't it? It'll be a memorable night, I think.' They sat down, gazing around them at the walls draped in Union flags, the people dressed in their finest, and the generous arrangement of raffle prizes donated by local businesses. The mayor and his wife passed by their table and climbed the steps onto the stage, where he tapped on a microphone to test it. He cleared his throat, and his wife pulled her stole round her shoulders as he launched into his opening remarks.

'Good evening, ladies and gentlemen – I would like to thank you all for attending tonight and for supporting this cause. We aim to raise as much money as we can this evening to enable the funding of a battleship for this area. HMS *Ribble* will be built and launched in one of our naval dockyards, but in order to make that possible, we need your contributions.' The mayor paused, looking around the hall. May followed his gaze: on all sides, hall attendants were quietly closing the doors and pulling the blinds down against the oncoming night. It was important to keep any light from leaking out.

'Aye, that's right, ladies. Don't let them bloody Jerrys know what we're up to! Now, later this evening we're to hold a raffle, but first, to start the night off right, we have our famous local Beresford Band. The bar is open, although we have no food this evening – I'm sure you all understand. Enjoy yourselves, but please dig deep into your pockets. It costs a pretty penny to build a battleship. Now then, lads – let's get on with it!' With that, he turned and gave way to the band leader, who took the microphone and waited for the portly mayor and his wife to leave the stage.

'I feel quite awkward, Trevor,' May murmured. 'I don't think I'll be able to bid for anything this evening – I don't have enough money.'

'Don't worry, I didn't expect you to. I don't even think I will have enough on me. We'll leave that to the wealthier guests, and I'll put something into that donation box by the entrance. This is just the start, anyway. It finishes in the coming year with the official Battleship Week, when we'll know if we've raised enough for the ship.' Trevor noticed the uncertainty on May's face. 'Would you like a drink? A sherry, or maybe a port?'

'I don't know; I get a bit giddy,' May said quietly.

'Go on. Just the one won't hurt, and then we'll have a dance. The band sounds so good.'

'Oh, all right – just the one.' May smiled up at Trevor. He was looking after her, and she was going to enjoy her evening. She watched him walk across the dance floor, nodding to acknowledge people he knew as he headed towards the bar in the adjoining room. People were starting to dance – a brisk foxtrot – and everyone was smiling and chatting. If not for the patriotic decorations and the scarcity of young men, no one would have guessed there was a war on. May tapped her feet to the music as Trevor returned with a small sherry for her and a pint of beer for himself.

Trevor handed over her glass and took a sip of beer. 'Not as good as the Vixen's, if you ask me. This tastes as if it's watered down. How's your sherry?'

'Lovely, thank you.' May beamed.

'Shall we show them how it's done?' He set the glass down and held out a hand to her. 'Not that I'm very good. I'll apologize for my two left feet before we even begin.'

'Neither am I, but yes, I love to dance.' May took his

hand and placed her other hand on his shoulder, feeling his arm encircle her waist. This was the closest she'd ever been to a man, and she felt a stir of excitement as their eyes met. Soon they were weaving their way round the room with the other dancers.

Two hours seemed to pass in no time as they danced the night away, resting every so often to catch their breath, but then unable to resist moving as the band struck up another well-loved tune. At ten thirty, the band announced that the last song would be a waltz before the auction was held, and everyone took to the floor with their partners. Trevor held May tight and smiled down at her as they glided across the floor.

May was almost dizzy with enjoyment. She had experienced the best night of her life, she thought, as Trevor nearly lifted her off her feet. Her father might not like him because he was the local bobby, but he'd been the perfect partner tonight.

The song came to an end and they returned to their seats as the mayor climbed onto the stage again, now accompanied by a local auctioneer to begin the bidding.

'I'm not bothered about sitting through this, but we'd better stay. It would probably be rude to leave,' Trevor murmured as the auctioneer held the first lot up for viewing.

'Donated by Mrs Sanderson – five pounds of good potatoes. Grand tatties, these are. Come on, ladies, no need to queue up at the veg stand come market day, and you'll be giving to this marvellous cause.' The auctioneer surveyed the room, rapidly taking bids as hands waved and shouts echoed around the room.

'A shilling from Mrs Baxter. A shilling and threepence, thank you, Mrs Bowman. One more bid, and then I'll put my hammer down . . . *Sold* to Mrs Baxter for one and six!' And he banged his gavel.

'They're only worth threepence!' May whispered, amazed.

'Aye, but they're all keen to show how wealthy they are. Shall we slip away? I know I said it would seem rude, but we've nothing in common with this lot. What do you think?' Trevor squeezed her hand.

'Yes, let's. I'm tired anyway, and these folk are spending my week's wages on a few potatoes,' May agreed.

They got to their feet as quietly as possible, hoping to make a discreet exit.

'Hey up, folks. Our local bobby has something else on his mind besides buying tatties. Now, don't you be doing anything we wouldn't do,' the auctioneer shouted as he spotted them edging their way out of the hall. The whole crowd turned to look; May felt her cheeks burning.

'Go on, lad. You get gone and enjoy yourself,' somebody called out as they hurried through the heavy door. 'Tatties can always wait!'

A short while later, May sank down gratefully onto the bench outside the churchyard near her home.

'Thank you for tonight,' she said as Trevor sat beside her and leaned back, holding her hand.

'No, thank you – I didn't want to go on my own. And you were so easy to talk to the other week, when I was having a bad shift. Folk think I'm tough and uncaring, but sometimes things do get to me.'

'Well, if you ever need a shoulder, you know where I am,' May said softly, looking at his handsome profile. She knew nobody spoke well of Trevor, but he had been good company tonight. 'I'd better go; else my father will be sending out a hunting party, whether you're the local law or not.'

'I don't blame him. I'd guard you and look after you as well,' Trevor replied. He leaned closer to her. 'Can I kiss you, May?'

'I think I'd like that . . . I've not had many boyfriends,' May blushed as he put an arm around her. They looked into one another's eyes. The evening had been perfect, and it felt natural that it should end in a kiss.

May relished the feeling of his lips on hers, and she sighed as she withdrew from his arms. Trevor was the first person ever to have kissed her that way.

He was still holding her hand. 'Friday night, I'll come by once I've finished my shift and see if you can come out the following week. Most likely Wednesday – there's bound to be something on at the picture house. That's if you want to walk out with me again?' He smiled. 'I'd better not make it Saturday night, as Flora will need you. I don't want to push it too much with her. The pictures are open most nights.'

May felt her heart beating fast at the idea of seeing him regularly. That would suit her mother, but perhaps not her father. As far as she was concerned, it was everything she'd been dreaming of.

'That would be lovely, the pictures – that would be a real treat. Next time I walk up into Settle, I'll look at what's showing.' May pressed her lips to his once more and whispered, 'Thank you. I've had a wonderful evening,' then picked up her handbag and gas mask and stood up to go.

'It's been just grand, May. Until next Friday. Now, please apologize to your parents for me for keeping you out so long. I've enjoyed every minute with you.' Trevor remained sitting on the bench as he watched May walk the short distance to her home and open the front door, closing it quickly to stop the light escaping after she waved to him.

It had been a wonderful night. May was blonde, good-looking, lively and good company, and she didn't seem to mind that he was the local copper. He'd make it his business to stop in and see her every Friday after his shift, then take her out one night the following week. That would also enable him to keep an eye on Flora's illegal trading at the pub; she'd been a bit too obvious about it of late. Trevor didn't want the docklands police to catch her and her supplier, pinching his glory before he had a chance to find out the whole picture.

He lit a cigarette and drew on it slowly, staring across at the blacked-out windows of the Cunning Vixen. It might look dark and empty, but he'd bet his bottom dollar that a few old soaks were still sitting round the bar with whiskies in their hands courtesy of the local milkman. He had warned Flora, but only because the Liverpool coppers were watching his every move, trying to catch the milkman and his contact in the act. Trevor was looking after his own interests. He had noticed young May Lambert for a while, but he knew that she'd have nothing to do with him if she suspected what he was up to. This way, he could monitor Flora's movements and nobody would suspect a thing, he thought as he smiled. He was having his cake and eating it. May was a very convenient cover for his operations.

With luck, there would be a promotion in line for him before long. 'Sergeant Whinray' – that had a nice ring to it. And one of the new police houses that had just been built would suit him very well.

'Well, you're late back. Have you had a good night? I hope he behaved himself.' Betty Lambert yawned and set her darning aside as she greeted May.

'Oh, Mam, I've had a wonderful night. We danced, we laughed, and he walked me home . . .' May swooned around the kitchen. 'He's taking me to the pictures next week – I can't wait.' She sighed and sat down heavily, kicking her shoes off and rubbing her feet. 'I think I'm in love.' She grinned at her mother as if she were drunk.

'It's early days yet, lass. He won't have shown his true colours. Let's see how he shapes up in the next week or so. I do like him, though – he's a good catch. Now, your father's in bed, and that's where I'm going too. Turn all the lights off before you follow, will you?' Betty got to her feet. She could remember being May's age, seeing a young man for the first time; she, too, had been swept off her feet. Then it had all come to an end when he'd run off with her best friend. 'Night, love. Don't stay up late.'

'I won't, Mam. I'll just sit here and think of Trevor,' May sighed. Trevor Whinray . . . who would have thought she'd end up walking out with the local copper?

Chapter 10

Matt Walker stepped off the train and put his suitcase down. So this was Settle! He breathed in the fresh air and looked around him, taking in the dome of Giggleswick Chapel in the distance and the expanse of open green fields around the busy little market town.

His mother had often spoken about this place, her voice laced with sadness as she remembered the life she'd left behind just before his birth. She had swapped her home in the Dales for a damp flat above a pub in Leeds, where she had worked as a barmaid while raising him. They had both remained there until her death eight years earlier, and then Matt had joined the civil service down in London. Now, thanks to his job, he was here on an extended visit to the place where his mother had always said she'd been happiest.

He watched as the train was prepared for departure, doors slamming shut, and the stationmaster blew his whistle to see the train on its way up to Carlisle.

Passengers who had disembarked with him were dispersing; locals hurried away over the barrow crossing while visitors paused to get their bearings. It was a quaint sight, a true country station – a world away from the metropolitan grime of Leeds and London. Settle station was lovingly maintained, its gardens filled with blooming flowers and hanging baskets adorning the ticket office and waiting room. The railway staff had a cheery welcome for everyone.

'That case looks a bit heavy, lad. Do you need a hand?' The stationmaster looked enquiringly at Matt, whose smart suit marked him out as a city man.

'Thank you, but I'll manage,' Matt replied, lifting the case and putting his coat over his arm. He followed the stationmaster over the crossing, along with a frail-looking elderly woman and a farmer who had just taken delivery of a crate of quacking Aylesbury ducks from out of the guard van.

'Have you come on holiday or business?' asked the stationmaster, as everyone safely crossed the track. He was wondering why a fit young man like Matt would be visiting Settle.

'Business – I work for the War Office. Perhaps you can help me. Could you direct me to Whitefriars? I believe it's rather a large house near the centre of Settle.' Matt set down his case again, hoping the stationmaster would tell him the way without asking what business he had there.

'Oh, you'll be the fella that's giving us another batch of these bloody prisoners of war!' The stationmaster's expression became a shade less welcoming. 'I've heard they're taking them in down there – not by choice, either. A house like that doesn't want the likes of them in it. I bet our lads won't be looked after as well by bloody Hitler.'

'News travels fast in Settle – even though that's supposed to be classified information until I've given it my blessing,' Matt said wryly. 'Local people will have nothing to fear from the men. They will not be politically active, and they're only here because of overcrowding at other camps. They'll be put to work helping out with local businesses and farms. They will be a boon to the community, not a burden.'

'That's what you would say. It's you lot that started this war. My lads are out in Germany,' the stationmaster growled. 'Why can't I bring them home and send a couple of this lot to fight in their place, if they're "not political"?' He turned away and started to walk back towards his office.

'Now, that would not make sense at all. I'll find my own way to the house. Thank you for your help.' Matt shook his head. He should have remembered how quickly bad news travelled in these little Dales towns, and foreseen that locals were bound to think the worst of POWs living in their community.

With a sigh, he lifted the case again and made his way out of the station and down onto a main road, which he followed until he came to the local police station. Pausing, he decided to go in and ask the way to Whitefriars once more. Hopefully this time he'd get a sensible response.

'Good morning, sir. What can I do for you?' Trevor Whinray looked up from where he stood behind the station's front desk. A smartly dressed man stood in front of him, carrying a suitcase.

'I'm in Settle on war business, so I thought I'd introduce myself as well as ask for directions.' Matt offered his hand to be shaken. 'I'm Matt Walker, working on behalf of the War Office, and I'll be seeing to the smooth transfer of Italian POWs into Whitefriars. Could you point me towards the house?'

Trevor came out from behind the desk and looked at him. Matt's arrival was expected, but the news about Italian POWs had not been welcomed by locals. There were already German POWs billeted at Horton, working in the quarry that had to be visited by the police to see if there were any problems. So far, there hadn't been any; but the Italians were going to be living in the centre of Settle, with local farmers encouraged to use them as cheap labour. It was a different set of circumstances.

He took Matt's hand and shook it.

'Aye, we heard you were coming. The sergeant will want a meeting with you. It's all right that these POWs are arriving in our community, but we don't know exactly what we are getting. Can we trust them?' Trevor asked. He knew the sergeant would be asking the same thing.

Matt nodded. 'We wouldn't send any that we couldn't trust to mix safely with the community. They will all be Category A and Category B prisoners. Category A prisoners are benign, no political views, men who have been dragged into the war under force, mainly from agricultural backgrounds or similar. Category B does show sympathy towards the enemy, but they pose no threat. The real fanatics are Category C – they're best behind wire fences. They will never be released until the war ends, and then some will be held to account. There have been no problems, as I understand it, with the German POWs further up the dale?'

'No; one or two have fought between themselves, but nothing untoward that I know of. I suppose if it's free labour for our farmers, that's better than having to keep them fed and them doing nothing. They would only start arguing amongst themselves then.' Trevor wasn't in favour of POWs staying on his beat, but there was nothing he could do about it. 'Now, you were asking the way to Whitefriars? Follow me and I'll show you.'

Matt followed Trevor across the tiled floor and out to the front of the police station. They paused under a huge yew tree, and Trevor pointed down the busy main street.

'Walk down into the centre of Settle and keep walking as far as you can see from here. Then on your left, after you've walked past the Royal Oak, you will see Whitefriars slightly set back from the road. You need to go through the main gates – there's always somebody minding them. Little do your Italians know, but they're going to be living in one of the finest hotels in the Dales. The garden and grounds around it are immaculately kept. Perhaps they'll be lending a hand with that work.' Trevor didn't think much of POWs getting free run of one of the bonniest houses in Settle. It seemed wrong to him that the War Office had taken possession of it.

'Thank you. They will appreciate where they're staying, believe me,' Matt said. 'I expect I'll see you again before very long. As you said, I've a meeting tomorrow with your sergeant and other members of the community to assure them nobody is under threat from those who will be living at Whitefriars. I aim to stop for a while, just until the first detainees arrive, to see how they fare.' He held his hand out again, and Trevor shook it with a little more warmth.

'Will you be staying there yourself?' he asked. He liked to know where any visitors to the town were staying.

'Just until they arrive at the end of the week – then I must find myself some lodgings for a month. There won't be room for me, and I'll be needed back in London once the men are settled.' Matt glanced at Trevor. 'You wouldn't know of anywhere? Could you recommend a place to stay?'

'Well, as it happens, there's a small pub in Giggleswick looking for a lodger. The landlady's husband has gone away to fight, and she's taking in a lodger to help with expenses.' Trevor smiled. He was helping Flora, but at the same time, hopefully, he would put an end to her illegal doings before she got caught by somebody who would treat her more harshly. He'd grown to admire her lately; after all, her husband was doing his bit. And she had to make a living somehow.

'Do you mean the Cunning Vixen, by any chance?' Matt asked with a smile.

Trevor was surprised. 'Yes, that's the one. Do you know it?'

'No, but I've heard of it from my mother. She knew this area well. I may just follow your advice.' Matt picked up his suitcase. He could hardly believe his luck. 'Thank you.'

'Tell Flora, the landlady, that I sent you. You'll be well fed and looked after there,' Trevor called after him. He stood for a moment, watching Matt disappear along the road. At least his money will be good for Flora, if nothing else, he thought as he turned to go back into the station.

Matt made his way up the broad drive that led to Whitefriars. It was a grand house, set in extensive grounds with trees and well-maintained lawns – in fact, it was quite spectacular. Smaller than some of the stately homes that had been commissioned for POWs or invalided soldiers; but all the same, grand. He mounted the immaculately clean steps and paused for a moment beneath the entrance columns, then walked through the open door into what had been the foyer. It was empty and silent.

'Hello? I say – anybody here?' Matt called quietly. He approached a large wooden desk, looking around him at the pictures of hunting scenes on the walls. After a moment, a door opened behind the desk and a middle-aged woman appeared.

'I'm very sorry; I've just been tidying the office in readiness for our new occupants. Have you been waiting long? I do hope you aren't looking for a room – I'm afraid the War Office has requisitioned us,' explained the woman. She wore her hair in tight waves, a neat twinset and a tense expression.

'Well, I hope that you do have a room for me – but I believe you're expecting me. Matt Walker, from the War Office. And you must be the owner, Mrs Bainbridge? I'm here to oversee the arrival of your new guests.' Matt looked at Mrs Bainbridge and noted her look of contempt.

'Guests! I would hardly call them guests. They are certainly not the sort of persons we usually have within these walls. Still, I'm doing my bit for the war effort. And at least the rooms will be used. There isn't much demand from holidaymakers these days.' Mrs Bainbridge sighed.

They both looked round as a uniformed soldier came in through the front entrance carrying a metal bedframe, which bashed against the paintwork as he started up the grand staircase.

'A little respect for my property would not go amiss,' Mrs Bainbridge called as she watched the squaddie lug the frame upstairs. She turned back to Matt. 'Four beds in a room – they're going to be like sardines! Didn't you consider the size of the house when you commandeered us?' Although she knew Matt was probably not responsible for that decision, she had to vent her frustration.

'I'm afraid those details were decided by others,' he replied ruefully. 'All I know is that our Italian POWs will be staying here, and that I've to make sure all is running smoothly before I return. Now, can you make room for me for the next two nights? After that, I will stay elsewhere in Settle, as your rooms will be full of POWs and their guards.'

'Yes; I've given you my daughter's room at the back

of the house. She is in Lincolnshire, doing her bit with the Land Army. My family is in turmoil as well as my house.' Mrs Bainbridge led him along a corridor. 'I'll show you to your room. Dinner will be at six o'clock tonight, so that gives you time to rest or look around.'

'Thank you. I'll take a walk around Settle before I change. I may go into Giggleswick as well – my mother lived there before I was born.' Matt followed her to a white-painted door that opened into a brightly wallpapered bedroom, with matching curtains and a quilted eiderdown on the bed.

'It's only a single room, but it's very quiet in here. You say your mother lived at Giggleswick? Whereabouts?' Mrs Bainbridge looked more closely at the young man, who seemed about the same age as her eldest daughter.

'She was the landlady of the Cunning Vixen – Maisy Walker was her name. I believe she ran it for a few years. Then she moved to Leeds.' Matt set down his heavy case with relief.

She nodded. 'I shall rack my brain and let you know at dinner time if I remember her. At least I'm still in charge of my own kitchen until Friday. Quite what the cook you have employed will be like, I do not know, but I can see that your POWs are not going to go hungry. We have taken delivery of an enormous quantity of provisions in the past few days.'

'They need to be fed. They will be earning their keep,' Matt said simply.

'So do our people, and some are struggling.' Mrs Bainbridge turned towards the door. 'Your bedroom key is on the dresser. I lock up the house at nine, but you may borrow a key to the front door if you expect to be any later. I shall leave you until dinner – six o'clock, sharp.' She left Matt to his unpacking.

He sat down on the bed for a moment and looked around. He had known that he wouldn't be welcomed in Settle with open arms, but things would surely change when the local people realized the Italian POWs were men just like their own – many of whom hadn't wanted to fight at all. Tomorrow he would inspect the quarters, meet with the staff and guards, and make sure all was in place for their unwanted guests. But now, once his few belongings were put away, he would walk into Giggleswick and look for a place to stay – somewhere away from his work and where, he hoped, he would be made more welcome.

Chapter 11

The Cunning Vixen was just as his mother had described it: a small, whitewashed pub set back from the road that ran through Giggleswick. It made Matt proud to think that she had once been its landlady. She had run the place all on her own while his father had been in the army – the father he had never known, as he'd died before Matt was born. Maisy had been left to raise him all by herself.

He smiled as he gazed around him. She had described the village cross, the domed chapel high on the hill, the primary school with children streaming out of its doors as the school bell rang at the end of the day. He had never quite understood why she'd chosen to leave, and that seemed all the more puzzling now that he was here: it was such a perfect English village, with flowerboxes, ancient houses and the odd sleepy cat dozing in a window.

It was nearing four o'clock now. There were still a few children and mothers wending their way home, and the pub's doors were closed. He should perhaps have waited until after dinner to visit, he thought; however, he might as well knock now he was here. Perhaps someone would be in there to hear him. He approached the entrance and knocked firmly on the heavy oak door.

A woman passing with a child called out, 'She'll be in the back garden, if you're looking for Flora. The pub's closed until six.' She dragged her little boy up the steep hill out of Giggleswick as he moaned about wanting to visit the sweet shop.

'Thank you,' Matt called after her, then turned back to the door as he heard the bolt being drawn from within. It swung open.

Flora looked down the steps at him. A man in a suit, she thought. Another one from the War Office, come to tell her how to do her job? She looked at his clean-cut features and neatly trimmed auburn hair.

'We're closed. Can't you come here during opening hours if you need to tell me something? Not that it will be relevant to us here. It never is.' She glared at the young man and began to close the door on him.

'Sorry, I'm not – An officer at the police station said you had a room to let? And I need one,' Matt quickly said. He smiled in relief as the expression on Flora's face completely changed and she pulled the door wide again.

'My goodness, I'm so sorry! I thought you were here from the ministry to tell me how to run my business. There was a little man here not so long ago, wasting my time and his own. And he got a soaking for his trouble,' Flora added, blushing.

'You didn't throw a bucket of water over him, did you? Because I will count myself lucky.' Matt smiled.

'Oh, no, I'd never do that. But the heavens opened up just after he left, and it was a wasted visit with what he had to tell me. Now, yes – I do have a room to let, and you are welcome to come in and have a look at it. Was it Trevor Whinray who told you about the room? And may I ask what brought you to the police station?' Flora stood aside to let Matt step into the main bar, where he stood for a moment, taking in the sight and smell of the room.

'We aren't going about this the right way, are we? You are going to soak me, and I've just walked out of the police station. I'd better introduce myself properly.' He held his hand out to be shaken. 'I'm Matt Walker, and are you Flora Whitaker?' She nodded, smiling. 'I went into the police station to ask for directions. Completely innocent of any charges.'

'I'm pleased to meet you, Matt. I'll be honest, I was hoping for a couple to take the room, or a lady. However, as long as you can pay the rent and keep yourself to yourself, I'm sure we will get along fine.' It hadn't escaped Flora's notice that Matt was well dressed and well spoken, and if Trevor Whinray had sent him, he should be all right.

'You'll not see much of me. I'll be at work during the day, and in the evenings I'll probably walk out around the Dales, clear my head.' Matt took in the ancient walls of the bar, decorated with horse brasses and paintings of the Dales, and drew in a deep breath of the beer-scented air.

'It's only a small place, but I run it well, even if I do say so myself.' Flora looked quizzically at her guest. 'No bags?'

'No; they are at Whitefriars, where I'll be staying until Friday. Then I will need somewhere else for about a month, or perhaps a little longer. I do indeed work for the War Office, but I'm not here to offer you any advice – I'm in charge of making sure the Italian POWs settle in and are well supervised, with no problems for them or for the locals.' Matt watched Flora's face for a reaction, wondering if she'd object to somebody from the War Office staying in her pub.

'Oh, I see – I thought you looked official when you stood on the doorstep. I don't mind, but you'll have to put up with the local banter, and some of my drinkers – well, they speak as they find. They may take a while to get used to you once they know what you do. Now, we both may be wasting our breath if the room is not right for you. You'd better follow me and have a look at it.'

They climbed the stairs. Flora found herself secretly hoping that he would not like the room. She didn't trust anybody who worked for the War Office, and it wasn't entirely a good thing that he'd already met Trevor. However, she needed the money, and beggars could not be choosers.

Matt didn't care what the room looked like; he intended to take it purely because his mother had once lived here. She had spoken so fondly of her years in Giggleswick, and now he was probably going to sleep in her old bedroom. He was going to be staying where his mother had found love. As he followed Flora to the bedroom, his head was filled with memories of her describing her past.

'Well, this is it. Not very large, but cosy enough, and it catches all the morning sun. I'm afraid the church bells may keep you awake until you get used to them. They chime every hour; the locals call them Faith, Hope and Charity, but most visitors just curse them. Especially those who are staying at the Hart's Head, the hotel on the main road. If this room isn't to your liking, I'm sure they will be able to fit you in.' Flora stood beside the brass bedstead and watched as Matt pulled back the curtains and looked out of the bedroom window.

'No, no, here is perfect, just right for my stay. How much are you charging per week? And can you provide breakfast and an evening meal?' Matt turned and smiled at Flora. She was quite a good-looking woman, the landlady of the Cunning Vixen.

'I was thinking of two pounds a week, if that's not too much. I can provide all meals and whatever you need, if you'd be happy to leave me your ration book? Unlike larger hotels, a pub doesn't have any special privileges.' Flora held her breath. She didn't know how safe it would be to express her frustration with Lord Woolton's rules, what with her new lodger being from the ministry.

'Of course you can. And I fully understand how difficult that must be. Some of the ideas they come up with at the War Office fail to consider the small businesses that keep this country running; I'll be the first one to admit that. How about you give me a bill when I depart and include everything you've provided for me? It would make your life easier and mine – I could pass it directly to my accounts department. Once I've paid it, of course,' Matt added, noticing that Flora looked a little worried at the thought of perhaps having to wait for payment. 'I'll pay three pounds a week in advance and will settle the balance when I go. That would suit us both, I think?'

'That should work out wonderfully. You'll not go hungry, and your room will be cleaned daily. And you could run a tab at the bar.' Flora grinned, relieved. 'Sorry if I seemed worried. I've to run a pretty tight ship here.'

'No need to explain. I'm fortunate to have good employment now, but believe me, I know what it's like to search around for money you haven't got. My mother, bless her soul, raised me on her own after my father died, so I'm used to making ends meet.' Matt hesitated. 'In fact, I wasn't going to say anything, but the main reason I want to stay here is that before I was born, my mother lived here. She was the landlady of this pub, just like you. Have you always lived in Giggleswick? Perhaps you'll remember her. She was called Maisy Walker. I think she ran this pub for a few years.' Matt watched her face hopefully.

Flora beamed at him. 'Yes, I remember your mother. In fact, I was thinking of her just the other day. She always smiled and waved to me as I passed by on the way to school – always made a fuss of me. I knew her well. Oh, I had no idea who you were; what a turn-up for the books!' Flora couldn't stop smiling; she had no problem with her guest now. 'Is your mother still alive? And forgive me, but I can't remember your father.'

'Mother died some years ago, and I'm afraid I never knew my father. He died before I was born. He was a soldier, I believe, according to my mother. I'm so glad that you knew her; you must tell me all you remember. She always spoke so fondly about living here.' Matt followed Flora as she made her way downstairs.

'When you come and stay you must have a good look round, now I know who you are. My mother and a lot of the older visitors will remember her. You'll have to make yourself known to them.' Flora leaned against the bar, still smiling. This was no 'man from the War Office' – this was Maisy Walker's son! Not that she'd ever known Maisy had a child, nor could even remember any mention of a husband.

'Thank you.' Matt paused, taking a deep breath. 'I knew I was doing the right thing in coming here. Perhaps it's providence. I believe your husband is in the army, is that right? We have a lot in common.' He smiled at her. 'Now, I must return and get ready for dinner. I've a feeling that my landlady at Whitefriars values punctuality, and she is not exactly delighted to have me as a guest. I can't say I can blame her; we are taking over her beautiful hotel and filling it with undesirables, in her eyes.'

'Oh, that will be Anne Bainbridge. Her husband is the manager of the Midland Bank. I'm afraid she thinks herself a cut above us mere mortals. She must have been devastated to have Whitefriars commandeered; no wonder you're looking for a different place to stay.' Flora smiled sympathetically at his expression.

'She says it as it is, I'll give her that. Poor woman, I rather feel for her. You can tell the place was beautifully appointed until the bedrooms were filled up with army bunks and the good furniture packed away. At least she's got Italians staying, not Germans; and they are all carefully vetted and completely trustworthy.' Matt made for the doorway. 'I'll see you on Friday, and I look forward to my stay. You must tell me all about my mother and introduce me to yours,' he said warmly.

'Yes, yes, I will. Will you be needing your evening meal on Friday?' Flora asked as she held the door open.

'Yes; but I don't know what time I'll be with you, so something cold? A salad, perhaps, or whatever you can muster up. I haven't got my ration book with me, else I would leave it with you now,' he apologized.

'That's all right. I can run to the first few meals. We don't go short of many things really, here in the country – unlike the towns.' Flora stood on the doorstep and watched her visitor leave. 'Don't walk back by the main road, take the shortcut. Past Belle Hill, there's a snicket you can follow that takes you out to King's Mill and Queen's Rock. It's a pleasant walk along the river, or you can cut through the town straight to Whitefriars.'

'Thank you, I'll do that. See you on Friday, Flora.' Matt waved and walked on, feeling pleased with the decision he had made. Flora was certainly very welcoming, he thought as he went on past the way he'd come and searched for the snicket she had described. He'd timed it badly, he realized as the mill bell sounded the end of the working day. Scores of working women began filing out of the Bridge End mill's doors, all chattering and walking arm in arm, in haste to get home and make their evening meals and enjoy their own time. Some of them looked at him and giggled, whispering as they glanced up and down. He raised his hat to them.

He was going to enjoy himself working in Settle. It had some wonderful sights, and everyone seemed more than friendly. Well, apart from Anne Bainbridge; but surely even she couldn't always be frosty.

'This is Mr Walker, dear. He will be staying with us until Friday afternoon,' Anne Bainbridge said to her husband as they gathered for dinner. 'He's in charge of seeing that everything goes well for the POWs.' They were in her plush wallpapered dining room, which held a fine set of Chippendale chairs; Anne was now dressed in an immaculate two-piece, with a string of pearls at her neck.

'Blasted Italians. To think they'll be staying under my roof! The lot of them should be shot.' Colin Bainbridge took the terrine of cabbage and piled his plate up, glaring across at Matt. 'You'd better keep the bally lot in order. I for certain will not be eating with them, else I'll say what I think of them.'

'You'll hardly see them, dear. We will be living in the coach house after Friday night and taking our meals there,' Anne explained to Matt. She turned back to her husband. 'Besides, Mr Walker assures me that none of them are dangerous, and they'll be assets to the farmers.' She sent Matt a warning look, hoping he wouldn't say anything to inflame her husband's dislike of anybody who was not an ally of the British forces.

'Thrown out of my own bloody house and living where the groom used to live. This world has gone to the dogs.' Colin scowled from under his bushy eyebrows.

'We're most grateful for the use of your beautiful house, sir. It won't be forever, I hope, and then once the war is over, we will see it returned to the state in which we found it.' Matt thanked Anne as she passed him a meagre ration of potatoes to go with his lone sausage. He picked up his knife and fork.

'I should bally well hope so. I'll expect compensation if it isn't. There may be a war on, but we must not drop our standards.' Colin shook his head. 'Never did I imagine the day would come when I had to make way for a horde of Italians in my own home.'

'They'll be looking after the garden for us, dear. That will be very useful. Since our gardener went away to fight, the grounds have been rather unkempt.' Anne tried to smile at Matt.

'Yes, several of the POWs are experienced in horticulture and agriculture, as I told you earlier, Mrs Bainbridge. I should think they'll be only too happy to tend to your grounds,' Matt agreed.

Colin grunted.

'Can you remember a Maisy Walker, Colin, who used to be the landlady at the Cunning Vixen? Well, this young man is her son.' Anne decided to change the subject as supper was nearly over. 'It must have been . . . nearly thirty years ago?' She looked at Matt for confirmation.

'Twenty-eight, to be precise. She often talked about how much she loved living here. I can't say I blame her, now that I've walked through Settle and Giggleswick.' Matt wiped his mouth with his napkin and sat back in his chair.

'Would that be the same Maisy Walker who left in disgrace, owing money at the bank? She's the only one by that name I can recall. She certainly had a reputation,' Colin said bluntly, unconcerned about offending Matt. He would gladly have seen the upstart War Office man out in the street if it were up to him, not to mention all the Italians.

'Oh, no, dear – I think you must have that wrong. She might have been a Maisy, but not Maisy Walker, of that I'm sure. Although I can't remember her at all,' Anne said vaguely, with a polite smile at Matt.

'Ah, well, it was many years ago,' Matt said mildly. 'Times change. If you'll excuse me, I think I will have an early night; tomorrow will be a long day. Thank you for a delicious dinner.' He pushed back his chair, bade his hosts good evening, and left the dining room.

He did not regret one bit that he would soon be leaving this grand residence to stay in Flora Whitaker's modest room at the Cunning Vixen. At least he would be welcome there.

Chapter 12

'I apologize for my husband's behaviour on your stay with us; he is taking it hard that we're leaving our house in the care of the War Office. He seems to think we'll never get it back.' Anne Bainbridge picked up Matt's empty breakfast plate. 'I'd take no notice of what he said – I shouldn't say this, but sometimes he gets mixed up about which customer is which. I keep telling him that it's time he put his feet up.' She sighed and glanced out of the dining room window, noticing five uniformed men walking up the drive.

'Don't worry, Mrs Bainbridge, I understand. Nobody likes their home life disrupted, especially when the house is so well loved. At least I'll be out from under your feet shortly. My time with you has been most enjoyable, I have admired your home, while I have been staying here.' Matt stood up, following her gaze. 'Ah, that will be Captain Bentham with his guards; he'll be making his office in your study. Have you met him? I believe he's a nice enough fellow.'

‘Yes, he’s been back and forward quite a bit, arranging the office as he wants it. He was writing to all the local farmers and businesses the other week, telling them of the POWs’ arrival and encouraging them to come forward if they need any help. He usually walks straight in and makes himself at home.’ Anne sighed again. Her life was being turned upside down, but at least nobody in her immediate family was fighting abroad.

Matt nodded. ‘I’ll go and see him in the office. The POWs should have started from the camp at Eden by now. They’ll be here by lunchtime, so I hope one of those other men is a cook – they’ll need feeding.’

‘That is the hardest part: leaving my kitchen in somebody else’s hands. I live my life in that kitchen. But the one at the coach house wants for nothing, and it’s cosy enough for the two of us.’ Anne’s voice quavered a little.

‘Your sacrifice is appreciated, Mrs Bainbridge. I hope the government’s compensation makes up for your loss of income. I was looking through the agreement this morning and hoped that we had been right with you,’ Matt said, trying for a reassuring smile as he held the dining room door open for her.

‘Oh, the money is not that important. We want to help the war effort, so we will grin and bear it. Now, I will take these into the kitchen and wash them up for the last time and then make myself scarce.’

Anne drew a deep breath and walked across the hallway, saying ‘Good morning,’ to the two soldiers who now stood at either side of the doorway. It was going to be a hard day for her. She had already watched as basic bunk beds were placed into the bedrooms and her furniture moved out to the stables; now the dining room was about to be cleared, with long tables and benches replacing her beloved Chippendale table and chairs. It was a travesty what was happening to her home. One or two of the less valuable paintings still hung on the walls; hopefully they would not be stolen or damaged, she thought as she put Matt's crockery into the sink.

A soldier in khaki trousers and a white shirt was looking through the stocked pantry.

'Good morning; I hope you will be happy in my kitchen. If I can help in any way, do let me know,' she said with a faint smile.

He turned and smiled back at her, holding a round of cheese in both hands. 'Thank you, ma'am. I'll find my way around eventually. I'm expecting some cutlery and pottery any time now, and a delivery of bread. Got to keep these Italians fed, whether the bloody Jerries feed our lads or not. I sometimes think they've never heard of the Geneva Convention, and that we look after theirs too well.' He set the cheese down on the scrubbed wooden table and gave Anne a sympathetic look. 'I'll take good care of your kitchen. I'll make sure it is respected and kept clean.'

'Thank you; that's very kind.' Anne finished the washing up and then walked quickly out of her house, head lowered. Behind her, she could hear the sound of furniture being moved in the dining room. She hoped it would not be too long before this war ended and her unwanted guests were sent back home.

Matt knocked on the open door of the study and looked in at the captain, who was seated behind a large desk.

'Good morning – I see that you have everything in hand for the new arrivals.' He extended his hand and introduced himself as Captain Dan Bentham rose to greet him. Bentham was dark-haired and clean-shaven apart from a rather dashing moustache, and smartly dressed in his uniform.

'Yes, sir. Good to see you again, sir. I was present at the meeting at Eden Camp, sir, if you remember.' Bentham shook Matt's hand.

'I do indeed, Captain. They spoke highly of you, so I was glad to hear you were chosen to oversee this camp. It needed somebody with tact and sense. In a small town like this, local sentiment has to be taken into consideration, and we must ensure that the POWs prove their worth in the community. We don't want people thinking of Whitefriars as a holiday camp for the enemy.' Matt pulled out a chair, gesturing to Bentham to sit down with him.

'Indeed, sir. I've already had letters expressing concern about the security of the house. Some have suggested we should run barbed wire around the outer walls and actually shackle the men. I have, of course, replied to explain that the POWs here are carefully vetted. However, I hope you don't mind, sir – I've arranged a meeting with some of the local businesses and dignitaries on Monday evening to allow all these matters to be aired. Perhaps we ought to have done that before the POWs arrived, but the wheels were moving too slowly in certain departments. On the positive side, we've had a number of requests for them to serve as farm labourers. Their arrival couldn't be better timed for the Dales – it's shearing and haytime coming up, so the farmers are busy.'

'I gather Mr and Mrs Bainbridge would like a helping hand with the gardens here, and that would show our appreciation for the sacrifice of their property. Now, why don't you take me through each individual man's file? And then we'll walk round the house together. I believe you'll be staying in the bedroom I slept in last night – I can tell you the bed is very comfortable. Have we a local lady to see to the cleaning and needs of those that are staying here?'

'Yes, two, in fact. A young woman from Langcliffe to do the washing and mending, and an older lady to do the cleaning. I was afraid nobody would want to work here, but when the pay was advertised, we had quite a lot of interest. The cook is one of our men from Eden Camp, a reliable sort. All is in hand, sir.'

Bentham's tone was polite, but he felt undermined by Matt's presence. He didn't need a man in a suit telling him how to do his job. This fellow seemed to know it all, he thought to himself.

'I'm sure it is. Now, take me through the prisoners that are arriving. Assure me that they are all Category A or B, and that we have no Nazi sympathizers about to be placed in our midst.'

'None, sir. I'll show you their files; all details are present and correct. Most of them should never have been sent to fight in the first place. They're lads from rural farms, bakers' apprentices . . .' Bentham took an armful of files out of a filing cabinet and placed them on the desk in front of Matt. 'One of them has only just turned seventeen. They'll cause no trouble. They will be glad of the chance to stay safe, earn their keep and put their heads down until the end of the war, when they can return home. I'll send for tea while you look through them. They make interesting reading.'

'Thank you. A pot of tea would be most welcome.' Matt picked up the first file and started to leaf through it.

For the next hour they worked steadily through the stack of paperwork, pausing only to pour the tea that one of the men brought in on a tray. Eventually, Matt closed the last file, shaking his head.

'Half of these poor souls didn't want any part of this war. Or so their files tell us; however, that does not mean we should be lax. You'll have at least four men on guard duty at all times?'

'Yes, and they'll each be escorted to their places of work. We're buried out here in the country, miles away from any port or route to their homes. The chance of anyone escaping, or even of wanting to, is remote. However, they'll be watched, and if anyone gives us any trouble, back they'll go to the camp at Eden. Conditions there are pretty rough compared to here.' Bentham watched as Matt straightened the files and passed them back over to him.

'As you say, we can only hope our own men are being as well looked after – which I very much doubt, based on what I hear.' Matt sighed. 'Right, let's walk round the house and grounds before they arrive. And if you think there's anything that could be changed for the better, don't be afraid to say so.'

Captain Bentham took exception to the idea that anything might not be correct. He glared at Matt. 'I think you will find that all is in place, and I have a list from the Home Office of what favours and benefits can be given to the prisoners. We are prepared for their arrival, and I hope that they will be accepted into Settle. After all, it is to everyone's advantage. We may not even win the war, and then the enemy will become our victors and we will be at their mercy,' he added as he made his way up the stairs, Matt following.

'God forbid. May this country never fall into the hands of madmen like Hitler and Mussolini. We must win this war if it's the last thing we do as a nation.'

'Yes, sir. It's a good job we have men in uniform keeping the country safe,' Bentham replied. He was determined to prove that he was worth ten times more than the War Office man, whom he thought of as no more than an office clerk.

Chapter 13

Flora's letter had greatly encouraged Bill, who was finding life in an army camp hard the second time around. He was feeling his age, and the pain of the shrapnel in his spine and back seemed to get worse with every day's manoeuvres. The young lads who had been recruited alongside him had already left for North Africa, and he had a suspicion that he was about to be discharged on grounds of ill health. The idea hurt his pride. He was as fit as any man, he told himself – and ready to fight for his country, if only given the chance.

He looked up from the muddy ground where he had just slipped and fallen. The rest of his regiment, dressed in full battle gear, was heading onwards to climb another obstacle, yelling as they charged the make-believe enemy. It had been a telling few weeks at Catterick Barracks. His body was reminding him he was no longer a young man. He let his head drop into the mud for a moment, only to lift it up and find a pair of polished army boots standing immediately beside him. His sergeant major peered down at him, and Bill braced for him to yell. Instead, the sergeant smiled in a rather sinister way. He bent close to Bill's ear and spoke in a whisper, his moustache twitching as if possessed.

'Had enough, Whitaker? Feeling knackered?' He glowered down at Bill with steely eyes. 'You will next week, when you're over there fighting for your life. But at this rate, you'd have all on to fight your way out of a paper bag.'

'Yes, Sarge, I'm knackered,' Bill replied as he struggled to his feet, wishing the sergeant would send him back to barracks. He needed a rest.

'Shall I go and run you a nice warm bath? Make some toast?' The sergeant put his head to one side and grinned. Then, in the loudest voice Bill had ever heard, he shouted directly into his face. 'You useless excuse of a man! You are a soldier now, not a pub landlord! Now, go – get on with it, lad, else you'll get my boot up your arse, and you will have something to complain about then!'

'Yes, Sergeant.' Bill picked up his rifle and ran onwards through the mud towards the next wooden hurdle. He had forgotten what bastards sergeants could be. He had also expected a little respect and perhaps even deference as a veteran of the last war, but none was to be shown. The sergeant continued to yell abuse at him as he struggled to the top of the log pile, hurling himself over only to land at the other side in absolute agony as the shrapnel dug into him. He lay back down in the mud and closed his eyes as the sergeant approached at speed.

'You useless bag of shit, Whitaker! Get up! Get up, I tell you!'

Bill just groaned. The man could yell all he liked. He couldn't, just couldn't move another inch. The pain down his spine was excruciating and he could hardly feel his legs. 'I can't, Sarge, I can't.' He looked up at the roaring sergeant with wild, worried eyes. 'I can't, I just can't. I can hardly feel my legs. I can't move them.'

'Of course you can, man! Bloody well get up and stop dodging your training! Get up! Get bloody well up!'

'I can't . . . I can't move.' Bill put his face down in the wet mud and wished the sergeant would bugger off and leave him lying there.

'MOVE!' The sergeant squatted down and yelled once more in Bill's ear. After a short pause, he seemed to recognize that Bill was telling the truth. Frustrated, he straightened up. 'Stay bloody still, man. I'll call for the medics. Old men are not meant for this amount of training. I don't know what you're doing here. All I get sent now is old men and boys still in their nappies.' He turned towards a nearby soldier who had finished the course and circled back to see what was going on. 'Stay here with Whitaker while I go for a medic.'

'Yes, sir,' Private Osmond said. He looked down at Bill, then crouched to talk to him. 'What the hell have you done, Bill?'

'I've hurt my back. I should never have joined up. I wasn't fit enough, and I knew it. I've had damage to my spine since the last time I was in the army. I never told them when I went through the medical. In normal life it's no bother most days, but with all this, it's been worse. Now I can hardly move my right leg. Feels like I've been shot in it.' Bill held his breath and tried to turn himself over onto his back, but without success.

'You shouldn't move. Stay still until the medics come,' Osmond said, pushing his glasses up his nose. 'You silly bugger, you shouldn't be here at all. You've been suffering ever since we got here. You should've told them instead of being so proud. I'd leave if I could get away with it. I hate this mud, exercise and being treated like cattle. I'd rather be at work in my office.' Peter Osmond was a quiet, studious lad, not an obvious choice for the army. He had been picked on by the sergeant from day one.

'Aye, but I felt it was my duty.' Bill sighed and covered his eyes with his hands. 'What the bloody hell am I going to do now? Flora will have more than enough to say about this if I've seriously injured myself. She told me not to come.' He tried to move again and let out a yelp of pain.

'Stay still, you're making it worse. They'll patch you up and send you home. I don't think you'll be leaving good old Blighty any time soon.' Osmond looked round towards the barracks. 'Hey up, here comes the cavalry. You'll have a free ride home on a stretcher. The sarge isn't looking too happy. He'll maybe regret his hard words.'

'I'll tell him it's not his fault. He might be a bastard, but he's usually fair and I deserved all his shouting.' Bill prayed that his injuries were not serious. He knew that it was all his own fault – he'd tried to act like a fit young man when he should have been in the cook house or stables. Anywhere but on the front line, where he had to prove his strength and fitness. He had been a fool.

The sergeant approached, his demeanour totally different from ten minutes earlier. 'Now then, lad, don't move. These two medics are going to lift you onto the stretcher and into the infirmary, and then the doc will look at you. Don't you worry. You'll be looked after.' His voice was softer than Bill had ever heard it.

'It wasn't your fault, Sarge. I don't want you thinking it is, whatever I've done.' Bill caught his breath, the sharpest pain he had ever felt surging up his spine as the two medics rolled him over and placed him on the stretcher.

'Aye, well, I was being a bit hard on you, but you looked fit enough . . .' The sergeant looked round at the rest of the squaddies; they had gathered round the medics and stretcher, murmuring amongst themselves. 'Ten times round the field, you lot. Now! Nothing to see here. Get on with it!'

The soldiers moved off and did as they were told, but they were blaming the brutal sergeant as they jogged in twos around the perimeter fence. He was a bully, and they all knew it.

Bill lay in bed and looked up at the whitewashed wooden ceiling of the infirmary, waiting for the doctor. The walls were white and stark, the smell of disinfectant filled the air, and a breeze blew through the open windows. Nurses had changed and washed him as if he were a baby, and now he was waiting to see what they were going to do to him next. He propped himself up in bed and dragged his legs into a sitting position as he heard the doctor come along the corridor with the matron by his side.

'Now, what have you been up to, Private Whitaker? I understand you have severe pain down your leg and spine. Lie back down for me, if you can.' The doctor watched Bill struggle to lower himself back down into the bed.

'Mmm . . . I'm just going to turn you over with the help of the matron. Don't you twist yourself, you need support.' The doctor gently rolled Bill onto his side and ran a hand down his spine before laying him back straight in bed, not wanting to make the injury any worse. 'There's an old scar beside your spine. Have you been injured there before?'

Bill looked down, avoiding eye contact, knowing that he was in the wrong if he admitted the truth.

'Aye, I have a piece of shrapnel embedded in there from the last time I was in the army. But it's never done this before,' he said quietly. 'I should have said at my medical, but pride stopped me.'

'You were in the last war, and injured? Now, why don't we have that on your papers? The recruitment officer has been lax. He should have given you a thorough examination when he learned that.' The doctor moved to Bill's feet and, without Bill seeing, pressed a pin into each foot. He noticed that his patient did not flinch when he pricked the left foot, even when he had nearly drawn blood.

'I never let him know,' Bill said miserably. 'It wasn't the examiner's fault. And I'm a year older than you'll have on my records there. When he said a lot of the service records had been lost in a bombing raid, I hoped I could blag my way into joining up again.' He sighed. 'I've been a fool.'

'That's of no consequence now. What is most urgent is to see just how much damage has been done. I'll be quite honest, Private Whitaker – Bill. I think you have injured your spinal cord. The shrapnel has probably moved and is resting on a nerve at the very best, but at the very worst . . . Well, we will have to see what an X-ray can show us and how you improve over the coming weeks. Army medicine has made great strides since your original injury, and we now have an MX-2 machine here at the infirmary. Now, I want you to rest today – and then tomorrow, when the pain has eased with the help of some painkillers I'm going to give you, we will look at the damage. I imagine, though, that your idea of going to fight for us in North Africa will have to be put on hold.' The doctor looked down at Bill. 'Have I covered everything, or is there anything else I can tell you?'

'No, Doctor, thank you. I know you'll do your best, and I'm in good hands,' Bill replied quietly.

'It's lucky that you've injured yourself further while still in the country. If you had gone out to Africa with your historic injury, you could have put other lives at risk. That is why we give medical examinations before recruitment. I will be having a word with the board of examiners. We may be short of men, but there's no point sending unfit soldiers to the front,' the doctor said sternly.

'I'm sorry, Doctor; it's all my fault. I should have known better than to cover things up.' Bill sighed as he watched the doctor and matron walk away. He was in pain and worried beyond belief. What if he could never walk again – all because of his pride and stupidity? How was he going to tell Flora? And how on earth would they manage if the worst came to the worst? Bill put his hand to his head, starting to realize just how serious things were. 'Nurse, could I have a pen and some paper? I'll write to my wife – she'll have to know that I'm unwell.'

'Of course. I'll get you some straight away, and I'll put a stamp on it myself and drop it in the post box just outside the ward.'

Bill lay back and stared at the ceiling for a while. Then he raised his head and looked at the two other soldiers on the ward. They were both young. One had broken his leg and was in traction, and the other was asleep. Bill breathed in deeply, thinking about what to say to Flora. She would no doubt worry about him, whatever he said, but he didn't want her to worry *too* much – after all, he told himself, the X-ray tomorrow might show him to be fine.

The young nurse returned with a smile on her face and a pen and paper in her hand.

'Can you manage to write it? I can do it for you if you wish,' she said politely.

'No, lass, I'll do it. My wife will only worry more if

it's written in somebody else's hand. I'll be in trouble enough as it is,' Bill replied as he took the writing paper and an already stamped envelope.

'I'm sure not. She should be proud of you, even if she's worried as well. If you need anything else, let me know.'

'Thank you. I will.'

As she walked away, Bill looked down at the blank piece of paper, wondering where to start. It was not the letter he'd been hoping to send home, and he knew it would change everything.

Chapter 14

Matt sat in a quiet corner of the Cunning Vixen. He had decided that on his first night's stay there, he would keep himself to himself. It had been a long day already, and after eating the ample portion of rabbit stew that Flora had made him, he felt dozy and content.

Earlier in the day he had watched the POWs climb down from the back of the army wagon and look around them in disbelief. They had been ragged and tired, worn out by fighting a war that was not of their making. Matt had stayed on site while they were fed and shown to their quarters. Whitefriars might be cramped with the beds packed in tightly, but compared to the high-security camp at Eden, it must have seemed like heaven.

There was still plenty to do. Even though tomorrow was Saturday, he would have to check in at the camp to make sure everything was running smoothly. He picked up his pint and took a long drink, closing his eyes.

‘Are you the new lodger, then? You’ll be all right with our Flora.’

Matt opened his eyes to see an elderly man with a weatherbeaten face standing near his table, giving him the once-over.

‘I am indeed, and she has made me most welcome,’ he replied, watching as the man pulled up a chair next to him, uninvited.

‘Aye, she’s a grand lass, is Flora. She’d do owt for anybody. Not a bad bone in her body.’ Frank settled into his seat and looked at the young man opposite him. He was definitely not a country fellow. His skin was pale and his hair slick, and even at this time of night he was still in his city suit. ‘I hear you’ve come to look after them Italians that are joining us up in Settle. I hope that they won’t bring any bother with them. You can never trust these foreigners, no matter what they say. Hot-blooded, that’s what they are.’ Frank shook his head.

‘They shouldn’t bring any bother to the village. They just want to see this war end so that they can go home. Most were labourers before the war began. They’ll be a good help to the farmers round about.’ Matt drained the dregs of his pint and set the glass down, wondering whether to have another before bed. He looked up as Flora, having spotted him without a drink, made a beeline for him.

She patted Frank on the back and smiled. ‘Hey up, Frank. Are you making friends with Matt? He’ll be stopping with us for a week or two. But knowing the local grapevine, you probably already know that.’ Flora smiled.

'Aye, I heard May talking to her copper mate. So, I thought I'd come and make myself known. The local copper drinking at the bar, and a fella from the War Office staying under your roof – I bet Bill would have something to say about that, Flora.' Frank gave Flora a wry smile and looked back at the new lodger.

'He'd not say a word against it, Frank Capstick, and you know he wouldn't. He'd probably be glad we've got Trevor Whinray calling in on us. And when it comes to Matt here, I'm sure you'll change your tune when you realize just who he is.' Flora glanced at Matt as if to check she wasn't speaking out of turn. He smiled at her.

'Oh, aye? Why's that, then?' Frank tilted his head enquiringly at Flora, then at Matt.

'My mother used to be the landlady here before I was born,' Matt explained. 'If you have been here at least thirty years, you will probably remember her. Maisy Walker, a tall woman with blonde hair? Her husband was in the army.' He sat back and watched as Frank cast his mind back.

'Oh, aye, I remember her. A good-looking woman – but don't tell Madge that, else she'll flatten me for sure. Maisy ran here for a few years. She could pull a good pint, much like yourself, Flora. Aye, I remember her. I can't remember her husband, though – but if he was in the army, he'd not come home much.' Frank shook his head. 'Bye, it's a small world. So, you took the chance of staying where your mother once ran? That must feel strange for you.'

'It does, but she always spoke fondly about Giggleswick

and Settle. So I was more than happy to see the latest POW placement when I realized where it was at.'

'Can I buy you a pint? Now I know who you are, we can have a right good natter.' Frank smiled at Flora as she nodded at her guest.

'May I say yes for another night? I was just thinking of taking myself to bed, even though it's not ten yet. This has been a long day with a lot to do, and we've a meeting to prepare for that the town council has lined up for Monday evening. But thank you – I'll buy you one tomorrow night? And as you say, we can have a catch-up.' Matt spoke warmly to the old man. He didn't want to seem rude, but he was truly exhausted.

'Nay, you're rite, lad, and even better if you'll be buying me a pint.' Frank smiled and watched as the young man got wearily to his feet, turning to Flora.

'Is there anywhere I might take my laundry in Settle or Giggleswick?' he asked hopefully. 'I'll need a clean shirt for work next week.'

'If you give me your things in the morning, I'll wash them through – anything you have. I've not got a set day for my own washing, it's whenever I can fit it in, so just let me know and I'll do it for you.' Flora picked up his empty glass and stood beside Frank as Matt thanked them both and disappeared up the stairs.

'Well, that's a turn-up for the books, good and proper. Maisy Walker's son! I'm damned if I can remember her having a husband. She never acted as if she were wed. But she must have been, else he wouldn't be here. Maisy Walker . . . now she was a woman.' Frank shook his head, casting his mind back a generation to Maisy's days in charge of the Cunning Vixen. 'It was Maisy who renamed this place the Cunning Vixen. Until she came along, it was the Three Bells – because of the church bells, y'know.'

'I remember her,' Flora smiled. 'She always made a fuss of me, but I can't remember a Mr Walker. I'll ask my mother next time I see her. I was hoping she'd have been in by now on a Saturday night – I keep telling her to come along and have a sherry while Bill's away. I don't need to tell you that she and Bill do not always see eye to eye . . .' Frank nodded in acknowledgement, and she sighed.

'She can be hard, can your mother. Takes all to heart. Your father had a lot to put up with, like I do with my old lass.' He looked down into his pint. 'But I suppose there's always two sides to every story. Happen she had a lot to put up with.'

'You'd be absolutely lost without Madge, Frank Capstick, and well you know it. But you're right about my mother. Once she's been slighted, she never forgets. I haven't time for that; I just get on with life, no time for grudges.' Flora patted Frank on the back.

'Aye, you take after your father; he was a grand man, taken from us far too soon. He'd have been proud of you, Flora. He really would,' Frank said, pausing for a sip of beer. 'Your mother was always terribly house-proud and loved her garden, like she does now; and your father, he just liked a good time with his mates. Like chalk and cheese they were – aye, like chalk and cheese.'

'Will you have another? It can be on the house if I can have one or two carrots from your garden. I've an extra mouth to feed, now I've got a lodger.' Flora grinned.

'Sounds like a deal to me. A bunch of carrots, and I'll bring you some radishes as well. One or two of them are starting to bolt, so they'll need eating.'

'A deal it is, Frank. Thank you.'

Matt left for Whitefriars early on Saturday morning, hoping that nobody had tried to escape as he was eating his breakfast of scrambled eggs at a table in the bar before heading up the road with his briefcase. Half an hour later, Flora was rinsing his shirts and underwear in the kitchen sink with her back door wide open when she heard a familiar voice.

'I hear you've got a lodger, Flora!' Ted the milkman grinned as he passed her the day's milk. 'Jenny Moon came out of her front door to tell me all about him as I left her half-pint on the doorstep. You're giving her plenty to talk about, what with Trevor Whinray courting young May as well. Her tongue's scarcely stopped its wagging.' He leaned against the wall and lit a cigarette, watching as Flora stepped into the back yard to peg her washing out.

'If she's nothing better than that to talk about, I'm sorry for her,' Flora said lightly. 'My lodger is a respectable young man. And I hope May finds happiness with Trevor – not that he's my favourite customer.' She and Ted exchanged a look as she pegged Matt's shirt onto the line along with his socks and underwear; then, balancing the washing basket on her hip, she went to stand beside him.

'That'll get folks talking – a man's washing out on your line. The knitting club won't know where to start this coming week,' Ted chuckled.

'Oh, let them talk. They know nothing. He's a local lad, anyway, even if he works for the War Office. And he's only staying until the Italians get settled in up the road. His mother used to be the landlady here – Maisy Walker? I can remember her. It's brought back memories. She always seemed kind, but no doubt they'll have some tales about her.' Flora paused, noticing Ted's worried expression. 'What's up? You came in laughing, and now you look like thunder. Is it because of him staying here? He'll not interfere with our dealings.'

'What dealings? We don't have any now, Flora. Customs and Excise and the docks police at Liverpool have been watching us like hawks. They've even had some of their lot mixing in, pretending to be dockers. My brother wrote to tell me not to show my face this weekend. They haven't caught him helping himself, but they've thrown six of his mates into the clink. He just hopes they won't blab or send the coppers knocking on his door.' Ted drew hard on his cigarette, gazing over at the church.

'Oh, Lord, that's not good. Will he be all right? And I hope they can't trace anything back to us?' Flora's face clouded over. She couldn't afford to lose her licence.

'He says they're good lads, they won't tell. But you never know. What with Whinray sniffing round here and my brother probably being watched, I think we'd be foolish to push our luck. I daren't ask my brother for any more.'

'Bugger – the whisky and ciggies have been such a help. It's not as if I was making a fortune, but it was a bit of extra money for all three of us.' Flora sighed. 'I must admit, I was wondering how long it would be before one of us got caught. Especially with Trevor dropping hints about when he was on patrol or not. I wonder if he knew something was going on – if he was in on it?' Flora frowned. She hadn't quite worked out why Trevor had seemed so open with his hints.

'Oh, he'd bloody know all right. They all cover one another's backs, whether they work in Liverpool or Timbuktu. You can never trust them. They've spoiled a good little money earner, and I only hope my brother won't get nicked. He can't afford to be a jailbird or lose his job. He has six kids and a missus to support.'

'I hope not an' all, Ted. Especially when nearly every other docker will have probably been doing the same thing. I'm going to miss my few bottles of whisky and the extra ciggies; my locals will, as well.'

'Aye, well, there's nothing I can do about it, I'm afraid. Not until all settles down again, but that'll take a while. At least you've got a lodger to help you out with your bills. I'll just have to put my milk up by a farthing a pint and have everybody moan at me.' Ted picked up his crate and headed for the garden gate, where his faithful old horse waited patiently with the milk float. 'Dobbin here will have to make do with fewer treats. It's going to hurt everyone, even this old fellow,' he said as Flora leaned over the garden wall.

'Nay, Dobbin will still have his treats. You love him too much to deny him his carrots.' Flora smiled, but inside she felt sick with worry. What if they did catch Ted's brother and her involvement somehow came to light? Trevor Whinray must know what was going on, though perhaps not every detail – and he'd used the information to blackmail her into giving May the nights he wanted to walk out with her off. Whatever he was up to, she'd have to be even more wary of him now, at least until everything had settled down. Thank heavens she had hardly any cigarettes left, and only one bottle of whisky. Soon there would be no remaining evidence of contraband in the pub, even if someone did come sniffing round.

'I'll be in tonight for my usual Saturday night pint, Flora. I only hope that copper isn't about. Makes my beer go flat just looking at him.' Ted nodded a goodbye as he urged Dobbin forward, heading for the next stop on his round.

Flora picked up her washing peg basket and went back into the pub. What with Bill being away, her new lodger, and now this worry about the police, she was adding daily to her worries. If only her life were easier. Perhaps Maisy Walker had got it right when she'd left the Cunning Vixen. It was a lot of worry, especially now, with a war raging and everything being turned on its head.

She found May seated at the kitchen table, a steaming mug of tea in her hand. 'I let myself in the front – I wanted another glance at the new lodger. I saw him last night and thought how handsome he was,' she smiled. 'But I couldn't talk to him much, because I thought Trevor might come in and get jealous.' May sat forward and poured tea for Flora. 'I heard you talking to the milkie. I don't much like him – he's always giving me funny looks, especially of late.'

'Ted's all right,' Flora said, sitting down opposite her. 'He just doesn't trust anybody, and I can't say I blame him. There's always folk owing him for their milk. As for our new lodger, you'd have to have been here a lot earlier to catch him. He's been gone a good hour. Anyway, you should only have eyes for that copper of yours, and he'll always be suspicious of you – he's suspicious of everybody. That's part of his job.' She took a long sip of the weak tea and sat back with a sigh. 'Ta, love. I need this. It's not even eight o'clock and I've already had enough of this day. Trevor isn't expecting you to come out tonight, is he? I could do with you behind the bar.'

'No, but he might pop in and see me after his shift. He's promised to take me to the pictures on Wednesday night, when Bob Mason does his shift. They're showing *Gone with the Wind*, so I can't wait – Clark Gable is so handsome. I've never been to the pictures with a man before, but I've seen them all on the back row and what courting couples get up to.' May blushed. 'I just hope Trevor doesn't get too amorous.'

'Don't let him do anything you're not happy with, May. Not that he will – he's not that sort, I hope. He's your first real boyfriend, so take it slow.' Flora saw May's blushes; she was only young. She could imagine that May's mother might not be easy to talk to about such matters. 'No wandering hands this time. There's plenty of time for that yet.'

'That's what I worry about. Will he break it off with me if I say no?' May bit her lip, her eyes on the table.

'Well, he's no gentleman if he does, and you're better off without him.' Flora smiled at her. 'Now, come on. You can start the day by tidying Matt's bedroom. He is handsome, you're right – and a nice man. Perhaps a little old for you, but I don't think he's married.'

'Oh, isn't he? I thought he might be,' May sounded more cheerful as she stood up to gather her duster and polish.

'Not that I know of. I'll find out, shall I?' Flora smiled. She was thinking that when she was as young as May, the world had been her oyster – if only she'd known it.

Chapter 15

Friday morning was starting to be frustrating as Trevor Whinray sat in the main office of Settle police station beside PC Bob Mason. Opposite them, their sergeant sat behind his desk in a stern mood.

'Gentlemen, the forces in Liverpool have informed me that they've arrested several dockers after catching them in the act of stealing contraband from container ships. Now, none of those caught are known to have links to this area – or so they believe. I want to look more deeply into that. I've asked you to join me this morning to find out what you know about dealings in this area. Whinray, you said you had your suspects. Can you prove anything? Don't hold back with what you know.' Sergeant Blake looked over his spectacles at the young officer who thought he knew it all. He didn't much like Whinray or his ways; most of all, he knew the young fellow would jump at any opportunity to replace him.

'Well, sir, I've been keeping surveillance on the Cunning

Vixen in Giggleswick. I believe the landlady there has been taking contraband from the local milkman. He has family connections to Liverpool; his brother is a dock worker there. I let it be known that PC Mason patrols in the area on a Wednesday evening, hoping that they might then be tempted to offload their goods that night, as they know my shift pattern too well. I've also become friendly with a cleaner and barmaid who works there, May Lambert, but she either knows nothing or doesn't want to say anything. I'm certain something is going on. I believe I spotted some bottles of whisky under the bar that should not have been there.'

Bob Mason laughed quietly. Friendly! Trevor and May were more than friendly, from what Trevor had told him. He'd been stringing her along to benefit him in more ways than one. The poor lass, she was being used.

Sergeant Blake looked at Bob. 'And you, Mason? Seen anything on your beat on a Wednesday – or any other night, come to that?'

'No, sir, it's always quiet. Giggleswick gives us the least problems in the area. The Cunning Vixen's always in darkness when I walk past late on my shift. The milkman from Giggleswick does have relations in Liverpool, but so does nearly everybody in these Dales. Half their families used to supply milk to the city, and some still do. May Lambert comes from a good family – she'll not be mixed up in anything. After all, she's only a young lass of eighteen. And I can't see Flora Whitaker risking her licence.'

'The Lambert girl's eighteen?' Sergeant Blake raised

his eyebrows. 'I hope, PC Whinray, that you are not seriously involved with her. That would be highly inappropriate, especially if you've been using her as cover for an investigation. We're not in the business of encouraging unwanted feelings in the fairer sex for the sake of information.' He looked hard at Trevor. It was possible, he thought, to be a little too eager for advancement in the forces.

'No, sir – of course not. We've just talked, and I have tried to win her friendship.' Trevor shot a look at Bob. Why had he gone and mentioned May's age? No need for Sarge to know that.

Blake sat back with a sigh. 'It sounds as if we're chasing Scotch mist. And the less we have to do with authorities outside our area, the better. Let's make for a quiet life. Our fight is with Jerry, not one another. You can stand down from watching the Cunning Vixen, Whinray. I doubt there was anything to report there anyway.' He nodded a dismissal and straightened some paperwork on his desk as the young officers stood to leave. 'And Whinray? Find a woman, not a young girl, to become friendly with.'

All the same, he thought as he watched them go, he might take a stroll down to the Vixen himself later on. Just to make sure all was well.

It had been one of those mornings for Flora. May had come to work in a mood, hardly speaking as she went about her cleaning, slamming things down and just grunting when spoken to. As opening time approached and May was about to go home, Flora decided to ask her what was wrong – although she had a pretty good idea already.

'I hope your face changes for the better when you're serving tonight, else the beer will turn sour,' she said, as May shoved the mop and brush away under the stairs and banged the cupboard door shut. 'Is this over your elusive copper? I noticed he didn't visit us the other night.'

'Might be. Not that I'm bothered,' May replied, though her cheeks were red.

'No, you don't look it. What's he done?' Flora sighed. 'Was he busy or something, so he didn't give us the delight of his presence?' She couldn't help but be sarcastic; she had been grateful that Trevor hadn't appeared at her bar. It had allowed her to get rid of the last few packets of illegal cigarettes.

'He promised he'd come in and see me on Friday night, but he never showed his face. And then when I got home, he'd put a note through our letterbox to say he was doing a lot of overtime and that he'd catch up with me sometime.' May gushed her words out and finished with a sob. 'He's had enough of me. I'll not be seeing him again, not to walk out with anyway. I don't know what I've done.'

'Come here, silly.' Flora hugged May. 'He's only said he's doing overtime. He will be busy sometimes, he's a copper. It'll be with the POWs being based here – they'll be on their toes until they know that lot has settled into the community. Now stop those tears; there will be plenty of chances to go to the pictures. If not with Trevor, I'm sure with another good-looking man.'

'No, Flora, it's got to be Trevor. I can't be unfaithful.' May blew her nose and looked at her all-knowing boss. 'What you say makes sense. That is what he'll be doing. I should have known that myself, what with your lodger staying here and saying that the Italians have arrived. He'll be back when he's not as busy.'

'Of course he will; and if he isn't, more fool him, and there are plenty more fish in the sea.' Flora held May at arm's length and smiled at her. 'Now, you get yourself home and I'll see you tonight. No more tears.'

'No more tears, I promise. He's just doing overtime. He'll probably call in here tonight,' May said hopefully as she made her way to the back door and home.

Saturday morning went by quickly. As the clock above the bar struck twelve, Flora opened the pub's doors ready for her afternoon drinkers. She put the hook through the back of the main door to keep it open and turned to see her mother crossing the road towards her.

'Are you coming to see me? That's a nice surprise. You don't usually come for a drink in the afternoon.' Flora smiled as Mary climbed the two steps into the pub.

'Yes, I have come to see you – to find out if what I hear is true. You've got yourself a single man as a lodger? What do you think you are playing at, our Flora! A single woman or a married couple is one thing, but a single man staying here on his own? You'll be the talk of the village with your Bill away in the army.' Mary Whitaker's face was flushed, and she had to catch her breath as she stood at the bar and chastised her daughter.

'Oh, Mam, stop it. If the folk of Giggleswick have nothing better to do than talk about my lodger, then I feel sorry for them. Besides, he's from the War Office and is here on business, settling the Italians into their quarters at Whitefriars. He's got to stay somewhere, so what's wrong with here?'

'You are on your own. That's what's wrong. Folk will talk!' Mary stared at her daughter. Sometimes it seemed as if money mattered more to her than her reputation.

'Well, happen this will make you like him staying here more.' Flora looked at her mother and hoped that what she was going to tell her would calm her down. 'It turns out that his mother was the landlady here when I was a child. I can remember her – Maisy Walker? She was a beautiful woman with long blonde hair. She always said hello to me and talked a lot to my father. I'm sure you will remember her. I bet Matt would love to talk to you. He should be back any time now. He said he'd be back for his lunch.'

'Maisy Walker . . . he's the son of . . . Well, I've heard it all now. Why has he come back here? And to think he's staying here – he must have a brass neck!' Mary shook her head.

'Why, Mam, I've always remembered her as a right kind person. She always made a right fuss of me.' Flora looked at her mother with surprise.

'Well, as you say, you were a child back then. You had no idea what went on behind these walls, and it's best that it stays that way. But I can tell you that his mother was nothing but trouble and left with her tail between her legs, owing money and breaking a few hearts as well with her wicked ways.' Mary shook her head and swore under her breath. 'If I were him, I wouldn't be making it known he was her lad. Lord, you are going to be the talk of the village. Tell him that the room will be taken next week and get rid of him.'

'Mam, I can't. He's staying at least a month with me. Surely, if what you say about his mother is true, then you can't blame him? He seems so proud and pleased that his mother was the landlady here. That's why he came looking for it.' Flora was troubled by the anger and sadness on her mother's face.

'He's nowt to be proud of – nothing at all. His mother was a hussy, and everybody in this village will tell you so,' Mary spat. Flora stared at her in astonishment. 'Tell him anything you like. But you don't want him staying here, Flora, if you know what's good for you both.' Mary backed away as far as the open doorway and paused there as if unsure whether to turn and leave.

'I don't understand, Mam. I've never known you talk like that about anyone. You've never even met him,' Flora said, bewildered. It was clear to her there was something her mother wasn't telling her, something about what had happened all those years ago. Mary had never much liked the Cunning Vixen, never taken to the idea of Flora running it, but nor had she ever been so openly disparaging of its previous landlady.

'For once in your life, do as I say! Get rid of him. Send

him back to Whitefriars. Surely they've room for him there.' Mary turned sharply away just as Matt appeared in the doorway behind her. She glanced up for a moment as he apologized, but she didn't speak. Pushing past him, she walked rapidly away in the direction of her cottage.

Matt glanced after her briefly and turned back to Flora, smiling as he stepped into the pub. 'Well, she didn't have much to say!' he remarked cheerfully.

'That's my mam,' Flora said softly, still collecting her thoughts. She took a deep breath and managed to return his smile. 'I don't know what's the matter with her; she's in a mood. Something's wrong, but she'll tell me eventually. To be honest, I'd better tell you that she's not well suited to find I've taken you as a lodger. She thinks –' Flora hesitated, her cheeks colouring. 'She thinks people will talk because I'm a married woman on her own with a male lodger while my husband is away. Says a lot for her faith in me.'

'Oh, I see . . . I never even thought. I can assure you that I would never dream – I mean, you are attractive, but as your mother points out, you are married. And I'm engaged, as it happens. However, if it eases her mind, I can certainly look for a room elsewhere,' Matt said awkwardly.

'No, it's just my mother. She trusts nobody and easily falls out with everybody. Now, I didn't know you were engaged. You must tell me all about your lady love while I make you some lunch. You're back a little earlier than I expected, so I've just opened the doors for this afternoon's customers.'

'I would like nothing more than to sit in that corner over there with a freshly drawn pint and wait for my lunch, so there's no need to apologize. And I completely understand about your mother. She must be worried that I could turn out to be a mad rapist. But believe me, I am quite content with my Beth, who will be awaiting me at Leeds station when I return.'

'I thought I'd make you pork pie, cheese and pickled onions, a ploughman's lunch. May went out early this morning and managed to secure two pork pies from the butcher's down the road – a real luxury,' Flora smiled. Matt took a seat at the table while she pulled him a pint of bitter and then brought it across to him.

'Perfect. Just what I need after a morning with the POWs. Some of them can't believe their luck at having landed in such luxury. Come next week when they're put to work, I imagine their views may change.' Matt took a long sip of his beer and looked out across the winding village street. He noticed Flora's mother standing over in the post office doorway, and she seemed to be looking directly at him. Surely she thought better of her daughter than to think Flora would have an affair while her husband was away?

As for Matt himself, there was only one love in his life, and that was his Beth. A date for their wedding had already been set, and he had left her in the village of Methley just outside Leeds to decorate and prepare their future home.

He took another sip of beer and returned Mary's gaze until she eventually turned away. He hoped there might be an opportunity for them to meet again. He could at least try to reassure her that he wouldn't be making any advances on her daughter, no matter how good-looking Flora was.

The bar gradually filled up with Saturday afternoon regulars. Matt watched as Flora pulled pints and chatted to the locals, making them welcome. She was a good hostess, and the pork pie and pickles she brought over certainly filled him up. He caught her eye as a lull came over the room, and she smiled and came to sit with him.

'So you're engaged, Matt? Have you set a wedding date yet?' Flora settled comfortably in the chair opposite him and looked at him with her green eyes sparkling.

'Yes – August first at St Mary's in Methley. Beth is very excited. We have been planning it for at least two years, but I've kept putting it off because my work has taken me all over the country. However, it's all planned now, and I hope to be based more in the Leeds area or at least in Yorkshire.' Matt sat back and looked at Flora. 'I believe your husband is at Catterick and is about to be sent to North Africa? It'll be a bit warmer there than in Yorkshire, I should think. Certainly a bit more dangerous.'

'Yes; he's still in training. I expected a letter from him by now, at least to tell me when he goes or if he'll be allowed leave to come home first. He always was a terror for not writing, even when we were courting.' Flora sighed. She had expected to hear from Bill before now, but she knew that he would be busy. And it was true what she said – he hated putting pen to paper. 'I'd better go and see if anybody else wants a drink before I call afternoon closing. Would you like another pint?'

'Just a half, thank you, and then I'm going to have a stroll up the hill to the chapel before writing a postcard to Beth. I bought one from the post office across the way – I thought she'd like to see what a lovely village this is.'

'A half it is; I'll bring it over to you.' Flora went back behind the bar, thanking one of her regulars as he set his empty pint glass down and bade her farewell until the dominoes match on Monday night. She was about to serve Matt when she half turned to notice the sergeant from Settle police station coming in.

'I'm on last orders and about to close,' Flora said politely as he came up to the bar. 'But you're welcome to come in,' she added quickly, although she hoped he wouldn't take up the offer. Already her drinkers were starting to melt away at the sight of an officer on the premises.

'You're on time with closing, I'll give you that, Flora. I just thought I'd have a stroll down this way. I usually leave this part of the world to my two constables, but it's a grand day, so I thought I'd pay a visit myself.' Sergeant Blake took his cap off and loosened his tie a little. 'It's a warm one out here for sure. May I trouble you for a glass of water? I'll not have a drink, as I'm on duty.'

'Of course; are you sure you wouldn't like anything else?' Flora stood with her hands on her hips and noticed that Matt was watching her with her surprise visitor. She felt a little thrill of nerves as Blake leaned over the bar, looking down towards her shelves. His gaze travelled across the large mirror behind her, where some of her bottles of spirits were kept.

'No, Flora, I'm fine with water. However, I would like to take a look behind your bar and down in your cellar. We've been told that black-marketeers are working in the area, and I know you won't be mixed up in it, Flora; but we've been asked to spot-check local inns. I hope you don't mind?' Blake didn't miss the fleeting expression of worry that crossed Flora's face.

'No, no, of course. Feel free to have a look around. I'm sure you will find nothing untoward here.' Flora opened the door that led behind the bar and lifted the cellar hatch, then retreated into the kitchen to gather her thoughts. She leaned against the sink and took a deep breath to calm herself, praying he would not see the bottle of McGregor's whisky that still remained on the very bottom shelf behind the bar. The cigarettes were long gone, and the whisky would have been too if he'd only chosen to pay his visit a day later. She felt her legs shaking. Sergeant Blake would know exactly which brand he was looking for, and he would also know the brand that the local brewery supplied. He was bound to see the bottle of McGregor's and ask questions. She took one more breath, let it out slowly, and returned to meet her fate.

'Ah, Flora, thank you for that glass of water. Most appreciated.' Sergeant Blake was leaning against the bar with the bottle of McGregor's next to him. 'I was naturally concerned when I came across this –' he lifted the bottle of whisky. 'However, Mr Walker, your resident here, says that he brought it with him from Leeds and that it is his private bottle.' Sergeant Blake looked across at Matt, who glanced up from the newspaper he was reading and nodded in confirmation.

'Yes – yes, it is. I perhaps shouldn't have it down here, but Mr Walker likes to drink down here and enjoy the company of the locals.' Flora's heart was in her mouth as she smiled nervously at the sergeant.

'Indeed I do.' Matt smiled as he put down the paper. 'It is amazing the gossip you hear when you're sitting here, just enjoying a tipple. Would you like a small snifter now, Sergeant? We will have a talk before our meeting at the Victoria Hall. Flora, do open the bottle up and pour the sergeant a drop.'

'No, no, there truly is no need. As a matter of fact, I don't like the stuff. I'm more of a brandy man,' the sergeant said, taking a drink from his glass of water. 'But as it happens, this is the brand we are looking for. Now that you know that, I hope you'll let us know at the station if anybody offers to sell you some.'

'I certainly will, Sergeant, and thank you.' Flora watched as Sergeant Blake put his cap back on and straightened his tie before taking another sip of water.

'I'll call in at the station on Monday, if that's all right with you, Sergeant. I'm sure there are matters we need to discuss regarding the POWs staying in Settle.' Matt's tone was relaxed but businesslike. He knew how important it was to sound as if he was comfortably across the situation at Whitefriars. Everything had to be seen to be running smoothly.

'Yes, I'll look forward to that. I shall be in my office all morning. We must show that we are united in our support of the placement of POWs here. No doubt someone will complain. I do apologize for thinking your whisky was contraband, Flora. I had to follow orders and check it out.' Sergeant Blake straightened up, glanced round the bar once more and then nodded to Flora and Matt. 'Afternoon.'

'Good afternoon, Sergeant.' Flora's smile was more genuine now. Relief flowed over her as she followed him to the open door, closing and locking it behind him as he went down the steps to the street. She sighed deeply and stood still for a moment before turning back to join Matt.

'Thank you. You really did not need to cover for me. I'd have managed to put him off the trail.' She smiled. 'How did you know?'

'I listen, wherever I go. I listen to what people are talking about. One or two of your locals have loud voices and loose tongues.' Matt grinned. 'Besides, I couldn't have my landlady arrested; my mother would surely come back and haunt me. I'm sure she's done much worse in her time, and it was only the one bottle.' Matt hesitated. 'I hope . . .'

'Yes, just the one.' Flora blushed.

'And you sold the last of your fags last night. I heard Frank Capstick telling his mate, to their horror.' Matt grinned.

'You really do listen to conversations!'

'Yes, but I keep to my own company. My mother always told me that was the best way to be. She used to say that gossip could break hearts, and that it was best not to spread rumours. She also told me how hard it was to make a living running a pub in the Dales. So I heard her voice telling me to intervene – the long arm of the law will survive for want of a bottle of whisky, and it wouldn't be worth the paperwork. It was my pleasure to help. There are far worse scandals than selling a drop of whisky to your best customers and a few fags here and there.' Matt rose from his chair. 'Don't you worry, Flora. Your secret is safe with me. Just be careful.'

Flora looked up at him. Now that she knew she could trust this man, she was wondering just what sort of man he was, apart from his work for the War Office.

Chapter 16

'For heaven's sake, May, will you stop sighing? If you want my advice, you're better off without him anyway. You hardly know him as a person. Anyway, he hasn't told you that he's finished with you – just that he's too busy to see you.'

Flora tucked Matt's sheets in firmly under the mattress. She had stepped in to help May tidy after passing his open bedroom door to hear the lass weeping as she made the bed.

'My father says it's a blessing,' May sniffed, 'because he was dreading having a copper in the family. And my mother's playing heck at him because she thought Trevor was a good catch. I can't do right for doing wrong, and nobody seems to care that I'm heartbroken. All they're bothered about is that my father's customers have been paying him at long last. And that's thanks to me and my new invoice system!' She plumped Matt's pillows violently.

'Well, I'm with your father on this one. You can never

trust a copper; they can never be your friend. I told you on Saturday night that Trevor's sergeant had been snooping round, looking for bottles of whisky he thought were here – I bet that's what Trevor has been thinking, too. But they aren't going to find anything here. Not now, thank heavens,' Flora added quietly. She glanced out of the bedroom window at the postman delivering letters across the street. He turned to head towards the pub.

'Oh, so you think he was coming here for the whisky instead of for me?' May sank down onto the bed. 'I'm never going to find a boyfriend. All the lads are at war, and if they aren't, they're already spoken for,' she sobbed. Flora sat beside her and put an arm round her shoulders.

'I didn't mean it like that. I meant he came across you because he was probably half on duty when he was standing at the bar chatting to you. He'll be back – and if he isn't, then he's not worth your tears. Now, come on; the postie must be downstairs. I've just seen him coming over the road. I'll put the kettle on, and we'll have a brew and see what he has to say.' Flora gave a cheery, reassuring smile, which May ignored, and stood up to go down to the kitchen, where she knew the postman would be waiting with her letters. He often stopped for a few minutes in the morning to share any gossip he'd heard on his round.

'Morning, Herbert, how are you? It's a grand day,' Flora called out as she descended the stairs. The postie was lurking at the open back door. He never came in unless invited, but when he did, he would stay a good ten minutes and watch her open her post if he thought she'd received anything of interest.

'It is that, Flora. You'd never think we were at war if you just looked up at those clear skies. I pity the poor devils elsewhere in the country, who are bombed regularly. They don't enjoy the peace we do.' Herbert smiled at her. 'Mainly bills as usual today – but there's a letter I think you'll be glad to see. It looks like that husband of yours has found time to write.'

Flora took the handful of letters – mainly brown envelopes, but on the very top was indeed a letter from her Bill. Herbert was looking expectantly at her, clearly hoping she would open it in front of him. 'I'll read it later, while I have my lunch. Would you like a drink, Herbert? You can stop and cheer May up, she's in the doldrums. *Man trouble*,' she whispered with a smile.

'You needn't whisper; I can hear you,' May said moodily as she came down the stairs. 'I've decided he's not worth bothering about, so I'm going to stop blubbing.'

'Is this our dashing PC Whinray that's causing your heartache? I've just seen him behind the desk at the station, complaining that he's to be on duty again tonight. Just to keep the locals feeling safe until they get used to these Italians staying in Settle.'

'He is? So he really is doing overtime? That's good to know,' May beamed. She could have kissed Herbert where he stood, holding his cup of freshly brewed tea.

'Bloody hell, I thought you'd be saying the opposite.' Herbert grinned and watched as Flora put her letter on the mantelpiece to open later. He wasn't going to get any snippets of gossip from her that morning.

'May thought he was making up the overtime to get out of seeing her. So you've made her day.' Flora leaned against the stone sink and watched as May went through to the bar with a duster and Brasso in her hand. With a bit of luck, Herbert's good news would mean that her bar railing got an extra good shine.

'Aye, young love. I've forgotten what that used to feel like. Me and my old lass just plod on, no more romance anymore.' Herbert sipped his tea contentedly and winked at Flora. 'How's the new lodger? Posh, I hear. Bill will be complaining, if I know him.'

'I haven't told him yet – I will when I reply to his letter. But my lodger keeps himself to himself, and that is just how I like it,' Flora said firmly. Herbert was an incorrigible gossip, and he was known for putting two and two together and getting half a dozen. 'Now, I've the bar to see to, Herbert, and I'm sure you have more post to deliver . . .' Glad as she was that the postie had lifted May's spirits, she really wanted to read Bill's letter in private before opening time.

'Aye, I'll be on my way. Hope Bill's all right. He'll be going abroad soon? You'll be hoping he visits home before that,' Herbert said as he started down the garden path.

'Yes, I'd love to see him. He's not been gone long, but it seems months to me.' Flora leaned against the door frame, waiting until Herbert had closed her garden gate, then rushed back to the mantelpiece for her letter. She sat down at the kitchen table, ready to take in every word Bill had written. She missed him every minute of the day and wished he were there standing behind the bar, gossiping, swearing and laughing with her locals; and in her bed at night. Her hands trembled as she opened the envelope and unfolded the letter.

Catterick Barracks
North Yorkshire

My Dear Flora,

Thank you for your letter. You don't know how thankful I was to hear from you and to read your loving words that have given me so much hope these last few days or so.

Now, I don't want you to worry you, my dear, but unfortunately, while I was training, I suffered an injury and find myself hospitalized in the army sanatorium. I was undergoing training and I fell awkwardly, damaging my back. (You were right, if it's any consolation, I should never have joined up.) I've been ordered to rest and keep still, which is easier said than done. However, they are talking of giving me a new thing called an X-ray, which will show them the exact damage that I have done to myself, and then I suppose surgery if they think it will improve my lot. I don't think this old soldier will be fighting any Jerries in the next few months. I'm hoping that they will be able to patch me up and then send me home.

Although at the moment, I'd be no good to you at all, as I can hardly move.

I've watched the young lads come and go and have realized just how stupid I was thinking I was fit enough to fight, like I was nineteen. But don't you worry, my love, they will put me back together and I'll be back with you before you know it.

How's the pub doing? Hope that you are keeping the regulars happy? I was sorry to hear about young Richard Taylor. His mother must be heartbroken.

The doctors and nurses here are wonderful, I'm well fed and looked after, and I know as soon as I'm able to I'll be returned home. So the war is over for me.

I love you, Flora – my heart will always be yours.

Bill

Flora turned the letter back over and read it through again. A tear ran down her cheek. Her Bill was injured – he was in the hospital, and she was miles away from him and unable to help him in any way. Having to lie still – and an X-ray? What was that? It must be serious, she thought. She sat back, sighing, and looked up at the ceiling, wondering just what it all meant. If Bill couldn't move, how was he going to get home? There was only one thing to do: she would go and see him. Surely she would be allowed a visit? Even if she wasn't, she was going to go, and nobody would stop her. The pub would just have to close while she visited the love of her life. Money meant nothing compared to Bill's health.

'What's up, Flora? Is it bad news? What are you crying for? Nothing has happened to Bill, has it?' May came back into the kitchen and looked at her with concern. Her hands were black with Brasso, and she pushed a lock of hair away from her face with the back of her hand.

Flora's voice quivered as she answered. 'He's injured himself – he's hurt his back. He doesn't exactly say how bad, but I don't think he can move. Said something about an X-ray. I can't just sit here and think about him; I need to go and see him. But the pub, I can't leave the pub closed. Oh, I don't know what to do, May! I'm worried for him. He should never have joined up; he knew he wasn't fit enough. Everybody thought he was putting it on when he struggled to lift everything, I know they did. I've heard them call him lazy, even my mother, but he and I both knew his back was damaged. He only went to prove a point – that he would fight for his country and stop everyone from thinking he was idle and hiding behind my skirts . . .' Flora paused for breath. 'I just don't know what to do,' she repeated miserably.

May washed her hands hastily at the sink and came to sit by Flora, taking her hand. 'You go and see how bad he is, that's what I think. I can look after the Vixen for a day or two. It can't go to the dogs in that short a time, and you'll only be worrying if you don't. Poor Bill!' She gave Flora's hand a squeeze. 'I really mean it – I can look after things here. And I'm sure Matt will understand, and he'll put up with my services.'

'Oh, I wish I'd never let out our room! Bill's going to come home and find he has no bed. What a blinking mess – but it doesn't matter as long as he's all right. That's all I care about.' She took a deep breath, letting it out with a sigh. 'I'll have a think, May, and I'll let you know what I decide to do. I'd hate to give you all the burden of running this place, even for a day or two. The locals will give you no problems, of that I'm sure, but . . .' Flora shook her head, overwhelmed. It was tempting to just close the Vixen's doors, but with Bill in hospital, they would need every penny of income.

Matt sat behind his desk in the office at Whitefriars across from Captain Bentham. He had now met each and every POW and was satisfied that they had been correctly categorized. None seemed likely to cause any difficulties for the Settle locals. All of them wore the standard grey POW uniforms, with the white triangle on the back of the jacket marking them as Italians and an armband of either grey or white identifying which type of prisoner they were. Most were from farming or industrial backgrounds. None were staunch sympathizers of the Nazis or Mussolini's regime. The captain had designated one man, who had worked as a chef in Naples, to work in the kitchens at Whitefriars, and he was happy to serve his fellow prisoners food that they would all recognize – rations permitting.

Now it was time to walk over to the Victoria Hall

and talk with members of the community about Settle's new visitors. If they were lucky, this would be an opportunity to secure employment for some of them locally. It was better that they were kept busy and mixing with their neighbours rather than sitting and squabbling with one another, and it also helped struggling businesses out with cheap labour and fostered goodwill in the town.

Matt and Bentham walked briskly across to the hall, where the POWs had already set out rows of chairs before some returned to Whitefriars. Later, they would find out if they were to be employed.

Matt nodded to Trevor Whinray, who stood guard on the steps of the building, and they passed through the foyer into the busy main hall. It was already packed with local people – farmers, shopkeepers, mill owners. Sergeant Blake held court behind a long table set at the front of the room, upon the stage, looking important with other dignitaries.

'You've got a good turnout!' Blake greeted them. 'There's nothing like curiosity to bring folk out, especially if they think they may be under threat from the enemy.' He nodded to Matt and Bentham as they took their seats alongside him. Bentham took his cap off and placed it on the table, looking around at the crowd. He knew that some of them had been dead set against having Italian POWs stationed in their quiet market town.

'There's no threat from the men who are staying in Settle. They're just glad to be away from the front line and out of the war,' he said, glancing at Matt.

'Right, let's get this under way. Have you everything

you need, Captain Bentham, for any questions that may be thrown at us?' Matt rose to his feet, and the crowd gradually settled as he called the meeting to order and introduced himself.

'Good evening. I'm Matt Walker, and I'm here on behalf of the War Office to help with the smooth integration of the POWs who are now housed at Whitefriars into the community. To my right is Captain Bentham, who is in charge of the operation. On my left, I'm sure you will all recognize Sergeant Blake. Now, the purpose of this meeting is to set your minds at ease about these POWs. We wish to make it very clear that the men pose no danger whatsoever to this community. In fact, we hope that they will be of great benefit to the town.' Matt paused, watching the crowd as they absorbed his words.

'We have twenty-four men staying at Whitefriars, none of whom are in any way connected to the Nazi movement or the followers of Mussolini. All of these men are to be trusted. Please feel free to come and talk with any of the POWs who are here with us tonight.' Matt indicated a row of five POWs who sat at the back of the hall, and smiled. 'They can speak English, although it may be a little broken, and they will do their best to answer any questions you might have. All of our POWs have come here directly from Eden Valley Camp. If any of them are to come and work for you, they will be transported back and forward to their places of work under guard. And now I shall hand the meeting over to Captain Bentham.' Matt sat down and watched as Bentham stood up and took the floor, explaining that he was in charge of arranging where the men would be deployed and how. He also outlined that it was up to each individual employer whether to pay the men for their work, but that it was expected they should be decently treated. Provided they did not step out of line, each man would have some spare time to himself. They were allowed to purchase an ounce of tobacco a week, and if they entered a pub, they could buy one pint. All POWs had to be back at Whitefriars by nine o'clock each evening, and a guard would be present there at all times.

There were murmurs in the hall as the crowd discussed this information, and a few people called out questions and remarks.

'That's all very well, but they could murder us in our sleep,' shouted a voice from the back of the hall.

Sergeant Blake stood up. 'We have round-the-clock patrols at the moment, just until we know what we have on our hands. I also have assurance from both of these gentlemen that none of you are at risk. The German prisoners of war based at Horton are causing no concerns at all – in fact, they have been welcomed into the community and are a boon to the quarry there.'

Matt looked at Sergeant Blake and thanked him.

A farmer sitting on the front row leaned forward and looked hard at Captain Bentham. 'And are they good workers? I could do with a farmhand. Haytime and clipping are nearly upon us.'

'We have farmers, cobblers, bakers, mechanics – all in need of employment,' Captain Bentham confirmed. 'And all to be trusted, else they would not be here. Go and speak to the men who are here tonight, or if you prefer, call in at Whitefriars and see me. Or give me your details this evening. Free labour, ladies and gentlemen. All you need to do is feed them and give them a bit of pocket money if you wish, for which they will be grateful. We will give you access to their files, and if any of them give you any trouble at all, we will take them back to Eden Camp. But I can honestly say that they are trustworthy, and that you will be doing your country a favour – not to mention yourselves.'

'Well, I could do with one of them,' the farmer replied, and then turned to his farming neighbour, who sat next to him. 'Jim, if I take one, you take another, and then we'll have enough men to gather the fell this clipping time. It'll cost us nowt after all.'

'What do you feed them on? They'll be used to foreign muck. My missus won't let garlic in the house,' Jim replied, and the room laughed.

'They will be grateful to receive just the same as yourselves. They will receive a main meal in the evening at Whitefriars,' Captain Bentham said. 'Bread and cheese will be good enough for their midday meal.'

'Go on, then, I'll take one. It makes a change to get something for nothing from this government,' Jim said, and looked at his partner in crime.

'Aye, I will as well. He can help me build a new dipping well for the sheep. I've meant to build one for a while but never had the time,' the other farmer replied, standing up.

'Right, come and give me your names, and then come

and see me tomorrow. We will give you two men who are used to farming. Although it may be olive or lemon farming,' Bentham added with a smile.

'Well, they'll just have to get used to our ways. I'd have thought owt was better than having your head showing on a front line at war.' Both of the farmers chuckled as they made their way to the table, followed by a few more people who had businesses. Free help was not to be sniffed at.

Matt sat back and watched as a steady stream of people moved towards the back of the hall to speak with the POWs he had selected to meet the public. He couldn't help thinking they looked rather like slaves at an auction, lined up in a row as they were; but he knew they would be well treated by the Dales folk. Farmers and businessmen came up to leave their details with Bentham and ask questions. The meeting had gone well, and everything was starting to fall into place.

Perhaps he wouldn't be needed for the full month at Settle after all, Matt thought. He might be able to get home more quickly to Leeds and his fiancée.

Chapter 17

Flora stood at the bar and watched as Matt ate his evening meal: corned beef hash, to be followed by spotted dick and custard. She was wondering what to say to him about her plan to visit Bill.

'You had a good meeting, then? All went well, nobody gave you any bother? Some folk are dead against POWs staying here, so I did worry about you.'

'Yes, it went extremely well. In fact, I don't know if I will need to stay with you as long as a month after all – I'll warn you now. Settle seems to have taken POWs in its stride with remarkable ease. I suppose it helps that there are already German POWs at Horton, and they've caused no problems.' Matt peered more closely at Flora, noticing that she was pale and looked as if she had been crying. 'Are you all right? Is anything wrong?'

Flora dropped her head and pulled out her handkerchief.

'I've had a bit of bad news,' she explained. 'My

husband – Bill – he's injured himself at the army camp at Catterick. It's his spine, and I don't think he can walk at the moment. I received a letter from him this morning. I can't bear to just do nothing; I've got to go and see him.' She let out a sob.

'Oh, that is unfortunate.' Matt set down his cutlery, the meal temporarily forgotten. 'Does he say how bad he is? Is he in the camp hospital? I'm sure they're doing all they can for him.'

'Yes, he says so; and that they're to give him an X-ray? I've never heard of that before; it sounds frightening. I should be with him,' Flora sniffed.

'Well, he's fortunate to be offered an X-ray. They must have an MX-2 machine at Catterick. Only a few places have those at the moment – most are portable and are being used on the front lines. They take photographs of inside your body, Flora, showing your bones and anything else that's solid within you. They're harmless and painless, so you don't have to worry about that. Once they can see what's wrong, they'll know how best to operate.' Matt picked up his knife and fork to finish his dinner. 'And I can tell you what they'll do next, too. They'll take him out of service and class him as an SOS – struck off strength – and put him, once he's recovering, in the RAC Depot. And there he will be, on an X list, for twenty-eight days, I believe. Then he'll either be sent home to you or sent for hospitalization elsewhere. The bad news is that they will not let you visit him while he is still in camp. No civilians are allowed in or out while we're at war.'

'But I must see him! He's injured!' Flora cried.

'Think of it this way: you wouldn't be able to if he were in a field hospital over in France or Belgium. It's much better that he's in Catterick, but he's still the army's concern until he is returned home, and what goes on in the camp is top secret. You could be a German spy, for all they know.' He sat back, looking sympathetically at her. There was one thing he could do to help, even if he couldn't get her into the camp. 'They've probably operated on him already, because they don't hang about. Especially if he was still in training when it happened.'

'Do you think so? Do you think he'll be all right?'

'I don't know; but I tell you what, when I go to Whitefriars in the morning, I'll use the military telephone there and ring a friend of mine at Catterick. He's a serving officer in charge of supplies there. I'll ask him to check up on Bill for you, how about that?'

'That would be wonderful. I must know how he is, if I can't visit him. Isn't it a good job that you came to stay here with me? I wouldn't have known what to do with the whisky, and now Bill's in the hospital – I can't thank you enough.' Flora stepped forward to take Matt's empty plate away. 'Thank heavens your mother was once the landlady here!'

Flora tossed and turned all night, thinking about Bill and the pain he must be in. She had told Frank Capstick and Robert Pitcher how injured he was after they'd finished their game of dominoes, and neither had sounded hopeful of a full recovery. Both agreed that Bill had been foolish to enlist again and play down his old wounds.

Her head was all over the place by the time May came in to clean on Tuesday morning. She decided that while May was there, she'd go and tell her mother about Bill's injuries – not that Mary could do anything, and Flora expected she would only have limited sympathy.

'Have you got packed?' May asked as soon as she arrived. 'When do you want me to take over? My mam and dad say that if there's anything they can do, just let them know, and they wish Bill the best.' May hadn't slept much herself, worrying over her rash offer to run the pub in Flora's absence. She hadn't a clue how to handle the brewery order or what to cook for Matt – and she would have to sleep at the pub by herself, with only him under the same roof. Her mother had been quick to point out that he could easily take advantage of her.

'I'm not going,' Flora explained. 'Matt says they wouldn't allow me into the camp, no matter how unwell Bill is. He has a friend who works there, though, and he's going to telephone him this morning. He says he'll ask him to go and see Bill and try to find out just how he is. I can't thank Matt enough for that.' She smiled at May, noting the girl's relieved expression. 'He also said that Trevor Whinray has been putting in a lot of overtime, and if you want to speak to him, he usually walks past Whitefriars around nine in the morning and three in the afternoon. You see – he's even good to you.'

'I really thought Trevor was lying to me, that he didn't want to see me again, but he isn't,' May smiled. 'It's a good job Matt Walker's staying with you – at least you haven't wasted a journey, and even better, you're going to find out how Bill is.'

'It almost seems like it was meant to be, for him to take the room. And he should be gone by the time Bill returns home. He was saying yesterday that he may not even stay the full month we'd agreed, because things are running so well at Whitefriars. So he'll be away by the time I get Bill back, and he's even told me about all the steps they'll need to go through before they discharge him, which puts my mind at ease. May, would you mind if I went across to see my mam for an hour? She doesn't know about Bill, and I need to talk to her anyway.'

'Of course not. Just leave me to it. Is there anything special you need me to do? It looks as if you've done most of the work in the bar. Either that, or you weren't busy last night.'

'I was up early. I couldn't sleep, so I thought I might as well clean. So many worries, and there will be more if Bill's unable to work. I just don't know how we'll manage.' Flora felt tears threatening to well up again.

'You'll cope,' May assured her. 'Now, go and have a chinwag with your mother. Everyone needs their mother to talk to. Even though all mine does is lecture me, I still know she's there for me.' She smiled.

'Oh, my mother's very good at lecturing. But sometimes I need her, and today's one of those days.' Flora sighed. 'I'll not be long.'

She approached her mother's cottage in trepidation. They hadn't seen one another since Mary's visit to the Cunning Vixen, when she'd taken Flora to task for taking on a male lodger. Hopefully she had calmed down a little by now, Flora thought as she went in through the open front door, knowing that her mother would probably be in the garden as usual. 'Mam, it's only me. Are you about?'

'I'm out here with Lottie. We're having a catch-up,' Mary called through to her daughter. 'It's too nice to sit inside, so we're enjoying the sunshine.'

Her mother was chatting to Lottie again? So they must have made it up – that was good news, Flora thought as she went through the house to the back garden. Outside, both women sat on a wooden seat just under Mary's kitchen window. The garden was humming with bees, attracted to the border of English marigolds that scented the air; further down the path, white butterflies flitted, looking for tasty cabbage leaves on which to lay their eggs.

'Bring a chair out and join us. We're having a good natter.' Mary looked up at her daughter and smiled at Lottie. She hadn't realized how much she had missed her old friend until Lottie had knocked on her door one afternoon. Seeing her face to face had filled Mary with regret for not giving her condolences for Richard's death.

'This is good, to see you two back talking – I know you've both missed one another's company. I'm so glad.' Flora brought out a kitchen chair and sat down with the women, wondering what had brought about the repair of their friendship.

'We've both been daft. We fell out over nothing, really – nothing important, in comparison to Lottie losing her Richard. She knew I'd be here for her, thank heavens, when she was feeling down. So she decided for us both to make amends.' Mary patted her old friend's hand.

'Well, I still don't know what it was all about, but I'm pleased you've made up.' Flora smiled.

'It was summat and nowt. It's not worth mentioning now, is it, Mary?' Lottie said quickly and smiled.

'No, not at all. It's in the past, anyway. And there is nothing I could have done about it,' Mary replied, frowning a little.

Flora drew a deep breath. 'I'm going to spoil your day with my news, I'm afraid.'

'Oh, why's that, our Flora? I hope that you're all right. I'm sorry I came across in a bad mood the other day; something was preying on my mind, but it's sorted now.' Mary's glance flickered once more towards Lottie before focusing on her daughter.

'Bill wrote to me at the weekend. He's injured himself at the training camp at Catterick. He's injured his spine and is finding it hard to move – he's in the hospital there.'

'Oh, my Lord. He may never walk again! I told him he was a fool to join up in his state. Let's face it, he's never been fully fit the whole time you've been married,' Mary replied, opting immediately for the darkest possible response to Flora's news.

'Eh, Mary, Flora doesn't want to hear that! I'm sure they will get him right, lass. After all, they deal with some terrible injuries. They'll patch him up, although they will probably send him home. His fighting days will be over.' Lottie regarded Flora with sympathy.

'He's to have something called an X-ray. Matt, my

lodger has explained it to me, and he's going to ring someone he knows at the camp and find out how Bill is. I was all set to go straight there and see him, but Matt says they wouldn't be allowed to let me in.'

'This Matt seems to know everything, doesn't he? A bit like his mother.' Mary pulled a disapproving face.

'Oh, so you do remember her? Why don't you come over and see him before he goes home? He would love to talk to you.'

'No, I'll not bother. The sooner he gets back to where he belongs, the better. You shouldn't have a man lodging when Bill is away. It's not right,' Mary said.

'Yes, I heard you had Maisy Walker's son staying with you – I haven't seen him, though,' Lottie said wistfully.

'Come across and say hello,' Flora encouraged her. 'He's usually in the bar of an evening. I'm sure he'd like to meet you. He says his mother loved her time living here.'

'I daresay she did, but she left plenty of trouble behind,' Mary muttered.

'What?' Flora asked, puzzled, but her mother just shook her head.

'She never paid her bills, dear,' Lottie said. 'The Cunning Vixen lived up to its name. When Maisy left, there were unpaid bills in her name all over Settle and Giggleswick. And there were other things, but we don't talk about those.' She glanced at Mary.

'No, we don't. In fact, I don't want her name mentioned in my house again,' Mary said firmly. 'Now, what are you going to do about your Bill, Flora? The sooner he can come home, the better, surely.'

'It depends on what I can find out tonight, when Matt has phoned the camp. But I'm going to write and tell him to come home, tell him how much I miss him. That's my job this afternoon, after I've closed the bar at three. I'll just catch the last post – although everything seems to be delivered or sent late to and from the camp. I suppose it's because they're so busy.'

'At least you still have his love, that's the main thing,' Lottie said quietly. 'I miss my husband and our Richard so much. They're never going to find his body. It's at the bottom of the ocean, and I'll just have to accept that. I hope you don't mind, Flora love, but I've changed my mind about a gathering in his memory. There are too many young men losing their lives at the moment, and my Richard is one among all of them. It wouldn't be right to only remember him. They are all heroes.'

'Oh, Lottie, bless you. You do whatever you want. Richard was indeed a hero, and he will never be forgotten in Giggleswick.' Flora reached for Lottie's hand and squeezed it. 'I'm so glad you're here with my mam. I know she missed you. It's just a pity it's the death of Richard that's brought you together.'

'Aye, you're right; that and other things. We should have had our heads knocking together.' Mary turned to Lottie. She had put on a good show of being an independent woman with no need of a close friend, but she had missed talking to her neighbour from the next row over. And all Lottie had ever done, really, was to speak the truth to her when they'd first fallen out.

Flora stood up. 'I'd better get back to the pub. I've left May on her own, although she's more than capable.'

'I'll come to the door with you, our Flora. Back in a minute, Lottie.' Mary followed her daughter through the cottage.

'It was a shock seeing Lottie there, but I'm glad for you both. You were such friends until after my dad's funeral,' Flora said with a sad smile.

'Aye, well, we've agreed to put that behind us. Both of us were in the wrong, so we will just have to try and forget what was said. Now, you tell me how Bill is as soon as you get to know. You must be worried to death. It's a good job all round if that Matt Walker is going back to where he came from and stops there; at least Bill will be able to come back to his own bed.' Mary looked hard at her daughter. 'Does he know you have a lodger? If I were you, I'd not tell him until he comes home. It'll only be another thing for him to worry about.'

'Mother, you have a poor opinion of me. Do you really think I'd jump into bed with Matt? I'm true to Bill and always will be.' Flora sighed. 'I haven't told him, but I mean to.'

'Aye, but you flirt behind the bar. I've seen you. Women don't like women that flirt. They give us all a bad name,' Mary said quietly.

'Well, if people are talking about me, I'm just sorry they've nothing better to do. Anyway, I'll have to tell

Bill, or else he'll wonder who this man is that's asking questions on my behalf. And then he will worry.'

'Well, I wouldn't tell him in a letter, and when he's not well. He'll start to think all sorts.' Mary gave her daughter a sharp look. 'Right, I'll get back to Lottie. We'll have a wander across to you for a quick sherry later this week, and then you can tell me how Bill is. Now, you take care. Behave yourself.'

'Mam, I always do. You know I do.' Flora would have liked a hug from her mother, but she knew that would never happen. Mary had never been one to show her affection outwardly. 'Take care.'

'You look after your Bill. And yourself.' Mary turned and left Flora to walk home and wait for Matt to return with his news.

Bill lay in his hospital bed, feeling like a pig that had been to the butcher's. He'd been exposed to something called 'radiation', which the nurses had said he could only have in small doses. He now had a six-inch scar along his spine, and although he couldn't see it, he certainly knew about it with the pain it caused as he tried to lie comfortably in his bed. He hadn't dared move his legs, but knew that when the doctor came round he'd be asking him to try.

He lay back and closed his eyes, thinking about Flora and their home at Giggleswick. She should have received his letter now, and she would be worried about him. He couldn't wait to hear from her and, hopefully, reply with good news – if the operation had been successful. He was annoyed with himself for bringing even more trouble to her door, all because of his pride . . .

'Private Whitaker – Bill Whitaker. Sorry to disturb you.'

Bill opened his eyes and saw a man in battle dress standing by the bed. He tried to prop himself up but decided against it as pain shot down his legs.

'Don't move, old man – just lie still. I can't stay long, but a friend of mine has asked me to find out how you are.' Captain Bruce Lewis smiled reassuringly down into Bill's pale face.

'A friend? Is he a friend of mine, too? I've only told my wife so far.' Bill was surprised and confused.

'It's your wife who wants me to ask. Flora, is that her name? Matt, an old friend of mine, is staying at the pub you both run. She asked him for help in finding out how you are.' Bruce sat down by Bill's bedside. 'He works for the War Office, so he was able to contact me and ask me to check on you. Put your wife's mind at rest. He said to tell you she sends her love.'

'I don't understand, but I'm grateful that you are here, and to hear that Flora is asking after me. I had an operation yesterday, and they think they've removed the shrapnel that has been lodged in my back these many years. But it'll be a few weeks before we know if it's been successful.' Bill wondered just how Flora had managed to get this well-spoken man in battle dress to ask after him; and how this friend of his, this Matt, had come to be staying at the Cunning Vixen.

'Sorry, did you say your friend Matt was staying with my wife, at the Vixen? She's never told me.'

'Yes, he's lodging there while working in Settle. That's all I can tell you, I'm afraid, my good man. Loose lips – you know the rest. Best to keep things as discreet as we can. Your wife will be glad to know you've come through the operation well. I will relay the good news back to her, and let's hope that you continue to make good progress.' Bruce patted Bill's hand and stood up as the matron came towards them.

'Captain Lewis, you are a surprise visitor; I didn't recognize you in your battle dress.' The matron made a fuss over the new arrival on the ward. 'I was just coming to tell Private Whitaker to rest.'

'I get the message, Matron, and I'm on my way. Now, I'm sure you are already doing an excellent job, but look after Private Whitaker. He's got a wife who needs him home once he's fit.'

'We will certainly do our best, Captain.' The matron smiled down at Bill. 'He's been a bit of a naughty man and never said his back had so much damage. Hopefully, life for him now will be a lot better.'

'Jolly good. I've heard he's a brave man, and that's what the army wants.' Lewis nodded at Bill. 'Message will be sent and cleared. You take care, my good man.' He turned and walked away, leaving the matron to tidy the bedclothes and take Bill's pulse.

'Captain Lewis . . . he's a captain?' Bill said.

'Yes; you must have friends in high places. Now, try

to calm down. Your pulse is a little high.' The matron glanced with concern at her watch.

'No wonder, with the news that I've just heard,' Bill whispered, gazing up at the hospital ceiling. The sooner he was home, the better. And who exactly was this man lodging with Flora?

Chapter 18

'What's this you're leaving me? I ordered barrels, not bottles. My lot'll not be happy with this.' Flora watched, hands on her hips, as the drayman from the local brewery traipsed up and down her cellar stairs carrying bottles of stout and bitter instead of the usual barrels he delivered on a Tuesday.

'Sorry, love, it's these or nothing at all. No metal for the barrels or hoops, so we have to change to bottles. This bloody war effort is taking every scrap of metal it can find. Garden railings are being taken down, gates . . . it's madness. I'm amazed the brewery hasn't been bombed yet. We've had a few near misses. The waterworks across from us got hit last week, and there was water everywhere! Everywhere except where it was wanted, putting out the fires. I tell you, love, you don't know you're born living out here. It's bloody heaven compared to Burnley.' He rested his elbow on the bar. 'Is he still away, then? Has he been posted yet? You know I'm here once a week if you're going short of anything.' He winked at Flora and tried to touch her bottom.

'If you mean my Bill, he's been wounded. In fact, he could be back any minute now,' Flora lied, stepping neatly out of range. 'So you can ask him if he's going short of anything. I'm sure he'll tell you straight.'

'Oh, I'm sorry to hear that, love. Wish him the best, and I'll be on my way.'

'I'll tell him you offered me your services. I'm sure he'll be impressed,' Flora called as the drayman made a quick exit and climbed into his battered Fordson flat wagon. It sounded as if it was on its last legs, backfiring as the driver changed gear going up Belle Hill.

He wouldn't have dared do or say that if Bill were here, she thought, heading down to the cellar to look at the crates of bottles. She knew all her locals would complain about them. They were no substitute for a pulled pint. 'Bloody brewery. Bloody war,' she swore. Looking around the whitewashed walls of the old cellar, she nearly felt like crying. What else could possibly go wrong?

'Flora, are you down there? I've come home a little early because I've heard from my friend at Catterick,' Matt called down the cellar steps. He peered past Flora as she made her way up towards him. 'Are you all right? Why bottles? Have they run out of barrels? That'll not go down well.'

'Oh, don't get me started on the bottles! But what did your friend say? Did he speak to Bill?' Flora crouched down to close the hatch, looking up at him with hope in her heart.

'Yes, he went to see him this afternoon. He's still in the hospital, and they have operated on him and removed the shrapnel. Bruce says he looks rather pale but was perky enough – not able to move at the moment, but the matron was looking after him well. He passed on your message that you gave me.' Matt blushed. 'It's rare I get to play Cupid.'

'And he's all right? Did he say when he's coming home? Can he walk?' Flora bombarded Matt with questions.

'Hey, I can only tell you what Bruce has told me. That he's in his bed, that he looks to be in a bit of pain and can't move much yet, but that he's in good hands. It's like I say, they will keep him in regardless of his progress so that they can monitor his fitness before deciding what's best for him. It is early days, but at least he's got through the operation. Bruce didn't stay long as he says the matron is a stickler. Worse than the drill sergeant, he said, so she must be bad.' Matt could see the worry on Flora's face. 'At least he's been operated on now. He should have had that done years ago. He must have been in some pain with shrapnel in him for so long.'

'I just hope he manages to walk again. He'll not be happy if he's in a wheelchair, and then what will we do when he comes home? It's all stairs here; we would have to move,' Flora fretted. It seemed she could only see the dark side of everything at the moment. The war was gaining pace; food was scarce; and now even her supply of beer had been hit. But Bill being injured was her main worry. He was her pillar, and she would not be able to run the Cunning Vixen if she didn't have him by her side.

'Look, don't worry. I'm sure Catterick will patch him up, get him walking and send him home to you as good as new. Bruce is only too happy to be our carrier pigeon. So, Bill knows that he's not on his own now.' Matt wondered whether to put his arm round Flora but thought better of it; it would seem a little too friendly.

'I know. Thank you for all that you've done for us both. How's your day been? I've only just closed from afternoon service. I was going to write to Bill, but then the man from the brewery came to deliver – not that it's what I ordered.'

'My day has been fine. We've placed nineteen POWs in various farms and businesses. The only ones I'll be struggling with are one who used to work in a bakery, and the youngest of the group who used to help his father in his joinery. So far, nobody in those two trades has shown any interest in taking them off our hands. The baker's helping out in the kitchen, so he's no trouble, but I would like to see the young joiner placed to work. At the moment, he's doing odd jobs around Whitefriars, but they will soon run out.' It was Matt's turn to sigh. He liked the young, shy lad, and he knew that he'd been treated badly at Eden Camp by the extremist Nazis there. He hoped to find him somewhere safe and make him as happy as possible, given he was working as a POW in a foreign land.

'Why don't you ask May's father, Harold? He's a joiner.

Your bedroom window looks out over his yard, and he always seems busy. May has just started doing his accounts and sorting his workload out when she's not here. You could always ask her first. Harold is easy-going, but his wife Betty can be a bit demanding. That's why May started doing the accounts – Betty was forever moaning about Harold being too relaxed to chase folk for payment.'

'I may just do that. In fact, would you mind if I brought the lad along for a pint this evening? Then May can meet him and perhaps give a good account of him to her father. It would do him good to get away from some of the older men. He's only young.' Matt suspected that Antonio Lugatti was not even eighteen by the looks of him, even though his papers said he was nineteen. He'd probably been made to fight even if he was under recruiting age.

'Yes, bring him along, but May doesn't work tonight. Bring him on Friday, when she's back behind the bar with me.' Flora looked gratefully at Matt. 'I'm so relieved that your friend has talked to Bill. I must go and write to him before we reopen for the evening. Is dinner at five all right? I have a rabbit cooking in the side oven with some carrots and potatoes that Frank brought round earlier. Thank heavens for his garden, else I don't know what I'd do! Although he'll be the first to moan about bottled beer in payment.'

'Oh, Flora, I don't envy you your lot. No wonder my mother left being a landlady and moved to Leeds. She, too, must have it hard. It's strange, when I mention her running here, the locals are hesitant to talk about her, although they do remember her.' Matt picked up his briefcase. 'Right, I'll do some paperwork in my room until dinner and let you get your letter written. Do wish Bill the best.' He made for the stairs.

'Thank you, Matt. I'll tell him,' Flora smiled. At least now she knew that Bill had come safely through his operation, and hopefully he would soon be home with her.

Flora sat down and looked out of the small study window. It was a lovely early summer's day, and the roses were just starting to bloom. Nature wasn't holding back, despite the feeling of sadness in the village. The hedges were green and white with blossom and in the stream, water-crowfoot was starting to grow where tiddlers hid for protection from the heron that often stood on the bank. The only thing missing was the village's youth, she thought as she put pen to paper to write to her Bill.

The Cunning Vixen, Giggleswick

Dear Bill,

It was such a shock to hear that you had been injured. I worried about you so much, my love.

By now, I know that a friend of Matt Walker's has made himself known to you. Matt is staying in the village, looking after some POWs that are housed in Whitefriars, and I've got to know him with his mother being the landlady here in the past.

He is kind enough to tell me that his friend will keep calling in to see how you are and that you can send messages through him. I was adamant that I was going to visit you, but I was told that it would be to no avail, as nobody who is not in uniform is allowed into Catterick Camp at the moment. I wish I could be with you, my love. There isn't a minute of the day that I don't think about you. Are you in a lot of pain? Are you able to walk? Have they said how long you will be in the hospital? I hope that you will be returning home as soon as you have recovered.

The locals are all asking after you, even my mother! She and Lottie Taylor have made up again and are now back thick as thieves. I don't know how it has happened, but I'm grateful that it has.

The brewery sent bottled beer this morning. They have run out of barrels, and the waterworks across from them has been bombed. Thank heavens we live in this part of the world, sheltered mainly from the war, apart from rationing and the loss of our men to the front.

My bed is empty without you, my love. I wish you were here with me. I miss your tender touch and your cheery smile. The Vixen is not the same without you behind the bar with me. I pray that you will recover, and then we can continue our lives together. If you need anything, let the gentleman who came to see you know, and I will try and send it to you. Please don't worry about me and the pub, we are both doing fine, just waiting for the day you return to us.

All my love

Flo

Flora read her letter through. She had thought better of saying that Matt was lodging with her in the pub. It was like her mother said – why give Bill something else to worry about as he lay in his bed? Not that she and Matt were up to anything untoward. He had been the perfect gentleman since he came, and anyway, he would be gone by the time Bill returned.

She sealed the envelope and kissed the back of it, then held it close to her chest. She missed Bill so much. The sooner he was home, the better.

Chapter 19

It was Friday afternoon, and May had just finished working her way through her father's bills and invoices. As she glanced up at the slow-ticking clock on the workshop wall, it chimed half past two.

She sat back and sighed, wondering whether to go chasing after Trevor Whinray. He might be working overtime, but surely he could still make time to come and see her, if only for five minutes? A night at the pictures the following week was looking less and less likely. She blotted the last of the hand-addressed envelopes and put a stamp on it, ready for posting along with all the rest, then pulled her cardigan on. There was just time to put them in the post, and then perhaps she would walk up to Whitefriars.

Stepping outside, she paused at the open front door of the cottage and shouted for her mother. 'Mam? I'm just going to post my father's bills, and then I might have a walk into Settle. Is there anything you want?'

'Well, there's plenty I want, but getting it is another thing,' Betty called from the kitchen. She came towards the door, wiping her hands on her apron. 'No, you're all right, my love. What are you walking up to Settle for? Has your father run out of stamps?'

'No, I just thought I'd have a wander. It's a nice day, and a walk will do me good.' May smiled and made to leave.

'Will your walk take you past the police station, by any chance?' Betty smiled.

'No, I don't think so, Mam. I'm not going to chase him – if he can't be bothered to come and see me, then why should I bother him?' May's tone was flippant. She wanted to make it clear that she didn't care one jot if she never saw Trevor Whinray again.

'Aye, and I'm the queen of Sheba,' Betty murmured, watching as her daughter headed up the road through the village.

Letters posted, May took the shortcut into Settle along the banks of the Ribble. She watched as children played in the clear waters, catching tiddlers in jam jars and throwing stones into the river, just as she had done when younger. It had been a wonderful childhood growing up the small village. She knew how lucky she was to still be enjoying the freedom of the Dales while people in towns and cities bore the brunt of Hitler's fury.

She turned from the pretty riverside path into busy Church Street and walked up quickly to the Whitefriars boundary wall, where she took the small walkway leading behind the gardens. If Trevor was indeed on the beat around Whitefriars, he would have to pass that way. She headed for a bench that was set back along the path with a good view into the gardens. Settling down there, she decided to wait for an hour. She wouldn't be missed at home until nearer teatime, and then she'd have to get ready for her shift at the pub.

It was a lovely day to sit and enjoy the sunshine. She looked up at the heights of Castleberg Crag, whose limestone rocks shone white in the sun and where a proud Union flag fluttered in the soft mountain air. Down below it, Settle was bustling with trade; May heard the town hall clock strike four as she sat back and turned her gaze on the gardens. She saw a young lad in what she took to be POW dress – grey, with a white triangle on the back of his jacket. He seemed to be mending the garden's bird table. As she watched, he hammered a loose board into place before securing the table back in its usual spot and standing back to admire his handiwork. May noted his dark hair and olive skin and found herself thinking that he couldn't be all bad if he was repairing a bird table instead of fighting on the battlefields.

That line of thought soon remind her why she was sitting there – and then she noticed Trevor approaching quietly, steadily, along the walkway. The silver buttons of his uniform glinted in the sunshine as he caught sight of her and stopped in his tracks.

'May, what brings you to be sitting here? I'm just on my usual patrol of the perimeter of Whitefriars, not that any of them are causing any bother – yet.' He stopped a little distance away. May patted the empty place next to her, inviting him to sit, but he didn't respond.

'I was posting some letters and bills for my father and thought I'd have a walk out. It's such a lovely place to sit here, with the gardens to look at and the crag above.' May looked up at the man to whom she had given part of her heart.

'You've chosen an odd place, especially with the POWs being stationed here. I know I've said they're no bother, but a young woman on her own – well, you never know!' Trevor replied.

'Well, in honesty, I knew that you'd be walking your beat this way. I wanted to see you and ask when we're going to go to the pictures? You can't be working twenty-four hours, seven days a week!'

He didn't look happy. She held her breath as he turned his head away.

'May, I'm sorry, but I've been thinking – you know, you are only young. I'm going to try and get a promotion to another station. I've outgrown Settle. I need some proper action in a town.' Trevor could see the disappointment on May's face, but he didn't acknowledge it. 'I'm sorry, but I'll not be walking out with you again. It is best that I don't have any commitments to anybody if I am to move. I might even enlist if the war continues. You will be better off without me.'

'I see.' May felt a lump come into her throat. Trevor had finished with her. She had never felt the pain of rejection before, but she wasn't going to let her feelings show. She swallowed hard. 'I understand, don't worry. I don't think we were that serious anyway. You're right to tell me now before we get to know each other better. I wish you well, Trevor; I know that you love your job.' May bowed her head, unable to meet his eyes.

'That's what I thought. You're a nice girl, May, but I need to spread my wings yet. Perhaps if you had been a little older and I were more settled. No hard feelings, I hope?' Trevor could tell that May was crushed, but he didn't attempt to comfort her.

'No, of course not, none at all.' May pulled a handkerchief from out of her sleeve, fighting back tears.

'I'll be on my way, then.' Trevor put his hands behind his back and walked slowly away, leaving May sobbing on the seat. But even as she wept, part of her was thinking that Flora had got the length of Trevor Whinray, and so had her father. Her heart might be hurting, but perhaps he was best out of her life.

'What's up with you, our May? Tha' looks as if you've been crying. Mother! What's wrong with her?' Harold Lambert nodded across the supper table at his daughter, wondering what could have happened while he'd been out at work.

'It's nowt, Father, don't be worrying. Our May is fine,' Betty replied as she dished up cabbage and potatoes to accompany their meagre slice of bacon. 'That Trevor Whinray has decided not to walk out with her again, that's all.'

'Mam, do you have to?' May sniffed. She lifted her knife and fork to attempt to eat her dinner. Normally she would have wolfed it down, but tonight she felt sick to her stomach at having lost her first love. 'It doesn't matter. He was too old for me, anyway – that's what he said.'

'Too old, my arse. He's a sneaky bloody copper. You wanted nowt with him anyway. That's good news in my eyes. I reckon nowt of him anyway.' Harold mixed his cabbage vigorously into his potatoes.

'He'd have been a good catch, but never mind. There's plenty more fish in the sea, our May,' Betty told her heartbroken daughter.

'But there isn't, Mam, not now! They're all at war!' May sobbed as she thought about the kisses and conversations she and Trevor had shared. They had clearly meant nothing to him.

'Somebody will turn up. I'm sure they will, our May. Now, don't take on so. No fella is worth your tears,' Betty said, glancing across at Harold as he shook his head.

'Aye, especially not a copper. You can never trust them,' he growled, and got on with his supper.

Later that night, all heads turned and the pub fell silent as Matt walked in with a young Italian POW by his side. Flora's regulars stared at the olive-skinned, dark-haired lad. He kept his head bowed as he let Matt lead him up to the bar.

'Two bottles of bitter, please, Flora. Antonio is allowed just the one, and if any other POWs come in, they are allowed just one pint also.' Matt gazed round the room at the local men, most of whom had turned their backs and were huddled together, exchanging meaningful glances. It was just about acceptable that the POWs were allowed to earn their keep; but being allowed to drink a pint in the pub, mixing with the locals, was a different matter.

Flora smiled at Matt and the young lad. She reached for two bottles from under the counter but found that May had already opened two and was passing them across to Matt and Antonio, along with glasses.

'I think I saw you in the Whitefriars garden this afternoon. You were repairing a bird house?' She smiled at Antonio, hoping that he understood her.

'*Si*. I help in gardens.' Antonio took the beer and glass and shyly returned her smile.

'Antonio is a joiner by trade. He's looking for a job, and he's the youngest POW we're holding at Whitefriars. I've brought him out with me just for an hour, as he's not been out in Settle or Giggleswick since he came.'

'Bloody w—,' one of the locals said quietly. The group around him grinned.

'Antonio was enlisted against his will. He's no threat to anyone. He'll be a boon to anyone who wants to take him on as a handyman. He's got real skills,' Matt said fairly loudly, looking round at the usually jovial locals.

Frank Capstick made his way up to the bar and stood next to Matt and Antonio. 'Tha's only young. Has Italy not got proper men to fight their war? I haven't no use for you, but I wish you well. Robert, Graham – have you two not got a few jobs you need doing? Give the lad something to do?'

Both men shook their heads and stared at the poor Italian, who probably felt as if he was being auctioned off. Matt caught Frank Capstick's eye in silent gratitude for his effort.

'What about your father, May? Could he not do with another pair of hands?' Matt watched May's face as she thought about how to respond. 'Do you think he could be interested?' he prompted gently. 'Both Antonio and I would be so grateful.'

'I don't know . . . I'll have to ask him. He is busy and has got plenty of work at the moment,' May replied. She looked at the young lad, wondering how much he understood of what everyone was saying.

'I good worker,' Antonio told her quietly, as he'd caught the word 'work'.

'I'm sure you are. I will ask my father.' May blushed as the dark-eyed lad smiled at her again. He was handsome – a lot more handsome than Trevor, she thought as she turned away and busied herself washing glasses rather than keep looking at Antonio. The locals, after the initial shock of seeing a stranger walking into their boozer, had restarted their conversations.

Frank, having finished his drink with his companions, returned to Matt's side. 'You'll find him somewhere. If he's a free worker and not a bad hand, happen Harold will take him on. I'll slip a good word in for him. Besides, looks as if May can't take her eyes off him. He'll have work come Monday.' Frank winked at Matt and then went back to his drinking group. He just hoped the Vixen wouldn't be overrun with too many POWs at once, all talking Italian.

Flora leaned on the bar and looked up at Matt. 'Well, you're certainly giving my customers plenty to talk about. And your Italian friend couldn't have come at a better time to take May's mind off her sorrows after Trevor Whinray's broken her heart.' They both watched as Antonio made his way to May's end of the bar, where he leaned in to listen as she tried to ask him where in Italy he was from. 'I don't know what her father will say, though.'

'I hope he'll take him on. He's a good lad; he needs a chance.' Matt took a long drink of his pint. 'I'll take him back to the camp once I've finished this, else your regulars will get a bit edgy. This is their local – no room for foreigners.' He grinned.

'They'll do as I say and make him welcome. He's only a lad, and most of them know it.' Flora straightened up and looked around her. 'They're all right now, anyway. Back to their usual conversation.' She smiled at Matt. 'I've written to my Bill and told him who you are; I'm so grateful to you.'

'It's nothing. My friend will keep an eye on him now and will let me know how he's doing. I'm just glad I can help. It seems I was meant to come here. No wonder my mother was so happy living here.' Matt reached for Flora's hand and patted it fondly, making her blush.

'Yes, I'm glad you chose to stay here. I hope all my future guests are as trouble-free as you! Although if Bill's to come home once he's fit, there will be no need to let the room again.'

'He'll be back with you, and I'll miss it here, but I'll always have the memory.' Matt finished his drink and glanced over at May and Antonio, still trying to hold a conversation. It was time to return home to his fiancée and his wedding plans as soon as possible.

'You can hold your noise, Frank Capstick. Our May has already tried convincing me to take the lad on. What do I want with an Italian POW working for me?' Harold frowned in concentration as he measured the new window he had made. He could have done without Frank giving his five-penneth about this Italian lad; he'd had more than enough of all that from his wife and daughter.

'Well, he'll be a good hand for you. Especially with big jobs like this one you've got on, making new windows for the schoolhouse. And another thing, Harold – if we don't win this bloody war, at least you'll look as if you're willing to adapt to their ways. We might have to work with the buggers in that case. Not that I even want to think that way.' Frank stood and watched as Harold shaved a sliver of wood from the frame, then stood back and looked sternly at him.

'Stop bloody swearing. We'll not lose this war. Not if all their soldiers are as young as this lad that you say I've to take on. I'm right as I am.'

'All I'm saying is that he would be a grand help. A gofer, if nothing else. He would save your legs and cost you nowt. That fella that's stopping at the Vixen says his father back in Italy is a joiner, so he'll know what he's doing.' Frank turned to go; he had tried his best to help everybody, and it was up to them now.

'I'll give it some thought. I maybe could do with him.

I'll see.' Harold sighed. 'Now, let me get on with this – I want to get at least this frame made before Monday morning.' He shook his head. Perhaps Frank and his May were right; he was snowed under with work, in all truth. Another pair of hands might not be such a bad thing. Especially if they were free. But a POW – now that did not sit happily with him.

Chapter 20

It was knitting club day at the Capstick house. Jenny Moon, Betty Lambert and Lottie Taylor sat in the back garden of the small cottage, enjoying the sunshine and the gossip while working on their gloves, stockings and scarves.

'Your neighbours aren't joining us this morning?' Jenny looked up from her needles as Madge brought out a jug filled with cool ginger beer. She began pouring it into glasses and handing them round.

'No – Sally and Brenda are doing something for the Mothers' Union. Probably looking at the new vicar and thinking how handsome he is. They were both giggling like silly schoolgirls when they were talking about him. He's not married, you know. Fancy sending a young, unmarried vicar to Giggleswick! He'll never replace Reverend Bacon – now, he was a true gentleman, and his wife was a lady. Kept herself to herself. Always turned down my invitation to join us for the knitting, but always told me we were doing a Christian job by looking after our boys. It was a shame he got moved to Bradford. I didn't believe the gossip about him for a minute.' Madge sat down to catch her breath and looked round at her little group of followers. 'Isn't it nice to have Lottie back with us? We'll cheer you up, Lottie. We are all here for you after the loss of your Richard.'

'That we are, Lottie. You were missed. I don't suppose you've heard any more about Richard? He may have survived rather than have gone down with his ship, You never know he might turn up like a bad penny. If he has drowned, do you think they will ever recover his body?' Jenny said, her words casting a little cloud over the group. 'He's not the first, and he'll not be the last.'

'Jenny, let's change the subject. Something a bit brighter.' Madge picked up her knitting needles and started clicking away. 'Mentioning Reverend Bacon, has anybody heard the outcome of all that nonsense about him selling the church silver off to a dealer? I can hardly believe it. He seemed such a nice man. Always popped by for a nip of whisky if we had any in.'

'Not heard a thing. It will all be rubbish; but his wife always did wear the best clothes. She was never a proper vicar's wife, never joined in with the jumble sales or jam-making. She would take some looking after. Expensive tastes, she had.' Jenny took a sip of her ginger beer. 'Bye, that's fiery. Could do with a bit more sugar, Madge.'

'And where am I supposed to get that from these days, Jenny? I've only been able to make that because Frank grew some ginger in his greenhouse that had come out of the school gardens. You can't get anything in the shops nowadays.' Madge sighed and looked across the bottom of the garden to where Frank was pottering in his vegetable plot. Thank heavens he could grow almost anything he turned his hand to. He definitely did enough digging; but whether it was 'for victory', as the posters said, was another matter. It was more for survival.

'Your Frank looks busy, Madge. He looks to have all sorts down there. You'll never go without anything that he can grow,' Lottie remarked, glancing up from her knitting with a smile.

'We'd have even more if he stopped trading vegetables for pints. He's got an arrangement with Flora at the Cunning Vixen. But I can't complain – at least he doesn't take his beer money out of my shopping money.'

'I bet he's not the only one with an agreement with Flora Whitaker,' Jenny said darkly. 'Have you seen the fella that's stopping there? Imagine her having a lodger, and what she could be getting up to while her Bill is away! And I hear that he's in hospital at Catterick as well.'

'Now, Jenny, stop it! You can forget any gossip there. I'm sure that there is nothing untoward going on between them,' Lottie said sharply. 'As for Bill, he got injured while out training. It's from an old wound. I don't think he'll be going fighting any time soon – in fact, he will probably be coming home. Mary herself told me when I had tea with her.' Lottie glared warningly at Jenny. The woman had a wicked tongue at times.

'Well, you would say that, now you and Mary are

back friends. She blows hot and cold with folk as well. You'll be calling her names next week, I'll bet,' Jenny retorted.

'No, I won't. We had a bit of a misunderstanding, but now, yes, we are back friends. Mary is fine; she just keeps herself to herself. She would hate joining our little group. She likes her privacy.' Lottie glanced once more at Jenny before focusing on her knitting again. Jenny had always been inclined to speak ill of Mary and her family, it seemed, although Lottie had no idea why. The rumours were that Jenny had been jealous of Mary long ago, when she had first married Fred; that he had been walking out with the two of them at once.

'Well, her lodger is Maisy Walker's son, who used to run the Vixen. My Frank says he's a good sort. He's been trying to find employment for one of those young Italian POWs, and he even brought him along to the pub on Friday evening.' Madge carried on with her knitting, hoping that this new topic would redirect everyone's attention.

'Maisy Walker; now, she was a case! I wonder if he takes after her. Because if he does, Bill had better be coming home as soon as possible. And fancy bringing a POW into a local pub like ours. You don't want his sort drinking with you,' Jenny tutted as she cast her stitches off. She held up the scarf she had just finished, assessing it. 'That'll keep somebody warm this winter. Do you think I should put tassels on the end, just to finish it off?'

'I don't think they'll be bothered about it being fancy, Jenny. Just practical,' Madge replied.

'Now, then, ladies, is the cauldron bubbling well? I can hear you all cackling from down the bottom of the garden.' Frank came and stood behind his wife's chair, grinning.

'Frank Capstick, you are nowt but cheeky, calling us witches. We are nowt of the sort. More like angels, that's us.' Jenny looked up at him. Frank always had a joke for them all, but sometimes she wondered if he really was joking or truly meant it.

'Are you all right, love? Do you want a drink of ginger beer and to join us?' Madge glanced at her husband, although she already knew the answer.

'Nay, I'm just going to have ten minutes with Harold. I can hear him hammering and sawing in his workshop, so I'll see what he has to say for himself. I'm wondering if he's going to take on that young POW who was in the pub. He'd be a fool if he didn't – he'd have no wage to pay, just need to feed him. And he's always saying he's got too much work on.'

'Well, I'd not want him in my house. He is still the enemy – and what if he pinched something?' Jenny looked aghast.

'I don't think this lad is your enemy. Happen Mussolini, Hitler and his Nazis; but this lad is just out of nappies and looks lost. He's only as old as our May. Poor bugger. You can tell he's been conscripted,' Frank replied firmly, addressing the main witch of the coven.

'They shouldn't make them fight that young,' Lottie said quietly. 'I hope Harold takes him on. It could be my lad, or anybody's lad, that has been made to fight and is a long way from home. We would all wish for our sons and husbands to be treated well if they were taken as POWs.' She hoped that would silence Jenny.

'Aye, that's right, Lottie. We should all show a little sympathy even if he is our enemy in name. Now, if you'll excuse me, ladies, I'll be on my way and leave you to your knitting.' Frank smiled at his wife's group of friends. He'd find better company with Harold and come back to his garden later.

He crossed the road and headed for the open door of his friend's workshop. 'Hey up, Harold. Thought I'd come round and see what you are up to. I can hear you banging and braying all the way over in my garden, so it must be something big.' He peered inside at Harold, who was stilling working on the new windows for Giggleswick School.

'I thought when I'd made these two windows and fitted them, that would see me done up at the school. But on Friday they told me they wanted *all* the windows replaced in one of the dormitories, so I'll have six more to make. It's grand I've got the work, but I'm going to meet myself coming back.' Harold stood up straight and took a breath. 'It's a good job our lass is doing my paperwork, else I'd never have a chance to look at it.' He pulled the flat cap from his head and used it to wipe his sweating brow before putting it back on.

'I keep telling you – you need an apprentice. That young POW would be just right. I know your May has said the same. He'd cost you nowt, except to be fed or whatever you wanted to give him.'

'Aye, so you all keep telling me.' Harold came out to stand with Frank in the sunshine. 'So much so that I went into Settle this morning and visited Whitefriars, and I asked that captain fella how I would go about taking the lad on. Only on trial, for now,' he added firmly, as Frank's face lit up with satisfaction. 'He might be telling them lot owt – he might not know a nail from a screw. I don't trust him. Nor them lot's records, come to that.'

'Well, from what I saw in the pub the other night, he looks a decent lad. Couldn't understand a word he said, mind, but he'll learn. And if he is a joiner, he should know what he's doing. I'm glad you're taking him on.' Frank patted Harold on the back.

'Aye, well, there's none of our lads spare to help with anything. It'll make May happy; she doesn't know yet, she's still at work in the pub. Just as long as they don't get too friendly. One minute she's broken-hearted because that Trevor Whinray has dropped her, and then she comes home and never stops going on about this Italian she's been talking to over the bar of the Vixen. I might live to regret taking him on. But as you say, he's free labour, and I'm desperate for another pair of hands.'

'It'll be right, Harold. I'm glad to hear that copper isn't walking out any longer with your May. He's sneaky, and she'd never have been happy with him. She's too good for him,' Frank said.

'Tell the wife that. She had them getting married and our May living as the sergeant's wife in Settle. But I'm like you; I'm glad it's come to an end. Can't stand the man.' Harold scowled.

'Just listen to us. I've left my garden because Madge has her circle of knitting friends round, and they were gossiping about everybody and driving me crackers. I come here, and we're as bad. D'you fancy a pint? Flora will just about be opening.' Frank winked.

'No, I'd better not; I need to knock on. If this lad's to help out, I'll have to make some space in the workshop before he starts. Besides, my old lass will have my guts for garters if she sees me sloping off to the pub at this time of day,' Harold said, although he felt tempted to keep his friend company over a pint.

'That's the joy of being retired. I can sneak out, and the old lass never knows where I'm at.' Frank laughed as he turned away to walk the few yards up the road to the pub.

'She'll play hell with you when she smells the beer on your breath,' Harold shouted after him.

'Don't get that close nowadays. Too old for owt of that,' Frank called back. He headed towards the open doorway of the Vixen, deciding it was his best option for refuge from the gossips – just for an hour, until they had all gone home.

Chapter 21

'That's good, Private Whitaker. Just a few steps more, then we'll take you back to your ward.' The hospital's physio watched as Bill gripped onto two hand bars and concentrated with all his might to take the steps he'd feared he would never manage again. The pain was manageable now, at least with the painkillers they gave him – he just had to get his legs working.

Effort was etched on his face as he advanced a few feet, holding on determinedly as he willed his limbs into action. Sweat dripped down his brow, and he grimaced as he reached the end of the bars and saw his wheelchair waiting.

'Damn it, I wish I could bloody well walk. I hate that thing. And I'm not going home in it.'

The physio took his arm and guided him gently down into the chair. 'Swearing will get you nowhere. And you won't be going home in a wheelchair. In another few weeks, your injuries will have healed and your muscles repaired. You just need to be patient,' she chastised him.

She draped a blanket over his knees and wheeled him across to an orderly.

'Another few weeks! I need to get home now. I don't want my wife to think she's married to a cripple,' Bill moaned, slapping the arms of the chair in frustration.

'She'll think no such thing. She will be glad to get you home alive and in one piece. She's blessed in comparison with many wives who will never see their loved ones again. Give it time, and you'll be fit as a fiddle. Now, I'll see you again in the morning; and no swearing, else I'll have to report you,' the physio added sternly, nodding to the orderly to take Bill back to his ward.

Bill muttered under his breath. It seemed as if the world was set against him, and he was making slow progress with his walking. Without medication, the pain in his back was still excruciating. However, he was grateful that he could at least put one foot in front of the other, no matter how difficult.

'There you go; back onto the ward for your dinner. And it looks like you have a letter waiting. News from home always cheers everybody up.' The orderly pushed Bill to the side of his newly made-up bed. 'Do you want to get into bed? Or shall I leave you in the chair?'

'I'm right here, thank you. In fact, if you wouldn't mind pushing me to the open doors, I'll sit in the sun and read my letter.' Bill reached for the letter, which he recognized to be from Flora. It was just the medicine he needed. He wanted to get home, but more than anything, he wanted to know about this man who was seemingly staying at the Vixen with his wife.

'All right, if you're sure. I'll come and wheel you back at dinner time.' The young nurse left him just inside the ward's tall glass doors, which stood open to let in the gentle summer breeze. It freshened the air inside and made Bill wish he could go home then and there as he heard the distant shouts of the sergeant yelling orders, followed by the crack of gunfire. He should never have enlisted, he thought for the thousandth time as he looked down at the envelope. Then he tore into it, eager for news from home.

He read and took in each line that Flora had written. He read about how she had contacted him; Matt Walker, son of an old landlady from the Cunning Vixen? He had never heard of her, nor him. And where exactly was this Walker fellow staying in Giggleswick? Flora never mentioned in her letter that he was staying at the pub, yet the captain who had come to visit Bill had said he was stopping at the Vixen. But there wouldn't be room for him, Bill thought. Unless Flora was sleeping elsewhere?

Doubts started to creep into his mind. What if Flora had always known this Matt Walker, and he had conveniently come back into her life as soon as her husband's back was turned?

He tried to concentrate on the rest of the letter – bottled beer; Mary back friends with Lottie . . . well, that was a miracle, he thought as he looked up to gaze out across the barracks. But there was still no mention of where this Matt was staying.

He began to imagine the worst. Was Flora being

unfaithful to him? But then, why rub his nose in it by mentioning the bloke? And then sending along that damn snooty captain, who had obviously been to private school just like all the nobs at the top of the forces? He gripped the letter in his hand. The sooner he could get back to Giggleswick, the better. Damn his stubbornness – he should have stayed at home in the first place, where he belonged.

'I say, old chap – are you all right? I thought I'd call in to see how you are and report back to Matt.'

Once again, Bill surfaced from a restless sleep to find Captain Lewis standing over his bed.

'Shame to wake you, but I'm expecting him to ring within the hour. Thought I could give him news of your progress.' Lewis pulled a chair up next to Bill's bed and sat down, placing his cap on his knee. 'Got a wheelchair there, have you? You must be moving better. That's good. Feeling all right?'

With an effort, Bill pulled himself upright in his bed. 'I'm getting there. You can tell your friend, and my wife, that I hope to be back home before long. She sent me a letter this morning.'

'Splendid. Are they looking after you well? Anything I can get you?' Lewis probed, undeterred by Bill's scowl.

'No. There's nowt I want but to get back home, and to be able to walk again. And I'll do both, if I have my way.' Bill fixed Lewis with a hard stare. 'This mate of yours – Matt Walker. Where did you say he was staying at? And how does he know my wife? She doesn't exactly make things clear in her letter. I didn't take much notice when you were telling me the last time.' Bill didn't really want to reveal his deepest insecurities to Captain Lewis, but he could feel his heart racing with anxiety, and there was nobody else he could ask.

'As far as I'm aware, he's staying with your wife at the Cunning Vixen. He says he's been made very welcome there. I believe he and your wife have a lot in common – now, I don't know exactly what . . .' Lewis noted Bill's grim expression and fixed stare. 'He's a jolly good chap, Matt,' he went on encouragingly, hoping to reassure the injured soldier. 'Always looks after everybody however he can.'

'Aye, I bet he does,' Bill growled. 'You can tell them both that I'll be back as soon as these legs can get me home.'

'Splendid, old chap. I'll tell them. But you will need your discharge papers first, and that may take some time. There are procedures; after all, this is the army.' Captain Lewis put his cap back onto his head and stood up, tucking his swagger stick tightly under his arm, every inch the officer.

'Bugger the discharge papers. Once I can walk, I'll get myself back home. I should never have been here in the first place.' Bill looked up at the officer. Lewis might be far above him in rank, but his days of tugging his forelock to his supposed betters had come to an end. It was time to sort his life out.

'Matron may have other ideas. You just build your strength back up again and get well. However, I will see what I can do – after all, as you say, you really don't belong with us. I'm sure your wife is running the pub well enough, and she will have Matt to help her for now. I'll be off to give them that update on your progress. Chin chin, old chap.'

Bill watched Lewis stroll out of the ward. Bloody military elite! They thought anything they fancied was theirs. If this Matt Walker had taken advantage of Flora's outgoing character and caring ways, Bill would bloody well set about him. And that would be sooner than any of them thought, if he had his way.

Matt sat down to his evening meal. Everything at Whitefriars was going well. All the POWs had been found placements – he could have done a celebratory dance when Harold Lambert had walked into Captain Bentham's office to see about taking on Antonio Lugatti as a worker. May must have some influence over her father, he had thought, as the local joiner sat down at the desk and completed forms for the lad to go and work for him.

He looked up at Flora and smiled as she set down his plate of mutton stew. 'Two good pieces of news this evening, Flora. May has convinced her father that he needs young Antonio – he'll start work for him this week coming. Although May's probably already told you that. And Bruce, my friend at Catterick, has visited your Bill again and says he's making excellent progress. The matron tells him Bill has no patience and will not do as he's told. He's been walking with help and is getting about in a wheelchair. It won't be long before he's back with you and able to walk unaided.'

Flora stood listening avidly, a hand to her lips. 'Had he received my letter? Did he say?' she asked eagerly.

'Yes; he said to Bruce that he had. Bruce also said he sounded puzzled about me staying here with you. Did you tell him I was letting out the spare room? I hope he doesn't think anything untoward is happening.' Matt raised his eyebrows.

'I should hope not – I must admit, though, I didn't mention that you were staying here.' Flora felt a surge of anxiety. She had only left that out so as not to worry Bill. He'd always been a jealous sort, even though she had never been unfaithful to him. On reflection, having had some time away from him, she'd been thinking lately that he was often unfairly quick to reprimand her for chatting with locals or customers. 'So, your friend has told him that you're lodging at the pub?'

'I believe he did; that was when he noticed a change in his mood. I hope Bruce hasn't caused any bother. Sometimes his mouth works faster than his brain. God only knows how he became a captain.' Matt sat back in his chair, frowning.

Flora sighed. 'I didn't want to worry him, that's all. I talked about you in my letter, but I didn't think it was a good idea to tell him you were staying.' She shook her head. 'I was going to at first, but my mother advised me not to. And I knew that he'd probably get the wrong idea. He can be so jealous.'

'Then I'd better leave. I don't want to cause any trouble

between the two of you – not that we're doing anything wrong. There's a spare room at Whitefriars. I will go and stay there; it will only be for a short while, anyway.'

'You will not – I'll write and tell him to stop worrying. That you are staying here, but as a guest only, nothing more. The stupid, stubborn man! He should have more faith in me; I have never been disloyal to him, even though he pushes me to the limit sometimes. He should never have volunteered, and then he would not be in the position he is in, and I wouldn't be running this place all on my own.' Flora felt like crying. She sank into the chair opposite Matt, dropping her head into her hands.

'Hey . . . hey,' Matt said soothingly. 'The last thing I want to do is make you upset. Shh, Flora; I'll not go if you don't want me to. But yes, you probably had better write that letter and explain.' He got up, placing a reassuring hand on her shoulder. 'My mother used to say that in a village like this, everybody always gossiped and put two and two together. I should have known better than to stay here when you were on your own.'

'That's their problem, not ours. We are doing nothing wrong. And we've become good friends while you've been here. I'll make it right with Bill, and if he doesn't want to believe me, then he's a fool and doesn't realize just how much I do love him.' Flora patted Matt's hand and looked up at him. She could never be unfaithful to Bill, and after all she'd done to show him her love, he should know that.

Chapter 22

The following Monday a noisy army truck pulled up outside Back Fold, and the rear panel was let down to reveal the POWs who were being delivered around the dale.

Harold Lambert came out of his front door as Antonio jumped down from the wagon and stood in front of the guards. He watched as Harold signed a form to take charge of him for the day. After handing the clipboard back, Harold studied the dark-haired young man who stood before him. Betty and May watched from the doorway.

'Well, you're here good and early. It's only just turned seven – you'd better come in and have a brew and let me finish my breakfast. I suppose you'll be with us at this time every morning. They must feed you early.'

'*Si*, six. Wake at six, work at seven.' Antonio smiled. He noticed May waiting in the doorway and grinned at her.

'Aye, well, you can have a brew and get to know the missus. She's the one that will be feeding you, but you'll work with me.' Harold gestured as he spoke, indicating to Antonio who was who and who did what, and Antonio nodded agreeably.

'Father, Antonio's English is nearly perfect – he knows what you are saying. I talked to him the other night in the bar, like I told you. But you probably weren't listening then.' May returned Antonio's smile as her father bustled her back into the cottage.

'Your father does not know, and I never say anything,' Antonio replied as he followed Harold and May into the family kitchen. 'I learn English in the other camp – you had to, to, how you say . . . live.' Antonio looked at the Lamberts and bowed his head.

'It's a good job you did, lad, because I can't speak a damn word of Italian. Now, do you drink tea? Betty will make you a cup before we start. Not that we can spare it.' Harold offered Antonio a seat at the table.

'No problem. My friend in the kitchen give me some. He said it would make me welcome in my new work.' Antonio reached into his pocket and took out a brown bag, which he put down on the kitchen table. 'British Army issue, very strong.'

'That's the way to make yourself welcome, lad. We're grateful for that. May, stop gawping at him and put the kettle on. Then you get yourself to the pub, and Antonio and I will see what he can do.'

'We make doors and windows, mend things?' Antonio asked.

'Aye – joinery. Making some new windows at the moment. You know how to dovetail joints?' Harold asked, interlinking his fingers.

'*Si*, joints, I know how to make. I work with my father back in Napoli.'

'Napoli? Naples!' Betty gasped. 'It must be beautiful. Blue skies and sea.' She sighed.

'*Si*, a lot warmer than Yorkshire. I always feel cold here.' Antonio reached for his cup of tea and tried not to look too long at May. She was very pretty, and she was the first girl to make him feel welcome in this country.

'Well, you'll be breaking a sweat with me, lad, when we get working, so you enjoy your tea. May, will you stop gawping at him and get yourself to work.' Harold scowled at his daughter.

'Gawping? What is gawping?' Antonio asked.

'Nowt for you to bother about.' Harold pushed his empty bowl of porridge to one side. 'Now, let's get you out of this kitchen away from these women, with their dreams of Naples. They wouldn't last five minutes there. You foreigners don't eat decent food for a start.'

'Food – pasta. My mamma's pasta, *bellissima*.'

'Aye, that'll do. Come on, let's have you making us some money. Naples can wait,' Harold said, heading for the kitchen door. 'Work, May.'

'I'm going, I'm going! I'll do your accounts this afternoon,' May promised as she picked up her gas mask.

'I thought you might. It'll be quiet for you, as I'm taking this one to Giggleswick School to measure the windows I'm replacing. So you'll have peace in the workshop.' Harold smiled as he saw his daughter's face cloud over. 'There will be no fraternizing in this house, madam,' he told her sternly. 'He's here to work, let me make that clear.' He glanced towards Antonio, who waited for him outside. 'Behave yourself. He's a bloody Italian, and don't you forget it.'

May looked at her mother as her father and Antonio left the cottage for the workshop. 'What do you think?'

'He is handsome, May. But like your father says, he's Italian – and the enemy. Don't get friendly. I must admit, though, when he said Naples, all I could think of was the sun and sea. I've always fancied travelling.' Betty sighed.

'Well, you won't be going there in a hurry at the moment. And I'd better get to the pub, as my father says. I'll see you this afternoon.' May grinned. 'Is it pasta for dinner? Whatever that is?'

'No, he'll have to make do on cheese and bread, but I'm grateful for the tea, although I think he may have pinched it. I don't know what the world is coming to. I only hope that we win this war soon, but that's wishful thinking on my part.'

'Never mind, Mam, at least we are reasonably safe up here in the Dales. Now, I'll have to go and see what Flora's up to today. No doubt there will be something happening there.' May kissed her mother on the cheek. She didn't often do that, but her mother looked so disheartened.

'Aye, go and see what she's up to today. She's a fair lass, is your boss,' Betty smiled. Flora was always ducking and diving and finding a way of making a bob or two, but she was a good'en, and she looked after May.

Once outside, May couldn't resist just putting her head round the workshop door and saying goodbye to her father, although it was really an excuse to have another look at Antonio. She didn't feel one bit concerned that thoughts of Trevor Whinray had completely left her head. She had concluded now that he had only been using her to spy on Flora.

'Bye, Father, see you this afternoon. Bye, Antonio!' May called to both men. Her father was bent over, demonstrating something to his new apprentice, and the smell of wood shavings filled the air.

'Aye, get yourself gone. We've already said bye,' her father growled.

'*Ciao, bella.*' Antonio raised his head from his work and smiled at May, making her heart skip a beat. He'd called her *bella* – now, what did that mean? She would have to find out. She smiled as she made her way to the pub.

'You look full of yourself this morning. A bit different to the other day,' Flora looked at her helper and smiled. If only she were her age again and had the worries that she had! Little did May know how much harder life was likely to get with age.

'Trevor? Trevor who?' May said as she put her apron on and hung her gas mask up at the back door. 'I've decided to put him behind me. Besides, who wants to be a policeman's wife?'

'Plenty would, seeing that you'd always have a good wage coming in and a roof over your head. Especially if he's a sergeant; they always get a house with their job,' Flora pointed out as she washed the beer glasses from the previous night.

'No – I'd like to see warmer climes, travel the world, when this war is over.' May looked dreamily around her before picking up the brush and shovel to sweep the stone flags of the bar area.

'This wouldn't have anything to do with Antonio, would it? Matt told me he was starting work this morning. You managed to persuade your father, then?' Flora smiled as she wiped her hands and left the glasses to dry.

'I hardly had to say a word! Gig School wants some new windows making, and he can't manage such a big job on his own. He had to find someone to help him. Antonio has arrived just at the right time in Settle.' May grinned. 'Flora, do you know what *bella* means in Italian?'

'I believe it means beautiful – yes, beautiful. I've heard it said in a film once.' Flora noticed the blush that had come to May's cheeks.

'Thank you, I just wanted to know . . . *Bella*,' May whispered as she grabbed the brush handle. She was thinking that her life was worth living after all – and she definitely would not give Trevor Whinray another thought.

The day went slowly for Flora; her head was full of worries. She kept thinking of Bill, knowing that he would be imagining the worst about Matt staying at the Cunning Vixen – he always did. He had never trusted her, not since the day they'd got married; it was just his nature. Sometimes it had been nice to know that he was so possessive, so protective of her, but this was the other side of it.

With being so busy, she hadn't got round to writing him another letter. When she did, she would reassure him that Matt was sleeping in their bedroom and she was sleeping in the attic – and also, most importantly, that he was betrothed and was one hundred per cent a gentleman. She should have done that in the first place, she thought, watching as May washed the dusters they had been using and pegged them on the outside line to dry. Flora had seen her humming happily to herself all day, and now she was about to go home. It was clear she was smitten by the Italian POW. Harold wouldn't be pleased – nor would her mother, Flora thought, as May came back in and took her gas mask from behind the back door.

'That's me done for the day, Flora. I'll go home and tackle my father's accounts. It's made all the difference, keeping those in line. At least my mother's not moaning as much now.'

'I bet they'll both moan if you get too friendly with that Italian. You behave yourself, May – you don't know the first thing about him,' Flora warned her friend.

'I do – he's from Naples. He got enlisted. He's one of four brothers, and his father is a joiner, just like mine,' May quickly replied. 'And he's got the deepest, darkest brown eyes . . . and he calls me beautiful. Nobody has ever done that.' She sighed happily as she made for the door.

'Italians are born romantic, so don't you forget that,' Flora cautioned. She followed May to the main door and propped it open for the day's customers.

'I won't; but there's no harm in looking when he's around home.' May grinned. 'See you in the morning.' There was a bounce in her step as she set off along the street towards Back Fold.

Flora stood for a moment and looked out on the scene as the clock struck twelve. Giggleswick was quiet, and she could tell it was going to be a slow day. Custom had dropped off slightly since bottled beer had replaced hand-drawn pints, and she knew some of her regulars were going up the hill to the Hart's Head, where he was still drawing draft beer. The landlord there had no problems – he was on the main road out of Settle and had several rooms to let that brought in a regular income. And he was tied to a different brewery than hers. She couldn't blame some of her customers for going there – she would, too, if she needed a good pint.

She went back inside, leaned on the bar and looked around the empty pub. Not even Frank was about to show his face at lunchtime – he had already mentioned that he'd be going to see about some plants at his friend's in Settle. After a few moments, Flora went to gather pen and paper from her little office and returned to the bar, sitting down at one of the tables to write Bill a letter of explanation. It was time to put his mind at rest. She sat tapping her pen, wondering how to go about explaining without making him even more suspicious.

'Now, then, you look a million miles away. You never heard me coming along, anyway.'

It was a voice she knew all too well. Startled out of her thoughts, Flora looked up as her old lover, Johnny Cowperthwaite, stepped forward from the open doorway. He approached the table where she sat. 'I thought I'd surprise you and bring you a present, one that I'm sure you'll be glad of. It's only an old boiler, but it'll be tasty. And I decided it was time I came to see you – especially seeing as I've heard Bill is injured.'

Johnny placed a dead, brown, feathered hen onto the bar. Its beady eye still looked lifelike. He took a seat across from Flora as she gathered herself to reply.

'Johnny – what a surprise! I haven't seen you for a good while. Sorry, I was miles away. I'm just writing to Bill. The pub's not busy, so I thought I'd drop him a line. It's good to see you. How are you?'

Flora and Johnny had courted for a good two years before she'd met Bill. Looking across now at his rugged face, she felt her heart beat a little faster. She still thought highly of Johnny. He was a farmer over on Malham Moor, and perhaps her mother had been correct when she said that Flora should have married him. Life would have certainly been more financially secure than with Bill, who had hardly a penny to his name.

'I'm grand. Keeping my head down and hoping that this bloody war will soon be over, so we can all get back to normal. You're right when you say you're dead in here today; tha's not got anybody in and it's nearly one.' Johnny looked around at the empty pub and sat back, looking at Flora. He still loved her – he always would. No matter that she was married and pretending to be happy.

'Aye, times are hard. There's no lads in the village, and the older ones are watching their pennies. Not to mention I've only got bottled beer at the moment, so I'm losing my regulars to up the road. You are only here because you know Bill's away, else you wouldn't dare walk in here as bold as brass.' Flora could read the look in Johnny's eyes as clearly as ever. She knew with certainty that he still loved her, but her love for him had cooled over the years; she knew she was married to the better man in Bill.

'Aye, I heard that the daft bugger had joined up and ended up in a hospital bed. How old does he think he is, nineteen? He should have stopped at home and looked after you.' Johnny shook his head, leaning back in his chair. 'Is he all right? I've heard he can't walk, is that right?'

'He couldn't a few days back. They've operated on him since and taken out the shrapnel that's been giving him problems ever since the last war. I understand he's nearly walking again now; hopefully, he will be back with me before long. The army will have no use for him now.' Flora looked down at her hands. She couldn't bear to meet Johnny's searching gaze in case she started to cry.

'Aye, lass, are you all right? You know I'm always

here for you.' He reached across and took her hand, squeezing it tightly.

'I know – you always are.' Flora wiped a tear away. Johnny had been able to read her moods, sensing when she was low or worried in the past. 'I'm thankful that we are still friends. I would miss you if you weren't in my life.' She smiled, fighting back tears.

'Aye, well; it's only because I'm a selfish bastard and hope that one day you'll see sense and come live with me. I'll be honest – when I heard Bill had injured himself, I hoped that it was to be fatal. Because I need you, Flora,' he said, pressing on despite the shock on her face at his words. 'I'll never marry another. My heart will always be yours – you should know that. I should know better; you are not the kind to hold a flame for another man while you are married to Bill.' Johnny paused to let his words sink it. Flora had rejected him for honest reasons – for the sake of the life she wanted to live, running her own pub in Giggleswick with the man who had won her heart.

'I know, Johnny. I did you wrong, but I'm no farmer's wife. It would never have worked. And then Bill came along, and I was busy buying here – you know I had set my heart on running it. And then you had your head turned by Gladys Middleton, and I thought that you were going to marry her.' Flora looked at Johnny. If she had chosen him, she would have had no money worries. She'd have anything she wanted. Her mother was right, she should have married him for security, but she couldn't have lived with a man she did not truly love.

'Aye, Gladys, the poor woman. I only turned to her out of spite at losing you. I treated her badly, and that's a fact. We've both been fools.'

He stood up and moved closer, embracing Flora as she rose to join him. She hesitated, then put her head on his shoulder. His tweed jacket felt comforting, as it always had, and she caught the scent of the wild fell land where he lived as he held her tightly. She closed her eyes. Johnny gently kissed her neck and whispered in her ear, 'I love you, Flora. I'll always love you. And I'm sorry I wished the worst for Bill.'

'I know. But I made my bed when I married Bill, and he loves me. I will always be faithful to him.' Flora leaned back and looked up into his face. To her surprise, Johnny lowered his head and brushed his lips over hers. Flora felt her heart miss a beat as she pulled back, looking into his blue eyes.

'We shouldn't – please, Johnny, don't do this to me. Bill is ill in the hospital. I know he's got his flaws, but he loves me, and it would break his heart if he knew that you were here. I love my husband. Please – don't.' She pushed Johnny away and stepped back.

'You're too good for him, Flora. He might love you, but he doesn't know you like I do and never will. Does he still hit you?' Johnny watched as Flora turned away, frustrated and with mixed emotions flitting across her face.

She shook her head. 'I'm sorry, Johnny. I care deeply for you, but my life is with Bill here at the Vixen.' She knew as she said it that she was breaking both their hearts again. And Johnny was telling the truth: he did know her better than Bill ever would. When they had been courting one another, there was not a secret kept between them, they had been so close, too close and too ambitious for love to last between them.

He shook his head. 'I hoped that you would see sense and realize we were always meant for one another. I thought with him being away for a while, you'd come to see how life could be without him. I've tried to stay away as long as I could, Flora, but I think about you every day and always will.'

Johnny watched as Flora retreated behind the bar, tears running down her face. She looked miserably at the dead hen lying there, then up at him.

'Our time has been and gone. I love you as a friend, but there can never be anything more between us. Bill is my man and always will be, despite his jealousy and anger.' Behind Johnny, a figure appeared in the open doorway – Matt, returning early from Whitefriars. Flora hastily wiped away the tears, sending Johnny a warning glance as Matt approached the bar.

'Everything all right here, Flora? You look upset.' Matt glanced at the unknown visitor. Clearly, he had walked in on a scene not meant for him to witness.

'Everything is fine, thank you, Matt. I'm just shedding a tear for this old broiler hen that my friend Johnny here has dropped in for us to put in a pot. She'll make a good dinner, but I hate to think she's given her life for us.' Flora picked up the hen and turned away, disappearing into the kitchen to collect herself.

'You're right about one thing, Flora – you never would have made a good farmer's wife. You are far too soft-hearted,' Johnny called after her with a quiet chuckle.

Left alone, he and Matt glanced at one another. Johnny turned to face Matt and extended a hand.

'You must be lodger Matt, the fella from the ministry that folk are talking about. I'm Johnny Cowperthwaite. Flora and I are old friends.'

'Yes, Matt Walker,' Matt said, shaking his hand. 'It's good to meet you. Flora has been a wonderful hostess, fed me well and made me most welcome. I don't know if she's mentioned it at all, but the reason I wanted to stay here was because my mother used to be the landlady here before I was born. I don't suppose you knew her, did you?'

Johnny seemed distracted, glancing over his shoulder towards Flora in the kitchen.

'I don't, mate, sorry. I live on Malham Moor. She'd have been here before I was old enough to go drinking down in Giggleswick. The Cunning Vixen has had a few owners, some good, some bad, but everybody should be thankful they have got Flora running it now. She's given a lot up to run this place and to be with Bill.' Johnny shook his head. 'No, can't place your mother. Must not have known her.'

Flora came back into the bar.

'Oh, well, there are a few of the older ones remember her, so that's good. It's in the past, anyway.' Matt nodded at Flora. 'I'm back early, Flora. I've been told to wrap things up here in Settle and report back to Leeds at the end of next week. They are happy that everything's gone well and that the POWs are all now placed.'

'So soon – I thought you would be staying at least another fortnight,' Flora gasped.

'The man will have to do what he's been ordered to do, Flora. You can't get the better of the government.' Johnny eyed the dashing young man who had been staying under the same roof as the woman he loved. He was glad to hear that Matt would soon be leaving.

'Matt will be returning to Leeds to get married; his fiancée is waiting for him. He's been the perfect guest while staying here.' Flora smiled at Matt and then gave Johnny a meaningful glance.

'That's what I like to hear – everybody happy. Or as happy as any of us can be under the circumstances. Now, I'll be away. My cows won't milk themselves, and it will be milking time by the time I've wandered back over the tops.' Johnny turned to Flora. 'I hope Bill continues to improve. And you know where I am if you need me.' He longed to kiss her again and comfort her. It was his love she needed, not Bill's; of that he was sure.

'Yes, thank you, Johnny. It was good to see you, as ever.' Flora's gaze followed Johnny as he left the pub. There was a short silence, and then she glanced at Matt. 'He's an old friend. We were close at one time.'

Matt nodded, searching for an ordinary remark to break the tension. 'I see you're having another busy day,' he said with an ironic smile. 'It's pretty quiet out there in the village as well.'

'Yes; I was just about to write to Bill, and then Johnny

walked in. He's not been here that long, and it was good to catch up. You said that you'll be leaving next week? That's earlier than you thought, but you'll be glad to be back home again. I'll have to let Bill know. If he's recovering, hopefully he'll be returning home soon.'

'Yes; sorry about that. It seems my work in Settle is done. Bill will soon be discharged once he gets anything like fit. They won't want him lingering in their hospital if he's of no use to the army. As I said, it usually takes them a month to sort the paperwork out, but I suspect because of his age and record they'll get on with it as fast as they can. They'll need his bed . . . Will you be glad to get him home?' Matt looked questioningly at Flora. He had never met Bill and had always assumed that the couple were close. However, after seeing the look Flora's old friend had given her, he wondered.

'I can't wait for him to be home. I'm going to make such a fuss of him.' Flora looked a little happier at the thought, and she smiled at Matt. 'What are you going to do this afternoon? I've a good mind to close up and take an afternoon to myself – after all, it's past one and nobody's in here.'

'I'm going to have a walk up Castleberg Crag. I've been intending to do it before I return home, and this seems the perfect day for it.' Matt hesitated. 'Lock the door and come with me, if you like? You can point out all the landmarks, and it'll be a memory for me of my time in Settle and Giggleswick. I don't think I will be returning once I've settled into my new life as a married man.' He looked at Flora hopefully. It would be good to walk with her and spend some time together before he took his leave of the village.

'Oh, I don't know . . . I should really stay open, but I'd love to go with you. I haven't walked up there for so long, and the view over the town is wonderful. I need to write this letter, though.' Looking out through the open door at the sunny street, Flora was strongly tempted to join Matt; the weather was glorious, and the pub was empty. The invitation was too good to turn down.

'Well, let's do it. I've a letter to write to my Beth as well, to tell her I'll be returning home soon. So we'll each post a letter to our loved ones and then take our walk. Go on, it'll do you good,' Matt grinned.

'I shouldn't; but yes, I will. We can both write our letters and then go.' Flora walked over to the main door and locked it shut. 'Thirty minutes – is that long enough for you? Then I must come back and dress that hen Johnny's left me.'

'Thirty minutes is fine, and I'll pluck and clean the hen later on. It's not a very pleasant job – I'm surprised he didn't do it for you,' Matt said, picking up his briefcase.

'That's the wife's job, if you farm,' Flora smiled. 'Thank you, though – I'd be grateful. I hate cleaning hens. Let me go back to my pen and paper and I'll finish my letter. Are you sure thirty minutes is enough?'

'Yes – my Beth will see the words "I'm coming home", and that's all she'll care about. I'm so looking forward to being with her again. I hadn't quite realized how dear to me she is,' Matt said quietly, smiling as he turned away to climb the stairs.

Flora watched him go. It was clear that Matt was deeply in love with his wife-to-be, and she hoped they'd be happy together. Meanwhile, a brisk walk this afternoon would surely blow any thoughts of Johnny Cowperthwaite out of her head – and then she could concentrate on her own true love, Bill, coming home.

Chapter 23

'There, that's our letters posted. Now, let's climb up there and look down over this beautiful town. I think the memory of it will stay with me for ever,' Matt said.

He and Flora were standing in Settle marketplace. The summer sun was shining on the whitewashed houses, and the main square was busy with shoppers and friends chatting. Above the town, surrounded by shrubs and trees, was the craggy outcrop that dominated Settle's skyline – still with a Union Jack flying proudly at the very top, where it had been ever since the start of the war. It would be a hard climb, but Flora knew that the views were spectacular once you reached the top.

The two weaved their way up through the cobbled streets of Upper Settle and then followed the winding path through the wooded slopes of the outcrop.

'There used to be a fairground that came here when I was young,' Flora recalled. 'I remember riding the hobby horses with my father watching me. It always came to the bottom just there, where the houses finish and the woods start.' She stopped to catch her breath, looking back to where they had come from. 'And before that, my mother used to say that there was a huge sundial on the crag side for the people of Settle to tell the time; but even she doesn't know if that was true or not. The truth has been lost to time.'

Flora took Matt's hand as he offered it to her over a particularly steep part of the climb. The terrain was rugged with loose stones, which made their feet slip as they both caught their breath and stopped again to take in the view. 'Thank you; nearly there now.'

Both smiled as they heard the sound of the flag billowing in the slight breeze above their heads. They made their way steadily over the limestone outcrops until finally they reached the enclave and the edge of the huge rock that hung over Settle. Standing next to the flagpole, they took in the view over the Ribble Valley and then sat down on a stone boulder, which made a convenient perch just below the fluttering flag.

'Just look at the view. Unbelievable – the people below us look like ants, and the village looks like a model. Look at the dome!' Matt exclaimed, pointing towards the green copper dome, green with verdigris, of Giggleswick School that dominated the skyline. They stood and gazed out over the panorama.

'You can just see the Ribble wending its way down Lancashire and Pendle Hill, and over to your right, the hills of the Lake District. It really is spectacular; I'd nearly forgotten just how beautiful it is. The last time I was up here would have been with my father, just before he died.' Flora felt a glow of pride in the loveliness of the area where she had grown up.

'Were you close to your father? You speak of him with fondness.' Matt looked closely at Flora. He had a secret – one that he had been hiding, and he didn't know whether he should tell her or not. He didn't want to mar the gentle pleasure of this afternoon they were spending together on top of Castleberg Crag.

'I was; he always spoiled me so much. He worked hard, but he also knew how to enjoy himself, from what I can remember. My mother didn't have an easy life with him – that I do know. That's why she is so independent now.' Flora hesitated for a moment. 'He liked his drink. He was never away from the Cunning Vixen of an evening; that's partly why my mother wasn't happy about me taking over as landlady there.'

'I see. I'd like to meet your mother properly before I leave,' Matt said quietly, his gaze still on the sunlit vista below them. He took a deep breath and let it slowly out. 'I . . . I think that it is time for me to come clean with you, Flora.'

She looked at him curiously.

'My work brought me here,' Matt went on, 'but I chose to stay at your pub, not by accident – I was going to track it down no matter what.' He paused.

'Yes, because your mother used to run it? I understand,' Flora smiled, but she could see the uncertainty on Matt's face now.

'It's more than that – I didn't know whether to tell

you or not. Although I think your mother already knows. Otherwise she would have been to see me by now,' he added.

'What do you mean? What's this got to do with my mother?' Flora was starting to feel a little alarmed.

'It's not your mother; it's your father. I really don't know if I should . . . The last thing I want is to upset you. It took me an age to believe it after my mother died.' Matt swallowed hard. '. . . Flora, I think that your father is my father, too. I believe that is the reason why my mother left Giggleswick. She left because she was pregnant, carrying me, and she had to leave quickly and in disgrace.'

He forced himself to look at Flora. Her expression was aghast.

'No – no. He was always true to my mother. You've got that wrong. You can't be my brother! You said your father was in the army!' Flora looked wildly around them as if seeking some kind of support. How could Matt suggest such a thing? Why was he trying to blacken her father's name and spoil a perfect afternoon?

'I'm so sorry, Flora,' he said urgently. 'I lied when I told you that. I was . . . curious about what sort of person you were, and I wanted to see where and how my mother had lived before she came to Leeds to raise me. Perhaps I shouldn't have said anything. But now that I'm going back home, I wanted you to know, and perhaps . . . we could keep in touch with one another? That is, if you want to?' He looked anxiously at her, wishing she didn't seem so distraught. 'I know – I'm sorry. I've made your father out to be a right rogue. I'm not surprised you don't want to believe me.'

Flora shook her head. 'I don't know what to believe. You're my brother!' She looked directly at him, and for the first time recognized the signs. They had the same red hair, the same shade of green eyes – her father's traits from his Irish ancestry.

'A big disappointment, I know, but I'm nearly positive that I am. After my mother died, I found some letters that your father had written to her in a box in her room. They did truly love one another, and your father even sent my mother money when he could afford it. He knew that I was his; my middle name is Towler, after him. My mother was determined to name me as his one way or another.'

Flora remembered seeing Matt sign his name – Matthew T. Walker – in her guest book.

'Your mother was always kind to me,' she said after a moment. 'She used to give me sweets, or a penny for the sweet shop. We used to always sit outside the pub when I went for a walk with my father. One day, I can remember her sitting on the bridge over the small stream while I caught tiddlers, and my father told me not to tell my mother.'

She drew in a steadying breath. A family secret had been let out of the bag. No wonder her mother had gone mad when Matt had come to stay at the pub! She knew just why he had come – and she must have known about him for years.

'Yes, she often used to mention a little girl with bright

red hair and green eyes who always had a smile for her. That must have been you.' Matt smiled. 'You are my sister; only half, but still my sister. I knew as soon as I saw you, but didn't know if I dared tell you.'

'I don't know what to say, or think. My father and your mother . . . I never thought anything about it. Nobody has ever said anything about it. But they wouldn't, would they? Not to me. Although I bet the Jenny Moons of the village had a good gossip. Is that why they always think I'm up to no good all the time?'

'Probably. Like father, like daughter, I suppose they're thinking. Although in your case, they couldn't be more wrong. You may have a warm heart, but I know that you love Bill and are true to him. It was pretty clear when I came in and found you with Johnny Cowperthwaite today that you'd been knocking him back.'

Flora blushed. 'Was it that obvious? He still holds a flame for me, and he does make me feel special. But it would never have worked out between us. I couldn't be untrue, as my father has obviously been to my mother. My poor mother – she would have had to put up with all the gossip. It's a wonder she can hold her head high. If there's one thing I've learned from listening to men's conversations in the pub, it is that it's always the woman's fault when things go wrong. Wives don't understand them, and the lovers are encouraging them.' She sighed. 'I can still hardly believe it. Surely I would have known? My mother would have said something.' Flora stared at Matt. Her thoughts were all over the place. She didn't want to believe him, but when she truly looked at him, there was no denying it. They were so much alike.

'I'm sorry,' Matt told her again. 'I know it will have come as a shock, but it's the truth. I just had to check everything out before telling you.' He took Flora's hand and squeezed it.

'Well, I have a brother. Never thought I'd say that.' Flora's head was filled with memories of her father smiling at Maisy Walker and whispering when he was around her. She should have known that they were more than friends. It was obvious now that Matt had pointed it out.

Perhaps she should say something to her mother – tell Mary that she had nothing to be ashamed of? That it was Flora's father's shame, not her own, that she'd been living with for so many years? Mary should have told her, she thought sadly, instead of hiding it.

As for her father – Flora would always love him, but now that she knew he had been lying and cheating behind their backs, she would never be able to think of him in the same way. She had always believed she was his beloved only child, and all this time, he'd had a son. Although she seemed to be taking the news in her stride, her head was still filled with doubts. Her understanding of her family was forever altered.

'Did you ever see our father? I can never remember going to Leeds. He never went out of Settle, really,' Flora said as they started back down from the crag, taking the easier path down through the Towhead Estate.

'No, never. But I do have a picture of him,' Matt said. He stopped as they came to the gateway onto the high road running along the back of Settle to nearby Langcliffe. Reaching into his breast pocket, he pulled out a faded photograph of a man in his forties, sporting a flat cap and smiling at the camera. He passed it to Flora.

Flora stared at it. Her father was there looking at her, smiling. It was the same picture that her mother had on the dresser in her front room. She turned it over and read the writing that she recognized as her father's on the back.

To my Maisy – Always remember me and know that I love you.
Fred xxx

'That's my father, and seemingly yours too,' Flora said softly. She gazed at the picture for a long time before looking up at Matt. 'Now, what are we going to do about it? Do we keep it a secret, or do we let it be known? I bet half of Giggleswick have put two and two together and got half a dozen, they always do. I wonder if some might have guessed who you really are, or perhaps they have forgotten? If your mother left when she was carrying you, perhaps nobody knows about you.'

'What would you rather do, Flora? It's all right for me; I'm going home soon. It will be you who has to live with it. Although . . . I know I said I probably wouldn't be back, but now you know who I am, perhaps I will.' He smiled hesitantly. It was a great relief to him that Flora had taken the news so well.

'I'll go and talk to my mother, tell her what I know.

There are some things she has said and done over the years that I understand better now. My poor mother,' Flora sighed.

'Do you want me to come with you?'

'Lord, no! Let me see how she takes it first,' Flora said wryly. She smiled at Matt. 'This has certainly been a day and a half, eh? It isn't every day you find out you have a long-lost brother. And that he's been staying under your roof! Bill certainly has no worries now.'

They made their way down Constitution Hill and back into Settle's market square, quieter now in the late afternoon sun. Matt turned back to look up once more at the high point where they had been sitting, silhouetted against the clear sky. Then he looked at Flora.

'I think we had better tell everyone just who I am, to stop the gossip. Else it's just history repeating itself.'

Flora nodded. 'I think so, too. But I'll go and see my mother in the morning and see what she has to say.'

Chapter 24

The next morning, Flora left May cleaning the pub and hurried over to her mother's house. She had tossed and turned in her bed all night – worrying about Bill misunderstanding Matt staying with her, and thinking about her father and his relationship with Maisy Walker. She was facing up to the loss of her rose-tinted view of her own childhood; what stood out to her now were the arguments she had overheard between her parents as she lay in bed pretending to be asleep.

She had a lot to ask her mother, she thought, as she knocked on Mary's door and stepped into her front room. There would be no hiding in her garden today. Rain was pouring down, and even thought it was midsummer, the wind was bitter.

'Flora? What are you doing coming round in this weather? I've even lit the fire, it's that miserable.' Mary looked up from her chair and immediately realized something was amiss with her daughter. 'Is Bill all right? He's not made a turn for the worse, has he?'

'No, Bill is all right as far as I know. He's learning to walk again and should be home before long, God willing.' Flora flopped down in what had once been her father's chair and looked across at her mother. 'Mam, did you know who my boarder is? Is that why you came across and told me to get rid of him?'

Her stomach clenched as she looked at her mother's face and saw the pain and anguish that Matt's presence had reignited there.

'So you've found out, after all these years. I was so determined to keep it from you. I hoped so much for you never to know; you loved your father so much.' Mary bent forward and moved some coals in the fire with her poker. 'How much do you know? What has he told you?' she asked quietly.

'Oh, Mam, you should have said. I'm a grown woman now – I can understand. Matt has told me what he knows: that my father is his father, and that his mother and my father had an affair while she ran the Cunning Vixen.' Flora looked at her mother. 'I'm sorry. I know this isn't easy, but I have to know if it really is true.'

'Oh, it's true all right, the hussy. She put her claws into your father as soon as she arrived in Giggleswick. And like a fool, he was flattered by her, with her blonde hair and lipstick and flirting ways. Bill thinks you're forward – well, you're not a patch on Maisy Walker. All the fellas used to nearly have their tongues hanging out over the bar looking at that trollop, and she knew it.' Mary's expression was bitter, and she shook her head. 'She was cheap and easy.'

Flora had never seen this side of her mother. Mary had always been hard, but never as bitter as she seemed now. 'I can't believe my father would be untrue to you. I always thought that you loved one another.'

'I tried to protect you as much as I could. You, thankfully, didn't know what was going on under your nose – as long as your father bought you sweets and took you to the park, he could do no wrong in your eyes. He was a fool. I loved him so much. I worked at the cotton mill, even though you were small, to make extra money for us, and he used to go and spend it at the pub. She even changed the pub's name because she knew she had all the men in Giggleswick eating out of her hand. You know it was originally called the Three Bells, not the Cunning Vixen? She called it that after herself.'

'I knew that was its old name; I didn't realize until recently that it was Maisy Walker who changed it. The old sign is still in one of the outbuildings.' Flora held her hand out for her mother to take, but Mary ignored it.

'Oh, she was cunning all right. When she left, she owed every shop in Settle and Giggleswick a small fortune. I bet your lodger, Matt, has not had many folk talking to him – they'll all remember his mother too well.' Mary shook her head. 'I knew nothing for months, your father kept it so quiet. I should have known better, the hours he spent in the pub.' Years of pain welled up in her, and she wiped her eyes with her handkerchief. 'What's he like, this Matt? Red hair, like you and your father. I saw him for a moment, but I've kept away because it'll bring back too many memories.'

'He's a right nice man, Mam. He must take after my father, because I don't think that he's got a bad bone in his body – though my father didn't do right by you, I can see that now. I couldn't believe it when he told me. It came out of the blue, and I didn't know what to say. My father – I always thought he was the perfect father and husband. And there was Matt telling me he was my illegitimate brother.' Flora wiped a tear from the corner of her eye.

'Aye. It's upsetting, and that's why I wanted to keep it from you. I fell out with Lottie because she tried to tell me what Fred was up to, and I didn't believe her. Then she got friendly with that load of gossips, and that was when we really fell out. I thought she would tell them everything. But she's never said a word, all these years – she's kept it to herself. Until your lodger showed his face, and then she came to warn me that he might be here to make trouble.' Mary sighed. 'She was always a good friend. That falling-out was another thing I can blame your father for. Anyway, we are back friends again now. Now, whether your father's old mates have twigged on to him being Matt's father is another question.'

'Oh, Mam, why didn't you tell me all this before? Matt isn't here to make trouble; he's just here to find out who he really is. I don't think he really wanted to tell me, but I'm glad he did.' Flora looked down at her lap for a moment, then raised eyes full of love to her mother. 'It must have really hurt when I told you I wanted to run and buy the Cunning Vixen. It must bring back memories every time you walk into the place. I'm sorry, mother.'

'Aye, I wasn't really happy, but your head was set, and I weren't going to stop you. And your father, well, you know how happy he would have been about it. Perhaps there's some justice in the world, with both of them gone. They're probably up there laughing at us.' Mary sent a glance heavenward and then shook her head.

'Oh, mother. What a life,' Flora sighed.

'It must have been a shock when he told you. Your father and you were so close – a sight closer than you ever were to me,' Mary said frankly.

'But we're close now, Mother. And I don't want you to blame yourself for my father being unfaithful. He always had a smile for everyone.' Flora looked at the photograph of her father on the sideboard, the same one that Matt had in his pocket.

'Aye, a flirt, and good with words – that's where you get it from. Not that you would be unfaithful to your Bill. You are not that sort, so at least there is a bit of me in you.' Mary smiled. 'So, if this Matt has told you all this, he must be returning home? Upsetting the apple-cart and then jiggering off back to where he comes from, just like his mother.'

'Yes, he's leaving next Friday. His job is done here at Settle. He's made sure the POWs have all got work and all is running smoothly. He's to be married shortly – his fiancée is waiting for him back in the outskirts of Leeds.'

'Well, I hope he's more loyal to his wife than his father was to me.' Mary's voice quavered suddenly as the old hurt welled up again, catching her by surprise. It had been hard, knowing that her husband had a lover on their doorstep.

'Oh, Mam. Come here.' Flora got down on her knees by Mary's chair and cuddled her. 'I love you. I wish you'd been able to tell me a long time ago what you had gone through.'

'What, and break your heart? I wasn't going to let your father's actions hurt you as well. You were still young and unable to understand that these things happen.' Mary kissed the nape of her daughter's neck. 'Now you know the family's dark secret. I'm amazed none of the local gossips have said anything, although your father was always very careful and didn't flaunt what he was doing – I'll give him that, at least.'

'Never had an inkling, Mother. And I still wouldn't if Matt hadn't broken the news to me. I must admit, I tossed and turned all night thinking about it. I felt so sorry for you.' Flora got to her feet.

'Don't feel sorry for me. What doesn't kill you makes you stronger. And at least I had one good thing from my marriage, and that is you.' Mary looked up at her daughter and smiled. 'What's done is done. We can all move on now.'

'No wonder I'm such a strong woman. I get it from you.' Flora returned her smile.

‘Aye, thank heavens you don’t take after your father. Else there would be problems at that pub.’

‘No shenanigans in my pub, Mother, and there never will be.’ Flora replied firmly. She could never be untrue to her Bill, no matter how Johnny Cowperthwaite tried to woo her.

May looked at Flora curiously as she walked back into the pub.

‘Are you all right? You look as if you’ve the weight of the world upon your shoulders,’ she observed.

Flora went behind the bar to get herself a glass of water. ‘Oh, May, why is life so damn complicated? I thought I came from a happy family – a perfect family – and it turns out to have been one big lie.’ She leaned against the stone sink and sipped the cold water, wanting to cry. ‘. . . I don’t know if I should tell you this, May – but I think I will. It needs to get out into the open, especially before Bill comes home. Else he’s bound to think the worst.’

‘What on earth are you on about? You are actually shaking.’ May was looking at her in alarm.

‘Matt is not staying here by chance. He’s staying here because his mother used to be the landlady – Maisy Walker. You know that much already, but there’s worse.’

‘Well, I didn’t want to say anything, but my mother and father have been talking about her. They remember her well, and not in a good way. She was a bit of a wild one, according to my father; and what my mother said about her, I can’t repeat.’ May sighed.

'Oh, it gets worse than that.' Flora took another deep drink of water, gathering her courage to tell May the full story. 'Maisy and my father were having an affair behind my mother's back, and the outcome of it all was Matt. She left here to go to Leeds and have him there, leaving a pile of debt behind her.' Flora noticed May's unchanged expression. She looked serious, but not shocked.

'Well, that's another thing that my mother and father said – that your father was never away from here. So I can't say I'm surprised; you and Matt even look alike. I'm surprised that you didn't see it yourself. I wouldn't worry about it, although it must have come as a heck of a shock to you. Your father's mates were bound to know. My dad had a good inkling, because he remembers seeing him coming here at night as he looked out of his bedroom window.' May's tone was matter-of-fact. 'At least he's all right, a decent bloke, and he's tracked you down.'

'Oh, Lord, what a carry-on. It seems I was one of the last to be in the dark about all of this. I keep looking at him and thinking, this can't be my brother! And yet, when I served him breakfast this morning, I did notice the likeness. He has the same hair, and the same nose . . .' Flora shook her head. 'It's taking me some time to get used to the idea. Not to mention accepting how badly my father behaved to my mother.' Looking at May, she could hardly believe how easily the whole situation seemed to have been discussed among the girl's family. All about Flora's beloved father and Maisy Walker.

'Is he staying much longer? And when he does go, is

he going to keep in touch? Come to that, do you want him to? I bet your mother really felt it when he turned up on your doorstep,' May said sympathetically.

'He's going back to Leeds next week. I don't know if he will keep in touch or not; he did say that he might. And as for my mother, she says she knew who he was as soon as she heard he'd been asking about his mother . . . Oh, May. My father's double life has been such a shock to me. I always loved him so much.' Flora sighed.

'Ah, well. Folk will talk for a while, and then it will be old news, and they'll find something else to talk about. I wouldn't worry about that, Flora. And look on the bright side – you are no longer the only one. You've got a brother.' May patted Flora's arm fondly and smiled at her.

'I don't know if that's news I wanted – but never mind.' Flora breathed in; she had to stop her fretting. 'I have more worries with Bill. I've a heck of a lot of explaining to do to him when he comes home.'

'Bill will be all right with everything once he realizes that Matt's your brother. It's a good job he is, really. It could have been a little awkward.' May smiled and looked at the clock. 'It's opening time, Flora, and I'll have to get myself home. Will you be all right?'

'Oh, Lord, so it is; I hadn't realized. Yes, I'll be fine. Thank you for listening, May. You must think twice about working here some days, with all you've to put up with from us,' Flora smiled.

'No, I love it. You are good to me.' May picked up her cardigan and gas mask. 'I'll go back – I hope Antonio's at work with my father.'

'Now, you behave yourself. Look what happens if you give your heart to the wrong person! Talking of Antonio and your father, could you tell them I've a small job for them, when they have time?'

'Yes, of course. And stop worrying, Flora. Everything will turn out right. It always does.' May departed with a cheerful wave, already looking forward to watching Antonio work alongside her father while she did the accounts.

Chapter 25

It was the Thursday night before Matt's departure, and the Cunning Vixen was full. Rain was falling hard outside and everyone had decided this was the best place to find company and sympathy, as the news of the war was becoming worse with each passing hour. Even though it was the middle of summer, Flora had lit the open fire, making the bar feel more welcoming as her locals sat around and talked.

'First Crete is declared to have fallen to those Nazi bastards, and now we are told that we're going to have to put up with clothes rationing. Somebody's going to have to stop them,' Robert Pitcher said. He looked across at Matt. 'And now his lot's bringing these Italians here and leaving us to manage them, even while Mussolini and Hitler are closer than ever!'

'He's only doing his job,' Graham Windle remarked. 'Besides, haven't you heard whose son he is? Some of us had a rough idea of why his mother upped sticks and disappeared from the village all those years ago. She was always too friendly with Fred Towler, let alone her habit of not paying her bills.'

'No; what are you on about?' Robert set down his pint and looked at Graham, perplexed.

Graham nodded towards Matt. 'He's Fred's lad. He's been here not only with work, but to look at the place his mother ran and to find his father's side of the family. Harold Lambert told me that Flora had no idea until last week. His lass said she was a bit shocked. That'll be nothing compared to her mother – she's a proud one, is Mary. When it all originally came out, she withdrew from everybody in the village.' Graham took a long sip of beer while his friend looked at him, aghast.

'Well, I never. I'd never heard a thing, and I've always lived here down near the beck. I used to see Fred often about here. But I never put two and two together.' Robert picked up his pint and looked over at Matt and Flora, smiling and talking across the bar as if they'd known one another for years.

Graham glanced round as the pub door opened. 'Bloody hell; I never thought I'd see this day. She and Lottie Taylor have not been in this place for years.' Robert turned to follow the direction of his gaze as Mary, with her best friend Lottie beside her, walked into the pub. She paused, looking round at the staring faces of the regulars.

'You can all stop your gawping.' Mary took her wet mac off and shook her headscarf from her hair. She reached for Lottie's hand. 'I knew this place would be full of you all tonight, bottled beer or not.' Her eyes found Flora behind the bar; and standing opposite her, the man Mary had come to see. 'You all like a good gossip, so I thought you could go home and tell it as it is.'

Mary approached the bar and stood before Matt. She had known instantly who he was the moment she'd first seen him: with his red hair, green eyes and slim build, he was the spit of her late husband.

'Mam . . .? What are you doing?' Flora said warily.

'I'm here to tell everybody that I always knew about your father and Maisy Walker,' Mary said loudly. 'That's it. Are you all listening? I've lived with the shame all these years, but not anymore. It wasn't my fault. And it wasn't this lad's, either.'

She glanced round at the silent drinkers, then turned back to Matt. 'I finally get to meet my husband's son. I always knew about you, although he thought I didn't.'

Matt met her gaze. 'I'm sorry,' he said. 'I've brought upset to you and your family, and I didn't mean to.'

Flora's heart went out to him. He looked so ashamed.

'Nay, it wasn't you. It was my daft husband and your desperate mother. She should have known he hadn't a penny to his name and would never leave me and our Flora. She picked the wrong fella. I've felt guilty all these years, thinking that I wasn't enough for my man, but not anymore. She even came between Lottie and me.' Mary nodded at her oldest, truest friend. 'But our friendship came through when Lottie knew I was going to be hurt. Not as much as she's been herself, mind, with her losing poor Richard at sea.'

The whole pub listened, rapt. This was better entertainment than any dominoes match.

'You wanted to know about your mother. Feel free to ask folk now. They have all been protecting me by not talking to you, but they don't need to do that anymore. The cat is out of the bag – or should I say the fox, as she renamed the pub after herself, the Cunning Vixen. She had a kind side to her and was a bonny woman, I'll give her that. Just lusted after men and money,' Mary said quietly.

Frank Capstick spoke up. 'Aye, she was a fair woman, was your mother, lad. Not one for Giggleswick, though; she brought town ways with her. She was best taking you back to Leeds.' He beckoned to Mary and Lottie. 'Now, Mary, it's grand to see you back in the pub. You and Lottie come and sit with me, and let's get back to how things used to be.'

With Frank's encouragement, his companions shuffled along to make room for the two women to sit down, now that they had set the world to rights.

'Thank you, Frank,' Mary said. She looked at Matt. 'Are you coming to join us? I'll not have you going back to Leeds saying you weren't made welcome by me. My Fred wouldn't have wanted it that way. He was heartbroken and sulked round the house for days when she did a runner with you in her belly.'

Around them, a quiet buzz of conversation began as people murmured to one another about what had just happened.

'I will, thank you. Flora told me that you're a strong

woman, and she was right; that speech took some grit,' Matt said. 'And now everybody knows who I am, and that your Flora is my half-sister, it's put the record straight – although my mother, no doubt, would have had something to say about it.' He smiled.

'She would that, and this time I would stand up to her. I was too young back then. I'll have a sherry, and so will Lottie. Come and sit with Frank. He always was a good friend, even if his wife does run that blessed knitting, gossiping club. She's not the worst one, though, is she, Lottie?'

'No, she tries to keep everybody in order. I only go because I think I'm doing some good for our lads.' Lottie looked at Matt. She, too, had recognized who he must be as soon as she had seen him looking up at the pub sign. She'd known that, like it or not, he was going to bring upset to her old friend.

'Ah, well, you are all doing a good job. And you need to share your troubles these days. I'll get the sherries, ladies, and come to sit with you.'

Matt winked at Flora as he returned to the bar. 'Two sherries and a huge helping of humble pie, please. Your mother certainly says it how it is.'

'She always has done. I couldn't be prouder of her than at this moment,' Flora replied. She reached for the rarely used sherry bottle. 'Thanks, Matt – that must have been hard to hear about your mother.'

'No, not at all. She was always looking for a fast way to make money, and she didn't care much for anybody. I knew she was lying about my father being in the army; she never showed me any pictures of him, and she changed the regiment every time I asked. My mother was only trying to protect me. I think she did feel ashamed that she'd given birth to me out of wedlock. She was a good mother, if nothing else. Perhaps your mother will tell me about my true father – I hope I take after him slightly. As long as I haven't inherited his roving eye.' Matt picked up the two small glasses and made his way back to join Frank, Mary and Lottie.

'You do take after my father; I can tell you do. A kind soul,' Flora said quietly to herself. 'But your mother was always good to me, so don't be too hard on her. You can't be responsible for who you fall in love with.' She turned to her next customer. 'Yes, a pint, is it, Graham? Sorry that we're still on bottles.'

'Doesn't make any difference to me. The Cunning Vixen will always be my pub.' Graham parted with his hard-earned cash as Flora passed him the open bottle.

'Now, that is where I am going to prove you wrong,' she replied.

'No, it is! You'll not get me going up the hill.' Graham looked shocked.

'Well, after Monday, you'll be drinking at the Three Bells. I've hunted out the old sign, and I'm going to give this pub its original name back. Harold is going to send his POW, Antonio, across to hang it back up. I think it's best if we put the past just where it belongs.' Flora glanced across to where her mother and Matt sat and noticed that they seemed to be getting on despite their differences.

'Back to how it should be.' Graham smiled and started to collect his round.

'Yes; and I had a letter from the brewery this morning. Our next delivery will be in barrels, you'll be glad to hear.' Flora grinned.

'That's good news! But bottles or barrels, we would still come here, Flora, when we can afford and the wives allow.' Graham looked apologetic. 'Not that you are a Maisy Walker – they all know that you're faithful.'

'Some do, Graham. Others believe what they want. I'm not that daft, but at least now I know why.'

Flora leaned on her bar, feeling that things were looking brighter at last. She had gained a brother, and thanks to Mary's bravery, her past was no longer a secret. All she needed now was for Bill to come safely home and the war to end.

Matt and Flora stood on the platform of Settle station, waiting for the Leeds train to arrive from Carlisle.

'Doesn't Giggleswick Chapel look splendid from here?' Matt said. 'Settle will always be dear to my heart. Would you mind if I came back to visit you once this war is over? And brought my Beth along?'

'Of course not – you're welcome any time. Little did I know, when you entered my pub, what a change you were going to make to our lives. But as my mother says, it's not your fault; it isn't really anybody's fault. I think my father genuinely loved your mother. He always seemed happy in her company.' Flora smiled. 'Well, it was either love or lust.'

'Yes, who knows? Complicated lives,' Matt agreed. He picked up his suitcase and mackintosh as they saw the steam engine approaching round the bend, billowing smoke out as it started to apply its brakes. 'Looks like my train is here. At least now you can tell Bill all about your lodger, and he'll be reassured that you've been faithful. He should learn to trust you.'

'He probably knows all about my father and has never told me. I'll have to tell him that I would never act like that – I couldn't break his heart. I expected a letter from him by now, but I've not heard a word.'

Flora stood back as the train pulled into the station and steam filled the platform. The carriage doors flew open, and the stationmaster yelled, 'Settle! Passengers for Leeds, Keighley and Bradford!'

'Well, it's been an eventful stay. Thank you. Make sure May behaves herself with Antonio, and thank your mother for being so understanding.' Matt leaned forward and kissed her on the cheek. 'Take care. I'll write – in fact, I'll send you and Bill and your mother an invitation to my wedding.'

'You take care, too. I don't want to lose you now that we've found one another!'

He boarded the train and shut the door behind him, moving down the carriage to find a seat. As Flora watched him – this man who had caused so much upset in her life – and wondered when she would see him again, she heard someone calling her name. She turned her head sharply.

'Flora! Flora, I'm here! How did you know I were coming home? I never wrote to tell you!' It was a voice she had missed for far too long.

The stationmaster blew his whistle for the engine to depart – and there, making his way through the engine's steam, was her Bill, propped up on two crutches and smiling. But he was also wondering about the man he had just seen Flora saying goodbye to.

'Oh, Bill, you are back! Oh, it's good to see you – you really don't know just how good. Have they let you come home? Should you be here? Is it not too early for you to be returning home?' Flora put her arms around Bill and hugged him delightedly.

'Careful, careful – I'm not used to these crutches yet,' Bill said, leaning forward to kiss her. 'I wasn't going to wallow in my hospital bed while my wife was running the pub and letting our bedroom out. They had to let me go. Besides, I'm on the mend now! Who was the fella you were seeing off? I don't recognize him.'

'That's Matt, the lodger. He's going home today.' Flora turned and waved to Matt as the train pulled away, and he returned the wave and smiled at the couple standing together. 'You'll never believe it, but it turns out that he's my half-brother. I'm sure the locals will tell you all about it.' Flora reached for Bill's bag, which the porter had brought out from the train, and put it over her shoulder.

'His mate that visited me told me that, when I was in my hospital bed. But I thought he was lying; so I thought I'd better get myself home.' Bill looked at Flora, wanting to believe all was well between them. He loved her so much.

'Oh, Bill! He is my brother – Matt Walker. And you

should know that there's only one man for me, and that is you, Bill Whitaker. And it always will be.'

'I know, Flora. Things will be different now. My back's not giving me as much pain. Time to make a new start and put the past well and truly behind us.' Bill looked at her with love in his eyes. He knew that he had been hard to live with over the years, but his time away had made him determined to go home and show his wife just how much he loved her.

'A new start, with no secrets. Just love.' Flora smiled as they watched the train disappear and Bill, with a determined look on his face, walked by her side down the station yard. It was the start of a new era, and the past was better left behind them both.

Wartime in the Dales

DIANE ALLEN

September 1939.

Friends Maggie Shaunessy and Lizzie Taylor are heartbroken to be evacuated from their Liverpool homes to rural Yorkshire.

Lizzie is sent to live with a vicar in the village of Gargrave, while Maggie finds herself delivered by chauffeur to Hawith Hall, the home of Lord and Lady Bradley.

Both the hall and the vicarage are far different to what the girls are used to, and both are very homesick – though Maggie finds friendship in the form of Alice, a young servant at the hall who takes her under her wing.

But change is coming to the Dales too, leaving the girls harbouring desperate plans of running away, back to Liverpool . . .

OUT NOW